The Challenge

The Challenge was named the year's best work of fiction for young readers in a 1960 competition sponsored by Gyldendal, the Danish publishing house.

THE
CHALLENGE

by POUL E. KNUDSEN

Translated by L. W. KINGSLAND

1963

The Macmillan Company, New York

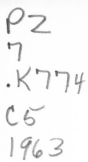

Original title: *Vaeddemålet*
© Gyldendal, Copenhagen, 1960
Translation © Methuen & Co. Ltd., 1962, 1963

Library of Congress catalog card number: 63-9595

First American Edition

The Macmillan Company, New York
A Division of The Crowell-Collier Publishing Company

Printed in the United States of America

Contents

The Challenge

1

Odbjørn Grows Restless

From the hills to the north of the stream came the sound of sudden hoofbeats, a hollow thudding as though from an underground smithy where demon and spirit of the earth sat forging swords of glowing iron amid a spray of sparks. The hillside seemed suddenly on fire as a cloud of dust drove over its carpet of heather.

There between the hill-slopes appeared horse and rider, the horse without saddle or girth or stirrups.

The horseman, twisting the long hair of the mane about his fingers, urged the horse with his fists now to the left, now to the right. Then he dug his heels into his flanks, bore downhill toward the fiord and vanished in a snow-white cloud of foamy spray.

"Halloo! . . . Halloo!" roared the horseman. The horse whinnied and galloped over the water-meadows, to and fro, zigzagging now this way, now that, as the horseman's shouts and peals of laughter sprayed out behind him with the stones and clods.

Well inland, he swung the horse around and made for the west, toward the sand dunes and the sea. The hoofbeats thundered heavily and hollowly on the ground. The wind whistled through the gray fringe of hair under the horse's belly. When he snorted, the west wind blowing through his nostrils sounded like a mainsail catching the wind. But his muzzle was soft and gray as dust.

The rider called his horse Graywind. His own name was Odbjørn. . . .

They had come to a halt right out on the dunes. Below them the surf rumbled with a hollow thunder over the beach. A spattering of sea foam drifted like flecks of wool about horse and rider, and Odbjørn's sand-gold hair whipped in the west wind. He often rode with Graywind among the dunes, letting time drift away on the wind.

Odbjørn the Nameless they called him.

As he sat there, his thoughts went back to the moment when, three years before, he first gazed upon those sand dunes from behind the dragon-prow of his father's ship as she stood in toward the coast.

Instead of sailing into the fiord and mooring alongside the jetty in front of Harja Hugwa's hall, his father Torvik had bidden his band of viking sea-rovers run the ship ashore a little to the north of the settlement. It happened a couple of days before the midsummer sacrifice, Odbjørn remembered. Harja's people had all been occupied with preparations for the festival, and so none of them saw the ship's warriors carry their chieftain ashore on a stretcher of hides and oars. Torvik lay with his eyes closed and face flushed, but it was not the glow of battle that brought the color to his cheeks and sent beads of sweat trickling down his beard. No, he was stricken with fever, and as Odbjørn followed with bowed head, the thought that his father might die shamefully on a bed of straw, instead of gloriously in battle, compressed his lips into a thin bloodless line in his pale face.

The men pushed on a little way up the coast and waded across the stream. Among the heather-covered hills they set the stretcher down on ground where they were sheltered from the wind and where their words would not be swept away by the rumbling of the sea.

"Believe me, Torvik, we were willing enough to wait till you get the better of the devil that's poisoned your body, but . . ."

It was the helmsman, Ulver, who spoke. Then he fell silent, as if to listen to the distant rumbling of the sea behind the downs.

Earlier that day a fleet of strange big ships had appeared out of the gray haze. They were ships with high prows and three bristling banks of oars jutting out from countless holes in their planks of golden oak. The oars rose and fell as if driven by an unseen power, and no one had been able to catch a glimpse of the rowers. But they saw a couple of warriors strolling about the deck, their burnished helmets gleaming like red flames in the morning sun, and the wind catching the black plumes that sprang from their crests. Beneath their cloaks the warriors were clad in scales—like fish.

Torvik's fighting men had been startled—perhaps they had come face to face with the wizards of Njord risen up from the deep with a heavy load of ill-luck aboard. When shortly afterward the ships vanished into the banks of mist, the men broke into a confused clamor and quieted down at last only when Harulf began to speak and told them there was no need to believe that the ships had been raised by magic or the powers of evil. They were made of wood and nails like any other ships, and came from a land where it was always warm and sunny, where mist and winter were unknown. This land, he had told them, was known as the land of the Romans, and once, he said, a Roman ship had been stranded down on the coast of Friesland. She had been laden with jewelry and vessels of silver and bronze which the strangers had bartered for amber and slaves. "Silver and bronze!" Ulver whispered, staring far away into the mist where the Roman ships had disappeared.

And so they had sailed northward after the ships in the hope that one of them would drop behind and they would be able to gain great plunder by falling upon her. But when the sun drew the mist off the sea the strange ships had gone.

It was then that they had begun to look askance at their chieftain Torvik who hung across the thwarts, doubled up and sick with fever. And Torvik had guessed his men's thoughts.

"That's how it is," he said. "Njord is ill-disposed toward me, and so he keeps the Roman ships hidden. Put me ashore now. And when you've met with good luck you can come back and fetch me."

It seemed to Odbjørn that his father was talking like an old woman, and his cheeks had burned with shame.

When they brought the sick man ashore, for a long time Torvik's gasping breath and the whistling of the wind were the only sounds to be heard. The men looked away over the hills or stood staring down at the heather.

"Now be off with you!" Torvik said. "When you've taken your booty, come back here again."

"That shall not be long," Ulver promised.

He turned away and walked over to Odbjørn. Torvik's son was sitting on the ground undoing a great bundle of hides.

"Odbjørn," Ulver said, "it's for you to command the ship now and be our chieftain in your father's stead."

"If I'd anything to say in the matter, none of you would go to sea again until my father went with you," Odbjørn answered, as he loosened the last thong and opened the bundle.

Before him lay a week-old foal shivering with cold under its ruffed gray coat. Freed from the thongs that bound it, the animal stretched its neck and tried to rise. Odbjørn put his arm under its jaw and helped it up. The foal stood straddling uncertainly on its long thin legs, and Odbjørn had to place his arm under its belly and support the tousled little beast to prevent a sudden gust of wind from bowling it over.

The day before they had taken plunder in a fight up north—chines of pork and legs of mutton, and a live foal which Odbjørn had wrapped in rags and hides.

"Everyone on board will obey your will," Ulver began again. "But no one can expect us to remain ashore doing nothing and let so rich a prize sail by."

As Odbjørn gave no answer, Ulver made a sign to the men. They drew their swords and saluted Torvik: then off they went in a compact band over the hills toward the sea. At the ford Ulver turned around.

"Torvik!" he shouted. "Before the moon changes we shall be back . . ."

The wind swept the words out of his mouth and scattered them over the hillside.

"Before the new moon!" he cried. "If all goes well!"

Odbjørn laid the foal on the ground and covered it with bits of hide. They were alone now.

But a little later Ketil and Aslak returned. The two old men trudged along with a leg of mutton wrapped in skin. When they threw their burden down, they were at great pains to make the most of their age and infirmities. Ketil in particular groaned heavily and said that he and Aslak were no longer capable of wrestling with the sea, and so if Torvik had nothing against it they would stay with him.

Torvik expressed his opinion that they had aged remarkably quickly. More than that he would not say, but a smile lurked in the depths of his beard.

He sent Aslak over to a large farmstead that lay a little to the south of the downs. Aslak was to ask permission to build a hut on the downs to shelter them from the wind.

Aslak went and came back, and during that brief journey he seemed to age even more.

The master of the farm, Harja Hugwa, had answered that he who begged a roof over his head was not so great that he could not ask his boon in person.

Torvik nodded.

"He's right," he muttered. "Carry me to the farmer's door."

But as his father was seating himself on Ketil's and Aslak's arms, Odbjørn jumped up and barred their way.

"I won't have it," he cried.

Torvik looked at him for a long time.

"We're guests and strangers here," he said. "Believe me, Odbjørn, I find it hard to bear, too."

Since that day Odbjørn hated Harja Hugwa who had thus humiliated his father, Torvik the Chieftain. Hugwa's son, Hjald, had since become Odbjørn's blood brother, but even in the very act of mingling their blood and swearing brotherhood, it occurred to Odbjørn that he was taking some small revenge on Hugwa, for if the old man should ever know that his son had sworn eternal friendship with Odbjørn the Nameless, he would certainly be grieved.

And now Odbjørn sat staring out over the sea which, three years before, had washed him ashore like a piece of wreckage, alone in the world and poor. His thoughts turned for a moment to Hugwa's daughter, the young maiden Groa, and he smiled. Then memories of that earlier time returned . . .

Harja Hugwa had given Torvik permission to build himself a hut. At the same time he sent an old bondswoman up into the heather-covered hills, and never asked for her return. Tova was the bondswoman's name. She applied leeches to Torvik's chest to draw the sickness out of his body. She sat the livelong day breathing on Torvik and rubbing her spittle into his cheeks.

In the meantime Odbjørn and the two old sea-rovers stacked turf on turf, and the walls of the hut grew up around the bondswoman and the fever-smitten chieftain.

Thrall and freeman from Hugwa's farmstead found excuses to visit the heather-covered hills, and folk came trailing from the farms in the hinterland to watch the strangers stack their turfs and build their hut. They concluded that Odbjørn had come from far away and knew nothing of the west wind, for otherwise he would not have built his hut to face the sea, thus inviting the cold and shutting out the sun. But they said nothing, for they could see by the look of him that he would not accept advice. At that time, on account of his defiant mouth and sharp gray eyes, he had already been given the first of his many nicknames. One and all, they called him stiff-necked—Odbjørn the Stubborn, they called the lad.

Before the hut was roofed, Torvik died.

Odbjørn set his jaw, and, dragging stones from the beach, lined a grave in the heather-covered hills. When they came to bury the dead, they heard not a whimper from him. When Torvik lay in his stone-lined grave, Odbjørn stepped down into it, loosed his father's sword belt and girded the sword about his loins. The bowl and beaker that Tova handed down to him he placed between Torvik's arms. As Ketil handed him the leg of mutton, the old man quivered and a half-choked sob broke through his beard. Odbjørn turned slowly around and stared at him with his sharp gray eyes.

But that same night the bondswoman found him lying cuddled up to the foal, with his arms about the animal's neck. Tova loosed his arms and, pressing his wet cheeks to her breast, stifled his sobbing so that no one might hear it.

It was of these things that Odbjørn was now thinking as he lay sprawled across the horse's back with his face buried in his stiff mane.

He would often lie like that among the dunes, dreaming himself far off on long voyages, plundering and looting far away from Hugwa's homestead where his word carried no weight, where a kinless man was counted no better than a thrall. And in his dreams he would come back a very different Odbjørn heading into the fiord behind the dragon-prow, an Odbjørn who was the equal of any man in Hugwa's hall. In his dreams, the wealthy farmer would bid everyone come to the sacrifice and the wedding feast of his daughter Groa and the chieftain Odbjørn. In the gray dawn the folk from the settlement would make their way to the temple of the gods, where Odbjørn would redden the sacred stones with ram's blood, while Groa knelt and scattered a handful of corn before the image of Frey. So Odbjørn would dream as the surf-laden west wind whined in his ears.

When the village folk saw him lying on Graywind's back out among the sand dunes, they shook their heads and gave him a new name. Odbjørn the Deedless they called him.

And that set them thinking of Thorkim, Hamund's son, who had spent the winter building a ship and getting a crew together. Before long Thorkim would be heading out of the fiord in his own ship. And like Odbjørn, he was only eighteen years old. But he knew what he wanted. Thorkim was a regular visitor in Hugwa's hall—and doubtless not just to admire Hugwa's beard . . .

The women laughed and whispered together over their

looms. Like the Norns, they dispensed weal and woe to
mankind. The thread of Thorkim's fate they spun strong
and long, but Odbjørn's was thin and short. Better for
him if the Norns cut short his life-thread right away.
Thorkim had been to Hugwa to ask for his daughter's hand.
It was said that the farmer had been friendly disposed toward him and promised him Groa as his betrothed when he
returned home from his voyaging.

That spring everybody talked about Thorkim and Groa.

Odbjørn's hands clutched like claws at the horse's
mane . . .

As for Thorkim's ship, it was built with timber from his
father's woods. Was Odbjørn expected to plait a ship from
heather and marram grass?

He had been to Thorkim to bargain for a place in the
ship, but Thorkim had answered that whoever wanted a
place on the rowing-benches must pay him a sheep for every
year of his life. The bondswoman Tova had seen the
wanderlust in Odbjørn's eyes, and she had offered to go to
Hugwa to borrow the sheep he lacked, but Odbjørn had
forbidden her.

As far as Groa was concerned, Odbjørn knew that
Hugwa's daughter held him in her heart and not Thorkim.
But that was something that he and Groa alone knew.

Odbjørn lifted his head and gazed across to the headland: he was looking to see if a green bough had been stuck
in the cairn out there, for if it had, it meant that Groa was
waiting for him behind the sand dunes. But there was no
secret signal calling to him just then. He smiled all the
same and his teeth gleamed like polished sea shells in the
sunlight.

"Groa," he whispered, but he did not hear himself speak,
for the west wind snatched the word from him as if it knew
that no one must hear that name from his lips.

Suddenly he jumped up with a start, for out there . . .

Far out where sea and sky met he had caught sight of a dark speck. It looked like a fly that had scrambled over the horizon's rim and settled down to rest on the lowest step of the gray-blue vault of heaven. He sat tensed and rigid, gazing out toward that dark speck which glided slowly nearer.

2

In Hugwa's Hall

But it was not Ulver. . . . Disappointment relaxed the tense muscles of his body.

The ship was now so close inshore that he could see the two banks of oars jutting out on either side. It must be a Roman ship—perhaps the same that the year before, around midsummer, had dropped anchor in the fiord with a cargo of gleaming bronze pots and pitchers, and brightly colored cloth, light as gossamer, so fine they could see one another through it as though through a haze when they held it up before their eyes. The women's eyes had grown bright as the cloth itself when they touched it. The Roman had a strange drinking-cup with him, too. It was transparent, and when you looked through it everything turned green—and if you dropped it, it would shiver into a thousand pieces. Hugwa had acquired one like it. It now stood on a shelf high up the wall for all to see that Hugwa drank from a cup made of something other than silver or bronze.

Odbjørn dug his heels into Graywind's flanks and rode inland, past the sacred grove where the wind sang incantations of rain in the rustling foliage. Behind the trees lay the temple of the gods and the tree of sacrifice with its whispering crown of pine needles that, like a flickering green tongue, lent voices to the images of the gods.

Out on the plain where the folk meet was held he turned and rode back to the beach. . . .

The Roman ship had come close inshore and was nearing the approach to the fiord. Odbjørn rode out on to the headland and as he watched the galley sail past the point, the shadow from the ship's lofty side swept over him like a cold wind. Upon that odd-looking erection amidships stood one of the strangers. He must have been the master of the vessel, for the upper part of his body was covered in iron scales that lay close to his chest like feathers on a bird, and on the iron crest of his helmet a plume of black hair waved in the wind. The Roman stood with folded arms staring straight ahead, as if he had fallen asleep and had not noticed that the ship would soon run aground. Odbjørn was just about to give him a shout to wake him up, when the fellow uttered a strange cry and a black iron cross slid down the bows and splashed into the water.

And now for the first time he saw that all the village folk had gathered in a crowd on the beach with Hugwa at their head. As the Roman ship swung around on her cable and lay across the fiord, he caught a fleeting glimpse of Groa, her bright hair flowing like molten gold over her shoulders. Then she was lost to sight as the whole settlement was hidden behind the vessel.

Never had Odbjørn seen so great a ship. It was something to be wondered at that a ship which stood so high out of the water could remain upon an even keel. But he was thinking only of Groa who had forgotten him and the cairn in her preoccupation with the Roman ship.

He rode home and sat down at the back of the hut—in a corner as dark as his own gloomy mood.

There Tova found him. She had been sitting in the stable and had heard Graywind thudding up the hillside. The sound of the hoofbeats was enough for her to guess that all was not as it should be with Odbjørn, and now she saw Ketil and Aslak sitting silent and bent in the straw. She clambered up into the hayloft and fetched down a hide bag.

"Have you seen the Roman ship?" she asked.

Odbjørn did not answer.

"It's high time you got yourself a cloak, Odbjørn. Winter can come on quickly. And we lack salt, too."

She opened the hide bag and poured a dozen small pieces of amber into her wrinkled hand. It was all she had gathered on the beach during the last two summers.

"Perhaps you could get cloth and salt for the amber," she said.

But Odbjørn struck her hand aside and scattered the amber over the clay floor.

"I'm not going begging with those scraps!" he shouted. "But perhaps I should trade Ketil and Aslak for rock salt— and you as well, Tova!"

The two old men shrank back into the straw and Odbjørn heard them whispering in the darkness under the hayloft.

He was suddenly overcome with remorse at having frightened them. He rushed out of the hut, threw himself on Graywind's back and rode down to the settlement.

Everyone who could drag himself along was inside the hall. Hugwa's housecarls had enough to do to keep people back from the long trestle table where the Roman and his slaves had unpacked cases and casks. Odbjørn stepped into the hall and forced his way to the table. On the sand-scoured trestle boards lay heaps of bronze vessels. Stacks of cloth were piled up to the roof beams, looking as if the end of the rainbow had dropped through the smoke hole. At one end of the table lay masses of red rock salt, and next to it were leather bags full of white powdered salt.

Hugwa stood there moistening his finger. He dipped it into the white powder, and as he thrust it into his mouth there came from deep within his beard the sound of satisfied sucking. They had lacked salt for a long time. Hugwa's finger flew from salt bag to mouth, backward and forward, like a bird building its nest in his beard, and many an envious glance was cast in the direction of Hugwa's finger.

Odbjørn had eyes for no one but Groa.

She stood leaning over the long table where gold rings and silver clasps lay glittering on a black cloth like stars in the sky on a winter's night. Now and then she leaned forward to stroke a trinket with her fingertips, and as she moved her hair fell over her shoulders like flowing molten amber.

As Odbjørn stood and witnessed the pleasure the glittering objects gave her, his cheeks grew hot with shame. His hands fumbled with his hide belt—but where others had a leather purse hanging, Odbjorn's finger wandered over a ragged tunic and lost itself in holes and darns.

Thorkim had entered Hugwa's hall accompanied by four thralls who trudged along bent double under creaking stacks of leather and mountains of skins. He was now standing at the end of the table bargaining with the Roman. He made for the pile of cloth. He threw what he picked out into the arms of one of his thralls. Then he sauntered off to the bronze pots.

"That one and that one," he said, as he heaved vessels and pots in the direction of the thralls.

The Roman followed him around and made a note in his wax tablets of everything that flew from the trestle table to the thralls. His small black eyes were here, there and everywhere. In between times he used his stylus to scratch his head which was covered in short hair like a black moleskin. Whenever Thorkim seemed to hesitate for a moment, the stylus remained planted, motionless as a post, in the cleft of his chin. He was smooth-shaven, but over his cheeks and chin there lay, as it were, the shadow of a pair of black raven's wings.

Thorkim did not look at the Roman. He barely looked at the things he chose, for he did not take his eyes off Groa. And whenever he spoke, his words seemed to be intended for her.

The Roman laid his hand on his shoulder and showed him the wax tablets. Thorkim brushed his hand away and turned his back to him.

"Roman slave!" he shouted. "Wait till I've finished!"

The words caused a burst of laughter to rise to the roof beams. And he shouted once again.

"Black Roman slave!" he shouted, glancing across at Hugwa's daughter. When Groa turned and smiled at him he felt himself grow tall enough to thrust his head through the smoke hole. Everybody saw how red his sharp cheekbones turned, and a whispering stole round the hall among the women. For everybody knew that Thorkim and Groa . . .

But Odbjørn clenched his fists until the knuckles gleamed white under the skin.

Neither did the Roman seem to find much pleasure in the burst of laughter and the peculiar whispering. He laid his hand upon his sword and made a sign to the Roman slaves.

Then Thorkim picked up six of the skin bags from the table and let them fall on the floor—six bags of the finest white powdered salt. He stole a glance at Groa to see whether she had noticed that in Hamund's household they never chose the second best.

He now decided to pay.

"Undo it," he said. The thrall opened a heavy skin bag—

and there lay pieces of amber as big as hen's eggs—bigger —as big as clenched fists.

For a brief moment the Roman let the light play on the soft golden amber. Then he tied up the skin bag and handed it to one of his slaves. He went over to Thorkim's pile of leather and counted out forty hides. He left only three behind.

But Thorkim nodded and walked over to Groa.

"Is it a clasp that's taken your fancy?" he asked.

He startled her and she dropped the trinket. Thorkim picked it up and weighed it appraisingly in his hand. It was a beautiful gold clasp, solid and weighty.

"It would look pretty on your shoulder when you fasten your cloak about your neck," he said. "Would you like it, if I made you a present of it?"

He turned to the Roman.

"Black devil, what do you want for this clasp? Is that enough?" he asked, pointing to the three hides.

The Roman laughed and shook his head.

"A slave then?"

"Slave," said the Roman. He knew that word. A smile spread over his face. "Slave," he nodded. A slave!

"Rudin!" shouted Thorkim.

One of the thralls stumbled forward, and then stepped sideways as if he were on the point of making off.

"You come here!" shouted Thorkim. He sprang forward and, striking the thrall across the face, sent him staggering toward the Roman.

"There . . . Take him—he's yours!" he shouted.

The people in the hall thought Thorkim's outburst of temper was the result of the high price he had to pay for the gold trinket. A thrall for a clasp! It was not to be wondered at that it made his blood boil.

But when he turned round to Hugwa's daughter his anger had blown away.

"Here, Groa. Take it," he muttered, as his hand closed over her fingers. Groa tried to imagine how beautifully it would suit her when it was placed, gleaming like a sun, on her shoulder. But she suddenly turned pale, for not two yards away Odbjørn stood staring at her. Never before had she seen his eyes so narrow, with such ferocity lurking behind them. A deep blush flushed her cheeks.

"No," she said. "No . . . !" She pulled her hand away. The trinket fell to the floor and rolled under the trestle table.

There was a deathly silence in the hall.

"You won't accept a trinket as a gift from me?"

Thorkim's voice rang out loudly in the stillness. The village folk saw that his narrow lips were bloodless and colorless.

"The thought does you credit, Thorkim," Groa said quietly. "But I can't accept your gift."

"Why not?"

Groa brushed her hair from her cheek and drew with her finger on the black cloth. But she did not answer.

No, for even the women of the settlement dared not let their lips form the words, not even as a whisper. But nevertheless they wondered if it could be true that the rich farmer's daughter had conceived an affection for this lazy young good-for-nothing from the hut in the heather—this Odbjørn the Nameless. Shame upon her if it were so!

There was a hush in Hugwa's hall. What would happen now? Would Thorkim bend his back and gather up his rejected gift? All eyes were upon Hamund's son.

Suddenly they heard a crash down by the gable end. It sounded as if roof and posts had come tumbling about their ears. And look! There was Odbjørn's horse coming through the doorway!

He had grown weary of standing all by himself out there in the yard, listening to the whistling of the wind in his fetlocks. And so he was now coming indoors, as his habit was at home in the heather-covered hills. But this time Graywind had taken a beam with him across his back. With a resounding crash Hugwa's doorway had been made bigger.

Freeman and thrall stepped hastily aside, giving way before the horse's heavy chest as it plowed forward through the hall like a ship's prow. Jagged bits of broken lintel slipped off the horse's back and landed on the floor in a succession of splintering thuds.

Hugwa was startled by the sound of hoof beats in the hall. The silence and the words between Groa and Thorkim had passed unnoticed, but the rumbling blows on the floorboards made the farmer stiffen just as he was about to thrust a white salty finger into his beard. He turned around, and the first thing he saw was the splintered doorframe. Then he saw Graywind standing behind Odbjørn and butting him like a ram. Rage came creeping up out of Hugwa's beard and painted his face blood red.

"May the spirit in the Tree of the Giants splinter your bones!" he bellowed. Broad-shouldered and heavily-built, he advanced upon Odbjørn.

"What's got into you? Are you stark staring mad, boy?"

With feet planted apart, he stood in front of Odbjørn. He had grasped his beard in his hand and pulled down his jaw.

"There will pretty soon have to be a limit to your impudence!" he shouted. "What do you mean by pulling down the gable end and dragging your flea-bitten jade into the hall! Do you imagine you're at home where man and beast feed out of the same trough?"

Odbjørn felt a multitude of eyes fasten upon him like pinpricks. His cheeks burned with shame. But suddenly he turned to Hugwa.

"At any rate, I notice you've got a swine walking about

your hall!" he cried contemptuously, nodding towards Thorkim.

An indrawn breath of fear passed through the hall.

Thorkim immediately whipped his sword out of its sheath. Those who were standing near backed away from Odbjørn, and he was left alone in the midst of a hostile crowd as Thorkim advanced slowly upon him—slowly and deliberately, with hatred gleaming in his eyes. His mouth with its narrow lips was twisted into a scornful grin. He had gripped the sword by its two-edged blade and handled it as if it were a stake with which he intended to give Odbjørn a hiding. But Odbjørn knew how swift Thorkim's movements could be. He would suddenly whirl the sword in the air, grasp the hilt and strike a deadly blow before his opponent was aware that anything had happened. Nevertheless, Odbjørn remained standing there with folded arms and looked Thorkim straight in the eye.

"Stop!" bawled Hugwa.

But Thorkim wasn't to be stopped—not before he was standing within two paces of Odbjørn. He drew his breath jerkily and heavily. Then Odbjørn saw it, the sign in Thorkim's face, an almost invisible twitching at the corner of his mouth. The sword whirled into the air—and then . . .

Odbjørn's sword flashed from its scabbard. Like a slashing whip, it met Thorkim's blade a hand's breadth above Odbjørn's head. He sprang aside beneath a shower of sparks—and more swiftly than a spark vanishes, he had raised his sword and lunged obliquely at Thorkim's shoulder.

But the thrust never reached its mark. Instead, it encountered Hugwa's broadsword from below, and it was like hewing at a rock. The sword flew out of his hand across the floor.

"Away with you!" bellowed Hugwa, and the spit sprayed out of his beard and caught Odbjørn across the face. "And keep away, so long as you can bring nothing but strife with you!" The farmer had raised his hand to strike, but when he met the lad's eyes he let his hand fall.

Odbjørn turned on his heel. With one bound he sprang upon Graywind's back, tugged the horse around by the mane and, as he thundered away over the floor, made the splinters fly about the horse's hoofs. Twice he swung the horse around in the hall. Shouting and bits of splintered wood and the screaming of women followed him on his way as he burst through the doorway.

3

Aboard the Roman Galley

For two whole days Odbjørn sat brooding in a dark corner up in the hayloft. Tova placed an earthenware dish and drinking cup in the loft as though for an invisible house goblin.

"Do eat now," she begged. "Do you hear me?"

But she got no answer.

Ketil and Aslak tiptoed about the place hushing one another, and they would stealthily plod some distance from the hut if they had but a couple of words to exchange.

Odbjørn would sometimes slip down from the hayloft on to Graywind's back and gallop northward along the coast. Afterward the horse would stand beneath the hayloft steaming with sweat, his flanks heaving like a pair of bellows.

He did not show himself in the village, and no one set eyes on him during the days that followed the scene in Hugwa's hall. And there was no one who missed him.

That day in the hall he had felt their hostility like a wall about him. If only a single one of them—Hjald or Groa—or Hugwa, perhaps—if only one of that crowd had stood by him, then he would have held out his hand and made his peace with Thorkim. But he was a stranger—a man without kin whose friendship no one valued.

But they would live to regret it one day—the day he headed into the fiord with a ship filled with warriors and oarsmen—as tightly packed as meat in a barrel of salt . . . Odbjørn sat up in the hayloft and swore vengeance on the settlement.

Then one morning Odbjørn came to a decision . . .

He rode around behind the village and out to the headland, where he stood hidden behind the trees, waiting till he saw the Roman come out of Hugwa's hall and go down to the beach.

He jumped off his horse and grabbed the Roman by his long red cloak.

"Take me with you when you sail," he whispered, his voice hoarse and breathless. The Roman fell back a step. What did this lad want? Then he witnessed a strange sight. The fellow crawled under his horse's forelegs and braced his back against the animal's chest. And just look if he didn't . . . ! The Roman opened his mouth, gaping with astonishment. This lad's slender body had raised the horse's forelegs clean off the ground!

"I'm strong," Odbjørn said. "I could be useful to you. Take me with you! Do you hear me?"

But the Roman did not understand the strange sounds that came tumbling, hoarse and uncertain, from the boy's lips. He shook his head vigorously.

Then Odbjørn clenched his teeth and leaped astride Graywind. At furious speed he galloped around and around the Roman, now hanging under the horse's belly, his head not a hand's breath from the whirling earth, now clinging to the horse's neck and raising himself upright on the animal's back. Then he jumped down and stood quivering and panting in front of the Roman merchant.

"Take me with you!" he begged, pointing to the Roman galley.

And then the Roman suddenly understood him. He pointed to Odbjørn, to the galley and the sea behind them. And he had taught himself a word or two of the language these skin-clad barbarians spoke.

"You—with me?" he asked.

Odbjørn nodded eagerly.

"Good," said the Roman. Then he pointed to the sun and the heather-covered hills, and uttered one or two sounds, a scrap or two of Odbjørn's mother tongue.

Odbjørn understood that the Roman ship was to sail early the following morning, before the sun had risen above the roof ridge of Hamund's farmstead.

He had told no one—neither Groa nor his blood brother, Hjald. He had not even told the bondswoman Tova that this would be his last night in the hut among the heather, that before daybreak he would be aboard the Roman galley. Nevertheless, the bondswoman woke up with a strange uneasiness in her mind, a feeling as if a great hand were clutching at her heart. Then all at once she heard the sound of hoof beats and she saw a dark shadow gliding towards the doorway.

"Odbjørn," she called, and as the shadow stiffened and came to a halt, Tova got up and tottered toward him. "Where are you off to so early?" she asked plaintively, her thin hands creeping uncertainly over his chest, her fingers clinging to his belt and the leather thongs that fastened his tunic, like hooks that would not let go—for she suspected the worst.

"I'm going away with the Roman ship," he said.

"No . . . no!" she groaned. "Don't do it!" And she would not let go of him.

"Be quiet, Tova, its no good," he said. "I'm only in the way here, a laughingstock for every bondsman!"

"Who dares to laugh at you?" cried Tova with a threatening ring in her voice.

"When I come back I'll endure no more contempt or ridicule! I'll build a hall where the hut stands, Tova, and you shall have young bondswomen to give you a hand in the house. The flames from your hearth will be reflected from hundreds of gleaming bronze vessels!"

As he gave her his solemn word, Odbjørn stood in the doorway of the hut, the moonlight painting shadowy lines on his pale cheeks. And all at once Tova realized, as if for the first time, that the boy was a boy no longer. Now she knew that she could not keep him back, and so she let go of him and stepped unsteadily back into the darkness of the hut.

"Wait a bit!" she cried.

He heard her pottering about the hearth, and then she came back dragging a heavy skin bundle.

"Here," she said, "here's something to keep you going for the first two or three days. You can never tell what queer food the strangers are used to!"

She fastened the bundle across his shoulders. In the hay Aslak moaned and turned in his sleep, and Odbjørn caught a glimpse of the pale old faces, like patches of mist in the darkness.

"Tell the two old men that when I come back they shall have a seat close to the hearth-fire in a hall that's free from draughts," he muttered. He half turned away from the bondswoman, as though he would turn his back in farewell and so slip out through the door. And then—for all her years of slavery, she now forgot herself—she drew the boy's head down and pressed his face to her wrinkled cheek.

"If only you find your way home again," she whispered, rumpling his hair. "Promise me you'll come back!"

But Odbjørn could make no promise, for something choked his throat and he was unable to speak. He pulled himself away from the bondswoman and galloped off down the depression in the hillside. A moment later horse and rider had vanished in the sea mist that hung like a pale silvery haze in the moonlight about the heather-covered slopes.

Close by the sacred grove he drew rein and jumped off his horse.

Up in the sky scattered clouds drifted across the face of the moon, and the sacred grove seemed one moment to withdraw into the darkness only to creep forward the next to meet him in the moonlight. He led the horse over toward the grove. On the edge of the wood stood the image of Frey, its grinning face in a half-circle of moonlight, and Odbjørn made a sweeping detour to avoid the goddess of fertility. Slowly and with some hesitation he disappeared into the darkness of the grove.

There before the temple gable stood the figure of the god Tyr beneath the heavy branches of the trees of sacrifice. To Tyr he was prepared to sacrifice and offer up the dearest of his possessions before he departed.

The horse pushed his soft muzzle into the back of Odbjørn's neck and blew a warm stream of breath through his hair. A cold shudder passed through him.

Above his head the wind soughed in the fir tops with the murmur of the sea. But sacrificial trees were green tongues that lent voices to the gods—it was Tyr whispering and moaning there in the darkness.

He slid his sword out, holding it close to his body so that Graywind should not set eyes on it.

"For success and prosperity in strange places!" he muttered. "For strength in arm and sword! For victory in warfare, and for much booty!" he whispered in a shaking voice. He took aim at the horse's neck and raised his sword.

The horse's quivering nostrils were examining Tyr inquistively, snorting and blowing into his wooden face. With the animal's neck stretched forward like that, Odbjørn would be able to strike through the vertebrae close behind the ears. Graywind would have a swift death. He would know nothing.

He stood with his sword poised. The blood ran from his arms until they tingled and stung.

"Strike!" whispered a voice inside Odbjørn—or perhaps it was Tyr's voice in the humming fir tops.

He shut his eyes so that he should not see the horse's shadowy back—but behind his closed lids he saw the foal Graywind lying wrapped in hides and rags.

"Strike then!" whispered the voice.

"No!" Odbjørn shouted, his voice rumbling through the trees of the sacred grove and returning like a hollow cry from the pillars of the gods standing round him in the darkness.

And at that moment Graywind whinnied.

Odbjørn started, and with one bound he leaped onto the horse's back.

"Here! You must be content with that! I ask nothing in return!"

He flung a handful of amber at Tyr's head, and the pieces hit the temple of the gods like drumming rain. As he swung Graywind around, the horse lashed out with his hind legs and struck Tyr. There was a noise of splintering wood as Tyr's image toppled over and crashed heavily against the door of the temple. In wild flight Odbjørn galloped in and out among the trees of the sacred grove, branches and twigs whipping his face and leaving it marked. Then suddenly he was aware of heavy raindrops on his burning cheeks.

A gale had blown up. As he rode out to the open meeting place, the wind met him, blowing a stinging rain into his face. The rain drove slanting in from the sea, weaving a gray net over the breaking day.

"The Roman ship will never get out of the fiord in this wind," he thought. But how could it be otherwise when he had offered Tyr nothing but a few pieces of amber—and given him a blow in the face with a horse's hoof in the bargain?

Dispirited and soaked to the skin, Odbjørn rode on toward the coast. He sat listening to the muffled thunder of the breakers on the beach, and he felt that ill-luck and adversity had already clung to him and would never more let go.

Over by the settlement he saw freeman and thrall seeking shelter under the overhanging eaves of the houses. Clad in hat and cloak, they stood huddled together, waiting patiently to watch the Roman ship put out to sea.

As Odbjørn turned off to ride around the back of the settlement, a horseman appeared from behind Hugwa's hall and made toward him. When, after a bit, the horseman rode up by his side, he saw it was Hjald, and although he was well hidden in hat and cloak Odbjørn recognized him. For a long time they rode side by side in silence. The sound of rain pelting down and hoofs sloshing through the sodden meadowland was all they heard.

Suppose it wasn't Hjald after all?

It might be Thorkim. He laid his hand on his sword hilt and glanced at the silent horseman. His cloak was turned up and covered his face—if, indeed, he had a face, for the rainsoaked hat seemed to rest on top of the cloak.

Odbjørn shuddered. He was on the point of digging his heels into the horse's flanks when the other drew himself up in the saddle and turned toward him. And it was Hjald. But his face was stern and his eyes flashed beneath the hat.

"Strangely as you behaved that day in the hall . . ." he began.

Odbjørn was silent.

"What did you mean by insulting Thorkim like that? What's he done to you?

Odbjørn compressed his lips and looked away.

"Answer me then!" cried Hjald, seizing him by the arm.

"Odbjørn . . ." His voice sounded differently now. "Do you realize you're driving everybody away from you with your pig-headedness? You'll soon have no friends left."

"I know. But you'll very soon be rid of me!"

"What do you mean by that?" cried Hjald.

At that moment he caught sight of the bundle hanging over his blood brother's shoulder.

"You mustn't!" he shouted.

Odbjørn turned and looked at him.

"What mustn't I?"

"You mustn't go with the Roman! That's what you're going to do! But I forbid you!"

"You?" said Odbjørn, and he saw a strange anxiety deep within Hjald's eyes. A mocking smile spread over Odbjørn's lips.

"Thorkim might refuse me a place in his outward-bound ship, but you, Hjald . . . You can't stop me sailing with the Roman!"

"Odbjørn, don't you understand . . . ?" Hjald hesitated. His lips were trembling, and once more Odbjørn saw the fear in his eyes.

"When your beard's grown a little thicker, you can let your mouth tremble like a woman's without anybody seeing it—but until then you should try to curb your weakness!"

Odbjørn's sarcasm brought the blood to Hjald's cheeks. He passed his hand over the downy growth that was his pride.

"Listen," he said. "I know Thorkim demanded a high

price when you asked for a place in his ship. All the same, you could have bought a place if you'd let my father lend you what Thorkim wanted. But you were too proud to do it. And I understand that. I understand, too, your wanting to seek your fortune in strange lands. But don't do it, Odbjørn! Wait till another time!"

"But why?"

"Because . . ." Hjald twined his fingers in his horse's name and hesitated a moment. "Just look at the sea, Odbjørn! You know well enough what it means. No ship will sail over the sand banks in this weather. But not a single man dares tell the Roman that! They're all afraid he'll think we're womanish folk, frightened of our own sea. So they won't tell him that none of us would venture to sail out of the fiord the way the wind's blowing now."

They had got down to beach. Beyond the headland the breakers were thundering against the cliffs. Even in the comparative calm of the fiord the sea was rough and the waves broke into foam over the horses' hoofs.

"It's certain death!" Hjald yelled into the wind.

"Perhaps it isn't for the Roman ship!" shouted Odbjørn.

He rode his horse out into the water and Hjald followed him.

"Promise me you'll take Graywind back to the hut!" he shouted.

Hjald nodded. His eyes were fixed on the golden-colored planks of the Roman ship and the countless oars that stuck out like spikes from the oarports.

"And if my father's helmsman, Ulver, comes back before I do, ask him to wait as long as I've waited for him!"

They reached the ship's side. Odbjørn's shouting had attracted one of the Romans. They saw his helmet bob up behind the bulwarks, and shortly afterwards a rope ladder was thrown down to them.

"Look there! Look, Odbjørn!" Hjald sprang back with a start.

A broad thickset man, his breast covered in scaly iron plates, had thrown a hatch open and crawled down into the hold.

"Just look!" Hjald pulled his friend over to the scuttle.

Down in the half-darkness of the hold they could just make out a tangled mass of arms and legs. At that moment a reddish light spread down below, and they saw that along each side of the ship ran two decks of massive oak. Fifty-odd rowers sat there divided between the rowing decks. A rank smell of sweat rose through the scuttle. The smell of sweat —and the clanking of chains.

"They're chained to the ship!" exclaimed Hjald. "If the ship goes down, then . . ." The thought terrified him and he fell silent.

One of the galley slaves had turned his face up toward them. They saw him screw up his eyes against the dazzling daylight from the scuttle. His face was gray and pale—like the light he so seldom glimpsed.

Down below a stocky warrior appeared from behind the ladder. He carried a hide whip in his hand. They heard him fill the hold with noisy shouting, and they heard the whip crack over the naked backs of the galley slaves. Muffled groans rose up through the scuttle.

The warrior with the lash returned and took his place on the lowest step, and when the two blood brothers looked up their eyes fell upon a Roman warrior who had taken his stand near the scuttle. The face under the helmet looked as if it had been made of bronze, so sun-tanned and lifeless was it. His brown eyes looked right through them. Up on the bridge amidships they caught sight of yet another Roman statue. The fellow, who was wearing a red cloak, was apparently the ship's master.

"Think about it again!" whispered Hjald. "They're quite

likely to pitch you down among the galley slaves as soon as
you're on the open sea!"

"It'll take more than one to decide that!" answered
Odbjørn.

"May Tyr stand by your side and add strength to your
sword-stroke!" Hjald held out his hand.

"I've splintered Tyr's face," said Odbjørn.

"That, too!" Hjald said quietly. "Then you've nothing
but my good wishes to keep you. My familiar spirit stand
by you when you're in need of help!"

Odbjørn watched Hjald slip astride his horse, take hold
of Graywind's mane and ride in toward the beach.

He stood and followed him with his eyes. And he saw
little knots of people gathering on the beach. But his eyes
did not find the one he was looking for.

4

Salute to a Hero

The Roman merchant had come aboard and was standing amidships in conversation with the master. Two Romans were by the tackle ready to heave up the anchor. And other Romans were standing about the deck, each at his station with his eyes fixed on the master. He was talking to the merchant, pointing out to sea and up at the sky.

"The strangers find it difficult to keep their arms still when they're talking," Odbjørn thought. "The master's throwing his arms about as if he were fighting for dear life with sword and spear at one and the same time!"

Odbjørn let his eyes wander over to the settlement, but he could see nothing of Groa, though Hjald must have told her by now that he had embarked in the Roman ship. His hand closed tightly around the mainstay. He turned his face into the gale and the stinging rain, but nothing would serve to cool the hot blood beating in his throat.

Suddenly a shrill screeching pierced the sound of the wind and made Odbjørn jump. He heard the high-pitched whine of the tackle, and then . . . The oars rose like the bars of a cage between him and the settlement and then disappeared in a swirl of foam alongside the ship. The galley trembled and swung around. Slowly she gathered speed, and the settlement receded—as if the halls and huts were moving slowly inland. Odbjørn ran aft and slipped behind the helmsman. He clung to the rail as the stern rose and fell, and it was the halls and huts, the whole coastline, that seemed to be rocking up and down. The settlement appeared and disappeared behind the bulwarks. But there was nothing to be seen of her, and the people were now growing too small to distinguish.

As the galley ran out into the open sea a thundering roar of surf closed in upon her. The prow was drenched in the heavy waves that crashed over her, and white clouds of foamy spray drove across the deck. The galley was brought momentarily to a standstill, as though by the spell of the sea. Loud shouts and the crack of the whip were heard from below, and the stroke increased. The oars clove air and wave furiously: taut as bent bows, they swept the foaming surf astern. The galley was under way . . . Slowly, and creaking in every joint, her stem plowed through the heavy seas.

The headland was now slipping past on the larboard side, the headland and . . . Odbjørn started.

The cairn . . . !

"Groa!" he shouted. The gale snatched the word from his mouth and no one heard him. He spun around from the rail and staggered across the pitching deck as though he would call all the world to witness the miracle he had seen —a green bough shooting from a gray granite boulder!

The branch on the cairn was Groa's signal to him—it meant that she was waiting for him in the wood behind the headland. But Odbjørn was aboard the Roman ship standing out of the fiord, and he could not . . .

The helmsman jumped out of his skin, unable to believe his own eyes, as he saw . . . Look if that wild barbarian hadn't jumped onto the rail!

The helmsman slipped the steering oar under his arm,

and with his mallet hammered the gleaming metal gong that hung at his side. The vibrant clanging cut through the gale.

"Seize him!" bawled the master.

Odbjørn saw two Roman warriors coming toward him, and one of them sprang forward to catch hold of him. And so he jumped . . .

The oars whirled around him like flails, and as one caught him a blow across the shoulder a sting of pain passed through his body like a quivering flash of lightning. The next moment the water closed over his head, and the blades of the oars, like so many hard hands, cast him aside through a whistling spray of white foam . . .

"And is that the only reason you put the signal on the cairn?"

Odbjørn's voice was dark with anger.

"Yes, that's all," she said. "Because I didn't want to see you drown. Hjald says the Roman ship won't get across the sand banks in this gale."

They were standing in the wood on the cliff top, Odbjørn and the girl Groa. The water was streaming from his tattered tunic and his cheeks were blue with cold. Groa stood thoughtfully raking the fallen leaves together with her foot. Thongs of pigskin crisscrossed her rounded calves, and a heavy girdle of silver gathered her woolen dress in about her slim waist. Suddenly she threw her hair back and looked up at him. Her eyes were dark and serious, but a roguish smile played at the corners of her mouth.

"Because I knew you'd come, Odbjørn."

He did not hear what she said. As he had tumbled down among the whirling oars, he already regretted what he had done, and the water roaring in his ears sounded like a burst of mocking laughter.

"I shall be a laughingstock for everybody now," he muttered.

"What does that matter? And Odbjørn," she said eagerly, "another time I won't stop you from going away. And I'll wait for you—I'll wait till you come back—I promise! Smile then! Do you hear me? Your mouth so rarely smiles, Odbjørn." She laughed mischievously and tried to lift the corners of his mouth with her two fingers, but Odbjørn turned away from her and went off through the wood. And he did not smile.

Nor did he when he caught sight of Hjald behind the wood. Withdrawn and silent, he walked toward Graywind.

"Don't ride down to the settlement," Hjald advised him.

"Why not?" asked Odbjørn, his mouth set obstinately in his pale face.

"Wait till tomorrow or . . ."

"Till they've forgotten the sight they saw when I deserted from the Roman ship! Is that what you mean? But I'll ride wherever it suits me!" he cried.

And Hjald saw him ride down along the foreshore toward the settlement.

They stood on the beach in front of Hugwa's hall and watched the Roman ship cross the first two sand banks without running aground. The ship had sailed a fair way from land and looked no bigger than a man's fist. From time to time a heavy squall of rain would draw a gray veil over the sea and hide the ship from view.

Many were of the opinion that in spite of everything the Roman would clear the banks, but when the older men heard that sort of talk it seemed to give them a pain somewhere inside. They laid their wrinkled faces to one side and nodded to one another to show they knew better.

"Everyone's bound to know that in this weather no one could clear that last bank!"

A shout went up that the Roman had disappeared—and it was neither rain nor the crests of the waves that hid her now.

"She's gone behind the bar!" yelled Vrage, Hunved's thrall.

They made their way to the point, clambering and running as if they were all arms and legs. When they reached it, they saw that the galley had swung broadside to the shore, her bows pointing to the north. And now they knew that the hand of Njord was on the Roman, for when Njord cast a ship broadside over the banks neither sorcery nor magic spell would avail.

A whisper went round that Thorkim was going to try running his boat out of the fiord to go to the Roman's rescue. And so he was . . . For when they got down to the fiord again they saw Thorkim standing in his ship with the steering oar clamped firmly under his armpit. He had braced one foot against the jetty to prevent the boat from being stove in against the posts. The men he had got together during the course of the winter for his long voyage were already sitting on the thwarts with oars raised and faces pale and resolute. Thorkim was in no hurry to slip his moorings, for there were still two thwarts standing empty.

"Four more men!" he called out. "There's room for four more!"

A dozen men fought and struggled to push their way forward and set foot over Thorkim's gunwale, and the planks of the jetty swayed beneath them.

At that moment Hugwa came out from the shore, bawling at them to make way. Behind Hugwa came six thralls trudging along with Thorkim's father. Old Hamund, who had lost the use of his legs, had had himself carried down to the beach on oak planks and thralls' backs to watch the Roman ship cross the banks in the teeth of the gale.

Thorkim was standing in his boat, talking, as men will, with the old men on the jetty. He stuck to his point, refusing to give way, and Hamund, proud of his son, nodded approval.

"I can make use of four men!" Thorkim cried. "Now, this minute!"

And there stood Odbjørn. He was right in front and stepped onto the gunwale, but Thorkim gave him a push in the chest with his steering oar so that he tumbled backward and landed on his back on the planks of the jetty.

"I can do without you!" he shouted. "I've no use for men who jump overboard as soon as the ship begins to rock!"

A burst of laughter greeted Thorkim's words.

"Hey, Odbjørn! Are you here again?"

"Who?" shouted a voice from the shore.

"Why, Odbjørn—Tova's young cub! Here he lies, back from his voyage to foreign parts!"

"Did you manage to catch a glimpse of the Roman coastline before you jumped overboard?"

He rose slowly to his feet. His cheeks were red with shame and his lips quivered, but his eyes were ablaze with fury. He could see nothing but grinning faces around him and the folk from the settlement standing shoulder to shoulder and barring his way. When they saw his eyes they looked away and glanced at one another with a smirk of derision in their beards.

Just as Odbjørn drew his sword, and in a furious temper was about to hack his way through the crowd, Hjald pushed forward and seized his wrist.

"Odbjørn," he whispered, "they'll bind you with cords and throw you alive into the bog! What else can you expect? Come to your senses, for heaven's sake! Put your sword up!" he whispered.

Then suddenly he turned and faced the men on the jetty. And if Odbjørn's cheeks were red as blood, Hjald's were deathly pale, like the mist that comes creeping in from the sea at daybreak.

"Make way for my blood brother!" he cried.

If only the gale had drowned his words! A gasp went up from the crowd. If only the gale . . . ! "Blood brother," he had said! Hare's blood had been mingled with Hugwa's. So much the worse for Hjald!

The men moved aside to make way for him. But as Odbjørn went by they turned their backs on him, and when his cloak brushed against them they spat on the planks of the jetty and muttered the name of Tyr.

Three times Thorkim turned his prow into the surf, but each time the heavy seas flung the boat back into the fiord. Only when he had tried the fourth time did he give up and beach the boat. The oarsmen's hands were bleeding, and Thorkim had held the steering oar so hard it had scored a red mark across his chest. Everyone could see that they had all done their duty, and Thorkim gathered a harvest of praise and glory for the deed, even though he had not succeeded in bringing help to the Roman.

The Roman galley was driven a fair way to the north. Toward evening a mountainous wave lifted the ship into the air and dropped her heavily onto the middle bank. They seemed to hear through the howling of the gale the rending of splitting timbers. For a brief second the galley remained on an even keel. Then she listed and heeled over. As the deck was turned toward the shore, they could make out three men clinging to the planks. The mast had broken off and driven its point into the sea bed some way from the galley, and there it stood poking up out of the water like the shaft of a spear.

The folk from the settlement expected every moment to see the ship break up, but she lay there for a long time lashed by the surf without budging from the sand bank. The heavy beating of the waves raised a white crest of foam over the capsized hull. The oars sticking out from the ship's side moved now and again, as if the galley were a great dying insect lying on its back and fumbling weakly for a foothold.

Odbjørn lay in the heather-covered hills and followed the galley's death struggle among the breakers. The sight of the oars, restless and groping in the air like the legs of an insect, brought to his mind the chained galley-slaves—for them there would be no rescue.

It had begun to grow dark.

Down on the beach a bonfire had been lit. The howling wind whipped the tops off the blustering flames and whirled tatters of fire up into the blue twilight sky. The folk from the settlement stood round silent and motionless, with the firelight flickering on their coarse cloaks. As the waves broke with a dull thunder on the beach, the water flowed like foaming blood, roaring and seething, into the red circle of firelight.

And then all at once something was happening . . .

Odbjørn jumped to his feet.

Beyond the galley a gigantic wave had risen, a rolling mountain with a foaming peak tossing and curling forward. The galley rose, sliding up the mountainous slopes of water. The wave lifted the ship off the bottom and carried her over the bar. The next moment there was a sound of splintering and cracking, followed by a heavy rumbling thunder. In the swirling foam they saw the capsized Roman ship rise. They caught a glimpse of the black keel timbers, and as the waves settled again they could just see an oar sticking up out of the water. It swept over the surface of the foam like the faltering leg of an insect. The Roman ship had disappeared.

But there in the surf . . . Look over there!

The gale carried a confused sound of voices up to Odbjørn. The people down on the foreshore were running this way and that, pointing excitedly toward the spot where the galley had disappeared. What was the matter with them? Odbjørn saw two men separate themselves from the crowd and set off at a run toward the village. And then he caught sight of the dark object out at sea. Close to the spot where the galley had gone down a man lay clinging to a piece of wreckage. Only now and again did he come to sight in the heavy surf, but the drifting timber, which Odbjørn recognized as the broken mast, rose above the foaming seas. The next time he caught sight of the dark object it was clear that the man was losing his hold on the mast—bit by bit the waves were dragging it from his grasp. One moment more and then . . .

Odbjørn dug his heels so hard into Graywind's flanks that he reared. He jerked and pulled the horse's head around until he had turned his muzzle into the howling wind.

"Come on . . . Forward!" he yelled.

And Graywind advanced.

With heavy hoofbeats and distended nostrils, the horse made his way down from the cliff. Odbjørn urged him forward, past the bonfire and in among the village folk who ran for dear life with the sand flying about their ears.

"Who was that?"

"That was Odbjørn!" came the answering shout.

"Odbjørn?" they gasped, with here and there a mouth left wide open like a hole in the beard.

"What's up now? What's he after?"

He drove the horse forward toward the breakers. But there on the beach Graywind dug his hoofs into the sand, swung round and galloped back over the foreshore, scattering the village folk like chaff before the wind. Odbjørn gave the horse free rein around the fire, and then he tried again. He threw himself forward and struck the horse across the muzzle.

"Come on then!" he yelled. "Come on . . . !"

But Graywind drove his gray-fetlocked feet into the sand and pulled up in front of the foaming breakers. Then Odbjørn took hold of him by the forelock and forced him backward into the sea, step by step, with the waves breaking over his hocks. He snorted and trembled and stopped short, but Odbjørn, leaning over backward and tugging at the forelock, forced his muzzle up until it pointed toward the scudding clouds.

From higher up the beach came a wondering murmur.

"What does he think he's doing, the mad fool? . . . The crazy lad, the . . ."

They clenched their hands and jabbed their neighbors in the shoulder with their fingers. The women bit their nails and dared not look—and yet they had to in spite of themselves.

The horse's hoofs were no longer touching the bottom. Odbjørn, clinging to his flanks, forced him around, and Graywind swam out with his nostrils above the foam-whipped sea.

Odbjørn was near the mast now—near the dark object. A heavy wave raised a steep wall of water in front of him, and the next moment the wave broke over him. Down and down he sank, gasping for breath, his mouth and throat filled with water. He put his hands out, clutched the horse's legs and pulled himself up. At the same time something heavy struck him over the hips, sending a dull pain through his body. The black object returned and gave him a blow across the shoulders, and as he stretched his arm out his hand touched the mast. The water closed over them with a hissing rush. Odbjørn was aware of a pair of strong arms locked about his neck, the mast slipped from his grasp and he was forced to let go of the horse. The Roman was crazed with fear. He clung to Odbjørn with a grip of steel, and as he dragged him down, Odbjørn struck out at his jaw—again and again until the Roman let go and slipped away from him. He just managed to grasp him by the tunic before he disappeared. Then he kicked out and seized Graywind around the neck.

Everything went black in front of his eyes and he vomited. Far, far away he heard the horse snort. Even farther away he heard the thundering breakers like a distant rumbling—he felt just as if he were lying in the straw at night up in the hut and listening to the breathing of the sea. Under both arms he was holding something big and heavy, something he knew he must not let go of. It was as if he were trudging home exhausted with a sack under each arm.

As he felt a jar go through the horse's body, he thrust a leg up over the animal's back, dragging the Roman after him. Graywind had firm ground under his hoofs, and his back rose slowly out of the water.

The horse came to a halt in the red circle of firelight. Sea water streamed from his dusky coat, streamed and dripped from his fetlocks and the fringe under his belly, the drops glistened like blood in the gleam of the fire.

The folk from the settlement had formed a ring around Odbjørn and his horse. Hjald was stroking Graywind's wet muzzle, and Une Ulfkil was standing there lost for words and patting Odbjørn on the knee. Then Hjald cried out, "You will all want to honor what we've all seen with our own eyes. Long life to my blood brother Odbjørn!"

Swords flew from their sheaths and the clash of blade against blade sounded like the screeching of gulls.

And there, a little way off, stood Groa. She withdrew her hands hesitantly from her face, which she had covered in her fear and anxiety. But she was smiling now. Tossing her hair back over her shoulders, she smiled at Odbjørn with eyes filled with pride and wonder.

But Odbjørn did not see her—he saw no one. He let the senseless Roman slide down onto the sand and brushed Ulfkil's hand away from his knee.

"Make way!" cried Hjald. And Odbjørn rode out of the crowd up over the dunes. Trembling with exhaustion, Graywind plodded on into the heather-covered hills.

But Aslak was home first!

The old man had been lying in the heather, following with his eyes everything that had taken place on the beach. Now he got to his feet and, rolling bowlegged over the hills, was the first to tell Ketil all that he had seen.

"There he is . . . There he comes!"

The two old men stood scratching themselves and grinning sheepishly. Aslak jumped forward first and took Graywind by the muzzle. But Ketil had now come forward and was there to help Odbjørn to the ground. And when Odbjørn put an arm over his shoulder to support himself, Ketil could not help a sly glance in Aslak's direction—and, sure enough, there stood Aslak green with envy!

"Odbjørn!" cried Tova, clapping her hands.

"You've got me back again. I got no farther than the headland this time," he mumbled.

More he could not say, his legs gave way under him and he collapsed in the hay at Tova's feet.

5

Hugwa's Vow at the Folk-meet

The moon was hanging in the sky like a golden sickle the night Odbjørn bore the Roman merchant from the breakers and saved his life. That night the water was emptied out of the Roman, and his clothes were dried by the hearth fire in Hugwa's hall. And as the days went by he recovered his strength again.

But he had hardly recovered when he underwent the same fate as the moon in the sky, which has scarcely grown large and round before it is on the wane again. The Roman sat in a corner of the hall wasting away in rivalry with the moon. A shudder passed through the women whenever they happened to look into his dark eyes, which, full of a boundless homesickness, seemed to stare straight through posts and walls right to the end of the world.

But they also got a lot of rough fun out of the stranger's queer habits. Hugwa's men told them that during the night the Roman would shiver so violently with the cold that the benches shook under him. They would hear him creeping about in the dark gathering skins together, and every morning they would hear a puffing sound under the pile of skins—it was the Roman blowing on his fingers to warm them.

During the daytime, when the sun was high, he would go around behind the headland and sit naked on the edge of the beach. Those who had lain watching him from the woods said that he would pour water all over his body and scrape himself with a piece of iron.

"You'd have thought he'd had enough water to last him a lifetime!" was Fakar the bondsman's opinion.

A queer fellow, the Roman.

Every morning he shaved his cheeks which grew thinner and thinner. And time and again he would clip the raven-black hair that lay close and short over his forehead. All in all, he was more concerned with his appearance than any woman. If he was not sitting staring listlessly in front of him he would sit preening himself like a hen.

Then one day the Roman rose and went into the heather-covered hills to Odbjørn's hut . . .

Aslak and Ketil spotted him in good time, and managed to scuttle up into the loft and bury themselves in the hay before the Roman even stepped over the threshold. There they lay poking their heads out, and from below no one could tell what was hay and what was beard.

He had come to thank Odbjørn that he was still alive. During the change of moon while he had been sitting in Hugwa's hall, he had listened to the talk and learned quite a lot of their speech. He spoke readily and Odbjørn understood everything he said.

But when the Roman asked if he would go with him and help on the long journey back to the Roman Empire, Odbjørn hardly dared to believe he had heard aright.

And yet there was no mistaking what he said. The Roman repeated that the overland journey was long and dangerous—especially, he said, through the dark German forests. There in the innermost recesses between the tree trunks many a Roman soldier had disappeared without trace. He said this so that Odbjørn could think it over. He did not want to hear Odbjørn's reproaches if the savage Cherusci piled stones and tree trunks on top of them and sank them to the bottom of the marsh. But, he said, if they once succeeded in reaching the Rhine, then they would be safe. And then he would find the means to reward Odbjørn so richly that he would be far more wealthy and powerful than Hugwa himself.

"And he who is wealthy," he concluded, drawing a deep breath, "he who is wealthy can buy swords by the hundred —and the hands to wield them. Wealth is power, and with power you find men ready to serve your purpose!"

Odbjørn nodded. The words left a deep mark in his mind—as a man will set a ship's course by cutting a notch in the rail, so he now saw the way along which he should direct his steps. For the moment his path lay southward through the German forests.

"It's a promise," he said. "When the moon is up again in a couple of days, I shall be ready to start."

The bondswoman Tova had been standing behind the door, but not until the Roman had gone did she come forth.

"His eyes are as dark as a bottomless pit," she said. "Don't trust his word!"

But Odbjørn set up a shrill wolf howl and, taking Tova by the waist, whirled her around till she grew dizzy. Then he set about Ketil and Aslak, and as he dragged them down from the hayloft they came flying through the air with their legs doubled under them like a couple of frogs. The old men hiccoughed with laughter, Graywind neighed and Odbjørn howled like a wolf. For a long time the hut in the heather was filled with the noise of their horseplay.

The next day Odbjørn went down to Hugwa's hall to talk to the wealthy farmer. And he was in luck, for he found Hugwa alone in the hall, sitting in the high seat between the pillars. He sat leaning over the table with his heavy head propped on his hands.

"Well, Odbjørn . . . Odbjørn Sea-Rider!" he said. But as he wiped the froth of beer from his beard he suddenly caught sight of Graywind, who stood with his head and neck thrust through the doorway.

"Didn't I tell you to keep that studhorse away from my hall!" he shouted.

Odbjørn sprang to the door and slammed it in front of the horse. And when he came back Hugwa saw that the lad was pale about the cheeks.

"Well, what can I do for you?" he asked.

"I . . . I'm going away with the stranger," Odbjørn began, and came to a stop.

Hugwa nodded. "And so?"

"Many months may go by before I return home."

Hugwa nodded again.

"And so I want to ask you, Hugwa . . . if you'll keep Groa for me as my betrothed until I come back."

"What? Are you proposing, lad?" bawled Hugwa. "Have you the audacity to ask for Groa's hand?" He jumped up, banging his tankard on the table and making the boards creak. "Have you the impudence to . . ."

Odbjørn drew himself up and looked Hugwa firmly in the eye.

"Yes," he said.

The farmer turned his back. For a long time he stood staring at the patch of yellow light that penetrated the oil-skin-covered opening in the wall.

"It was a great deed you did that day among the breakers . . ." He was silent again, and Odbjørn heard the wind whistling through the cracks in the oilskin. "But do you think I'll hand my daughter over to live a thrall's life in a hut among the heather!"

"No," said Odbjørn. "When I return home I shall build a hall with a storehouse and a kitchen . . . and a long ship in the fiord . . . and . . ."

"I can see you expect to become a great man in foreign parts! But I shall have to disappoint you, Odbjørn. I've already as good as promised Groa to Thorkim when he returns from his voyage."

The farmer fell silent, and once more Odbjørn heard the whistling of the wind through the oilskin, but this time it sounded like a hiss.

Hugwa suddenly turned around.

"Listen . . . Ride up to Witulf the Priest . . . and over to Thorkim. Summon them both to the folk-meet! Didn't you hear what I'd said?" he shouted, taking a step towards Odbjørn. "What are you waiting for?"

Odbjørn jumped. Then he turned and set off at a run through the hall.

Close to the image of Frey, Hugwa drew rein and halted, and there they settled down to wait for the priest. Thorkim had ridden up to Hugwa's side, and every now and again he leaned over toward the old man and said something to him. But Hugwa did not answer. He sat heavy and round-shouldered in his saddle, gazing with unseeing eyes over the meetingplace.

A little way off Odbjørn sat astride Graywind, his hands clammy with sweat. He had no idea what Hugwa had in mind—neither he nor Thorkim knew what was going to happen. Perhaps someone had discovered Tyr's image, smashed and splintered, in the sacred grove? Perhaps they suspected him?

Hugwa straightened his back and sighed so heavily that his horse shifted.

Witulf now came riding across the flat open space where the folk-meet was held, his priest's dark cloak flapping like raven's wings at his back. His horse, a black jade, lean and spavined, hobbled toward them.

Odbjørn dried his hands on his horse's mane. He could feel drops of sweat tingling like pinpricks in his hair, but he dared not wipe the sweat off his forehead.

Witulf was now near enough for them to see the sooty streaks that darkened the deep furrows in his cheeks. Witulf was both priest and smith, and the swords he forged went through helmet and mail as if they were nothing but turfs and grass-sods. He muttered incantations over the glowing iron; and when the blade hardened, the power of the god Tyr resided in the metal.

"Well, Witulf's here now!" said Hugwa.

"What am I?" shouted Witulf, holding his dirty smith's hand behind his ear, for the blows of the sledge-hammer had dulled his hearing.

"Here!" thundered Hugwa. "You're here now!"

"Yes . . . yes," Witulf nodded, "I'm here now . . ."

"I've asked you to come so that you can call upon the gods to witness the challenge I now make Thorkim, Hamund's son, and Odbjørn the Nameless, whose kin no one knows."

Witulf rode closer to Hugwa, his hand cupped behind his ear.

"What's the matter with Hamund?" he shouted.

"There's nothing the matter with Hamund! It's about Thorkim and Odbjørn!" Hugwa bawled.

"Good, good . . . Thorkim and Odbjørn, then. Swear your oath, Hugwa, and give your challenge. I'm listening."

Hugwa tightened his reins, backing his horse so that he had all three of them in front of him.

"Odbjørn and Thorkim," he said, "you've both been to me to ask for Groa as your bride. But I've given my word to neither of you." He took a deep breath before he continued. "You are now departing, going each his own way to win fame and fortune in strange lands. Hear, then, what I swear before gods and men! To whichever of you returns home with the greater following—with the more armed men at his back—to him, and to no other, will I give Groa to be his promised bride.

"I give you both from now until we celebrate the spring sacrifice for the second time. You must both be back again by then. That night you must appear here at the folk-meet with the men who've sworn allegiance to you. Here before the image of Frey the folk from the village will gather, and Witulf the Priest and I will count your honor and worth by the number of men you have gathered about you in foreign lands."

"That night the grass of the meetingplace will be wet with blood!" snarled Thorkim, his thin lips frozen tight between hollowed cheeks. He rode his horse close in to Odbjørn, forcing Graywind to stamp backward into the undergrowth of the sacred grove. But Hugwa rode in between the two young fighting cocks.

"Blood will not flow that night!" he said. "And to avoid strife, you and your men, Thorkim, will ride up to the folk-meet from the village, and Odbjørn and his band will come from the north over the hills."

"Band!" Thorkim sneered. "All the men Odbjørn will muster will be the two old dodderers, Aslak and Ketil! But perhaps he'll bring the bondswoman Tova along with him, too!"

The blood mounted to Odbjørn's head and his hand went to his sword, but Hugwa's command stopped him.

"Hold your hand!" he shouted. "And now remember what I've said! When we celebrate the spring sacrifice for the second time, we meet here again. Now ride your separate ways and depart in peace!"

For a brief space the two young men glared into one another's eyes. Odbjørn's cheeks were flushed and hot, Thor-

kim's blotched with gray like a stormy sky, but the eyes of
both were full of hate and enmity.

"Off with you now!" shouted Hugwa.

Thorkim swung his horse around and galloped away over
the grass of the meetingplace.

Graywind trotted northward behind the sacred grove
and over the heather-covered hills with an Odbjørn who
was dreaming of all the deeds he was going to do in other
lands. The sound of the horse's hoofbeats changed in his
ears to the stroke of creaking oars, to the heavy measured
tread of warriors in their hundreds. A red mist shimmered
before his eyes as he reveled in the intoxication of power,
and once more he heard Hugwa's voice: "To the one who
returns with the greater number of men under arms . . . to
him will I give Groa . . . to the stronger . . . to the one who
comes to the folk-meet on the night of sacrifice with the
greater following."

6

The Price of Betrayal

The next day Odbjørn came down from the heather-covered hills and entered Hugwa's hall, and there in the darkest corner his eye fell upon the Roman sitting silent, gazing at a knot in one of the posts that supported the roof. He started as Odbjørn laid a hand upon his shoulder.

"I'm ready to go with you now," Odbjørn said. "If it suits you, we'll leave in the morning and journey southward."

If it suited him! He threw his arms round Odbjørn and hugged him.

"Even before Apollo drives his chariot of fire over the horizon's rim, I shall be ready and waiting for you!"

Odbjørn shook his head in mystification.

"Why!" said the Roman. "Before the sun is up . . . I stand ready and wait outside Hugwa's hall. Still dark . . . yet I stand and wait! You understand?"

Odbjørn nodded in silence and disappeared.

The Roman was restless. Hugwa sent him out to the bondswomen in the storehouse, and there he packed himself a parcel of meat done up in skins—the tough sinewy meat these crude Cimbrians wolfed down. His stomach turned at the mere touch of the sour lumps.

During the evening the Roman went out to Hugwa's stable and saddled the horse the farmer had given him. A thrall had stuck a torch in a post and left him, and as he crouched down tightening the girth firmly under the horse's belly, the wind, the eternally blowing wind, whined through the wooden walls of the stable. The flame wavered and shadows glided like great black hands over him.

"By holy Jupiter, what a country! . . . cold, raw winds . . . And the people! . . . dressed in nothing but skins and coarse woven cloth, brown and gray like the earth beneath their rawhide shoes and the driving clouds above their long-haired heads!"

The Roman gave himself a shake as he struggled with the clumsy iron buckle.

"Just look at it—that's what they call a saddle! A lump of stiff leather, with a couple of iron rings on two strips of hide!" And that lad, that new companion of his, he used neither reins nor saddle!

Suddenly a cold shiver went through him. The stable door had swung open, and the wind came howling in from the black night outside, whirling chaff and straw through the stable. Then the door slammed with a bang. The Roman looked up from under the horse's belly, and an icy shudder ran down his spine from the roots of his hair. The stable was empty—the door had opened and shut, but no one had come in.

He lay listening to the wind whistling through the cracks and crevices. The blood seemed to freeze in his veins, for somewhere behind him there was a rustling in the straw—it sounded like a stealthy footstep. Yes, there was someone creeping toward him . . .

He drew his dagger from its sheath. Anything might be expected of these savage barbarians. The footsteps had stopped now . . . No . . . there was the rustling in the straw again.

The Roman sprang up and wheeled round. And there
. . . in front of him . . .

"What do you want?" he gasped.

The fellow did not look as if he were contemplating
murder or assassination. He held out his hands to show he
had nothing in them, and as his thin lips parted to lay bare
his big teeth the Roman recognised him. He was the one
he had done a lot of business with that day a long while
ago, the one who was willing to barter a slave for a trinket
he wanted to give the farmer's daughter—Thorkim, his
name was. The Roman thrust his dagger back. Thorkim
turned his back to him and stood patting the horse a moment. Then he turned around again.

"You're leaving with Odbjørn," he said. The Roman
nodded, marveling at the hatred that left Thorkim's voice
hoarse and breathless. Suddenly he thrust his hand beneath
his tunic, and the Roman sprang back with his hand on his
dagger. But the other shook his head and beckoned him
to step nearer.

"Look!" he whispered, holding his hand up to the flaming torch. He held a piece of amber, and inside the golden
amber the Roman could see a spider and a gnat . . .

Once, thousands upon thousands of years before, the
spider had crawled out over its web and approached the
gnat that lay twisting and turning in the tough silken
threads. But just as the spider was stretching its groping
legs out after its prey a drop of resin had slipped over them,
enclosing them within its gluey substance. With the passing of time the resin had turned to amber, and inside the
golden red stone the spider still sat stretching its legs out
after the gnat, just as it had done that day thousands of
years before.

That piece of amber was worth its weight in gold.
Polished smooth, it would be a precious jewel. The Roman
put his hand out for it, but Thorkim's hand closed over
it, and he smiled mockingly.

"What do you want for it? I've nothing to offer you!" the Roman moaned, apparently on the point of bursting into tears.

Thorkim's fingers opened again, and the Roman craned his neck forward. Yes, as sure as his name was Serbulus, there were two tiny creatures inside that lump of amber!

"Look," whispered Thorkim, "if you were that spider now, and . . . and Odbjørn were the gnat . . ."

"What then?"

"Why, then the amber would be yours!" Thorkim cast a glance round the darkness of the stable, and then he bent down toward the Roman. "If you'll see to it that Odbjørn never returns home from the land of the Romans, then it belongs to you," he whispered hoarsely.

The Roman merchant appeared not to have heard what he said. His eyes were fixed on the piece of amber. But suddenly he held out his hand.

"Yes," he muttered, "yes, give it to me . . . I promise you . . ."

"Swear by Tyr!"

"By Jupiter, I swear . . ."

"I don't know him! Swear by the god Tyr!"

And so the Roman swore by the god of the Cimbrians.

"Here!" Thorkim threw the amber into the straw at his feet. "But if I see Odbjørn once more, I'll thrust a sword through your body if I should ever meet you again!"

"I promise you he shall never come back. You'll never see him again!"

The Roman breathed on the piece of amber, polished it on his sleeve and held it up to the flaming torch.

"By Jupiter, I promise you . . . !"

Hjald Hugwasson went with them a short distance on their way to the south. The Roman merchant rode in front and left them to themselves, yet they did not exchange many words during the last hour or two they were together.

Hjald called to mind that Groa wished to be remembered to him. Odbjørn nodded and grew red in the face.

"She's made herself a chain of sixteen glass beads," Hjald said, turning his head away. "One for each changing of the moon," he said. Every time the moon was full she would break one of the bits of colored glass and rejoice in the passing of time that would soon bring him back again.

Odbjørn nodded again, and now his ears were as red as his cheeks.

By the stream to the south of the great marshes Hjald took his leave.

"Light the beacon fire when you return," he said. "Then I'll ride out to meet you."

Odbjørn promised he would. He gave Hjald his hand, and the two blood brothers parted. Hjald stood watching the two horsemen ride southward. Odbjørn raised his sword above his head, and when, a moment later, the two men disappeared behind the hills the sword blade seemed to be sinking slowly into the ground.

7

The Beginning of the Journey

For three whole days they rode south through the land of the Saxons. It was like riding over a vast green ocean where bushes and scrub were small waves rippling and lapping on the surface of an otherwise calm sea. They had an uninterrupted view all around the horizon, and so could avoid huts and villages in good time.

Odbjørn learned two or three new words of the Roman's tongue from time to time, and the Roman two or three of Odbjørn's in return. By exchanging words in this way and mixing them together they managed to understand one another.

And he heard many strange things, did Odbjørn. This Marcus Serbulus had travelled widely on his journeys and had much to tell. And Odbjørn listened readily. But he had an impression that the Roman spun him yarns and told him a pack of lies.

Before they reached the mighty river Rhenus, the Roman said, they woud have to cross two large rivers that ran northward toward the luckless German Ocean that had wrecked his ship. These rivers were called the Albis and Visurgis. The latter ran through the dark German forest, and within that unknown wilderness there lived a savage tribe—the Cherusci, they were called.

Odbjørn noticed that the Roman's cheeks grew pale at the very mention of the name.

Somewhere or other within the forest lay the Teutoburg. Every Roman soldier sent into that murky wilderness bore the Teutoburg in mind—but no one knew where it lay.

"Shall we meet your countrymen in the German forests?" asked Odbjørn.

"As soon as we're across the Albis we may be lucky enough to run into Roman soldiery," nodded Serbulus. "Many years back, the great Roman general, Caesar, conquered the whole of Gaul beyond the river Rhenus. Now the Emperor Augustus has given his army commander, Varus, orders to lead our troops forward to the Albis."

"Your land is big," said Odbjørn, looking sharply at the Roman.

"Big?" cried Serbulus. "The divine Emperor Augustus rules over the whole world, from the rain-drenched forests of Germany in the North to the scorching sandy deserts of the South! Over all the lands around the Romans' own sea! The Roman soldier stands on guard in Spain, in Macedonia, in Thrace, in Judaea, in . . . Briefly, the sun rises and sets within the Roman Empire! What's the matter? Where are you off to?" he shouted.

Odbjørn had turned his horse around.

"Since your land's so big, you can't possibly lose yourself," Odbjørn retorted sarcastically. "There's no need for me to go any farther with you!"

And the Roman was hard put to convince Odbjørn that it was not his intention to pull his leg. But he came to grief later when he told Odbjørn that in Rome they built houses that went right up in the air, houses that contained as many rooms as there were cells in a beehive, and each room as big as Odbjørn's hut in the heather. Close on three hundred people could live in one of those houses, he said.

"Are you sure you mean three hundred?" asked Odbjørn, slackening his speed. The Roman gave him a side-long glance.

"Well, perhaps I've made a mistake," he said.

The next evening they sought shelter under some bushes, but before they lay down to sleep Odbjørn asked if they still had a long way to go before they reached the Roman Empire. He had been sitting and staring at the wan sickle of a moon, and he had tied sixteen knots in one of the thongs that bound the strips of hide about his feet. Every time the moon shone round and full in the sky he would undo a knot, and in that way he would be able to keep an account of the passing of time.

"The way is long," mumbled the Roman, half-asleep. "First, we must go up the Rhine . . . then over the Alps, and then . . ."

"The Alps?" asked Odbjørn. "What are they?"

"Mountains," yawned the Roman. His voice sounded heavy and hollow with sleep, but Odbjørn prodded him.

"Yes, but what are mountains?" he asked in exasperation.

"They're . . . Well, yes, they're where the earth rises up in the air and stretches into the sky."

Serbulus heard a rustling in the bushes, and he jumped up wide awake. Odbjørn was on his way over to the horses. He went after him and seized him by the arm.

"By Jupiter, I swear it's true—every word of it! Mountains are masses of stone and rock piled up so high that you have to throw your head right back to see the top of them!"

He shook Odbjørn by the arm and at long last got him to dismount.

But the next day Serbulus kept his mouth shut, and when Odbjørn tried to question him he shrugged his shoulders and remained silent.

Late in the day they reached the broad stream of the Albis. There they dismounted and walked along by the water's edge to find a ford where they could cross, but the river flowed wide and sluggish between its low banks, and from its steady, even current they concluded it was everywhere deep and impassable. The Roman was of the opinion that they should take their time over it and fell trees to build a raft, but Odbjørn said he had no intention of felling trees with a knife and sword.

"We'll let the horses swim us over the river," he said.

Serbulus turned pale as he gauged the width of the river with his eye.

"The current's stronger than you think," he muttered. "And if we're going to put to sea on horseback at every opportunity . . . it'll end up as a bad habit."

They turned around to go back and fetch the horses. And it was then that they caught sight of the horsemen . . . They had drawn up in a circle about their horses and were apparently so taken up with the riderless animals that they had not yet caught sight of their owners. Odbjørn and the Roman hastily slid down behind the bank.

"What do we do now?" wailed Serbulus.

"We shan't get across the river without the horses," Odbjørn muttered. He raised his head and took a good look at the strange warriors. Most of them were armed with long lances firmly fastened around their shoulders, and they were wearing close-fitting leather helmets that hid their hair. Odbjørn noticed that they seemed to be in disagreement over something or other, and from time to time they pointed in the direction of the river.

"They'll start looking for us soon," he whispered.

"Don't complain," grumbled Serbulus. "You came along of your own free will!"

"Have you heard me complain?" Odbjørn crawled nearer. "Listen," he whispered. "I'll try to get hold of the horses. Crawl behind that bush, and then I shall know where to find you again. Keep in readiness. I reckon we'll have to get away smartly."

Odbjørn crawled up over the riverbank.

"What are you going to do?" Serbulus's voice was hoarse with anxiety. He was startled to see Odbjørn get up and walk across the meadowland toward the strange warriors. They had caught sight of him now. Slowly they turned their horses and faced him. He saw a couple of them bend their bows above their heads and fit an arrow to the string.

He stopped short and whistled. It sounded like the shrill complaint of the gray plover piercing the thunder of the breakers. Graywind was accustomed to obeying that whistle. Odbjørn whistled again, a sharp penetrating note. A wave of uneasiness passed through the band of horsemen, and an arrow whistled close by his ear. At that moment he saw a gray chest pushing its way through the encircling horses. They were trying to stop Graywind.

"Come on!" he cried. "Come on . . . !"

He spun around and set off at a run . . . Behind him he heard the heavy rattling thunder of galloping hoofs like a pile of bricks collapsing about his ears. The noise was coming nearer . . . steadily nearer. And just as he was expecting the point of a lance to pierce his back at any moment, he saw a gray muzzle shoot past over his shoulder. He seized the mane and swung himself up. A howl of disappointment rose behind him. He drummed his heels into Graywind's flanks and galloped in a wide circle over the stretch of meadow.

The yelling warriors were following and gaining on him. And Graywind seemed to have no more strength left: his body was shaking spasmodically as he plunged on with arched neck. If he went on like that, they would be overtaken any moment.

"Come on!" he cried. "Come on now . . . Come on!"

He turned off sharply and made straight for the river and the bush where the Roman lay hidden. By doing that he would shorten the way, but at the same time the distance between him and his pursuers would shrink appreciably. He heard the horse breathing heavily above the rumble of hoofbeats.

"Come on . . . Come on . . ." He threw himself forward onto the animal's neck, yelling in his ear. But it made no difference . . . no difference at all . . . Then all at once he realized what was the matter with the horse. They had fastened a hobble around his legs. Graywind had burst the thong, but a strip of leather still hung between his hind legs and his left foreleg.

"If he tries to leap from the riverbank with that thong between his legs, he won't have a chance," he thought. "Then it'll all be over with Serbulus the Roman and Odbjørn the Nameless, and our travels will come to an end by the great River Albis, on the boundary between the Saxons and the Longobards."

The river was drawing closer . . . the river and the bush . . . And if he couldn't free Graywind from the thong before he reached the bank . . .

"Serbulus!" he shouted. "Jump into the river, Serbulus! Jump!"

The Roman's head popped up from behind the bush and disappeared again. At that moment an arrow sang between Graywind's ears and stuck in his mane, hanging there like a hairpin in his thick locks. Graywind twitched his ears viciously.

Odbjørn slipped from the horse's back and hung down under his belly with his head close to Graywind's thundering hoofs, soil and grass flying about his ears. Knife in hand, he groped after the cracking thong of leather. Heaven and earth were full of flying sods and thumping hoofs, and between the horse's gray fetlocks he could see the bush, upside-down, growing bigger and bigger . . . Graywind was close to the riverbank. Two . . . three bounds at the most . . . and then . . . he caught hold of the leather thong and slashed at with his knife . . .

Graywind leaped . . .

They seemed to hover in the air, Odbjørn clinging to the horse's side and not knowing whether or not he had succeeded in cutting the thong. He caught a glimpse of the Roman standing in the river up to his waist in water.

The horse's hoofs landed with a squelch in the mud of the riverbed. And he didn't stumble, he . . . Odbjørn went under in a cascade of white foam and the brown waters of the river met over his head. When he came up again, he saw the Roman's beringed hand in the horse's mane.

"Hold fast!" he yelled.

"I wasn't thinking of doing much else!" Serbulus gasped, his head bobbing up and down behind the horse's neck and his black hair stuck stiff and short to his forehead.

From the bank the warriors followed the horse's struggle with the current. They had hung their bows across their shoulders, having no desire to sacrifice their arrows to the river. On top of the slope behind the warriors stood Serbulus's horse, and from his saddle hung the provisions bag which they had failed to take with them.

8

Is It the Buccina?

On they went through the land of the Longobards, but now they had no food, and only one horse which they took turns riding.

As long as Serbulus was seated on Graywind's back his tongue was never still. Now that they had the River Albis and endless stretches of unknown country behind them he was no longer afraid that Odbjørn would turn back. He would now have to put up with listening to the truth about the Roman Empire! That wild barbarian from the raw wind-swept coast at the uttermost limits of the earth should now hear about the wonders of the world!

Serbulus told him about the Roman army that had subdued the whole world with all its peoples. He described the division of the army into centuries, maniples and cohorts, which together formed a legion of some six thousand men welded together by an iron discipline.

"Should a Roman legion turn its back upon the enemy, every tenth man is taken from the ranks and put to the sword," he said with a gloomy air. Then he began telling him about stone-throwers and catapults, battering-rams and siege-towers.

And then it would be Odbjørn's turn to ride, and Serbulus would lapse into silence, for he had more than enough to do merely to keep up. Hunger gnawed at his innards, and he would grow dizzy and have to cling fast to the horse's mane.

Then they would change over again, and Serbulus would slowly recover and begin talking about the master of the world, Augustus Caesar, and about Rome, the city of white marble on the seven hills, with its massive columns like trunks of oak, its temples so spacious that every single one of them could contain three halls the size of Hugwa's . . . He told him about the paved military roads, highways that stretched to the ends of the world, about bridges and . . .

And then he would fall asleep with his arms round the horse's neck, and Odbjørn would escape his rambling talk.

For four days and nights they had been pushing southward. On their way they had passed two rivers whose names the Roman didn't know. He thought they must be tributaries flowing north into the great River Visurgis.

Serbulus did not talk any more. Odbjørn had to shake him into wakefulness when he wanted him to show him the way. The Roman would stare at him for a moment as if he were trying to remember who he was and then collapse onto the horse again. Then he realized that Serbulus was not long for this world. And Odbjørn himself . . . His eyes were blurred by a shimmering red mist, through which the bushes moved slowly around him and the scattered trees heaved like masts on the deck of a huge ship, tilting and rising steeply up toward the sky. His stomach felt hot and burning, and his mouth was running with water. For four days they had been living on grains of wild barley, bark and leaves.

"I think I could even enjoy some of the northerners' salt meat now," were the last words Odbjørn heard Serbulus mutter painfully.

He stopped and shook the Roman till he woke. He bawled in his ear that they must swallow some berries and eat if they didn't want to go on till they dropped. The Roman seemed to obey, and when Odbjørn saw him slip down from the horse he started crawling around gathering cranberries. But when his hands were full and he turned back, Serbulus was leaning against the horse fast asleep. A broad grin spread over Odbjørn's hollow cheeks. He gave Graywind a whistle, and as the horse moved toward him Serbulus dropped to the ground as though felled and woke with a start.

"It's best to lie down when you go to sleep," Odbjørn laughed.

They ate the cranberries and then staggered on toward the south with their arms thrown about Graywind's neck— neither of them had strength enough to swing a leg over the horse's back.

One morning Odbjørn saw the horizon covered with blue-black storm clouds. Serbulus admitted that it might look like clouds, but it might equally well look like a foaming sea frozen into immobility just as it was breaking over the rim of the horizon. In fact it was neither the one nor the other.

"That's the German forest," he whispered. "Somewhere deep within its wild recesses the Cherusci live. They say a Cheruscan can't live without the eternal rustling of the tree tops in his ears. Once he leaves the forest he pines away and dies."

Serbulus spoke as though in a dream.

"Once, when I was younger, I went into the forest with four slaves," he said in a low voice, "to barter for skins among the savages. A Roman patrol went with us. We crossed the Rhenus and penetrated the forest, and there we stayed for forty days without running into a living soul.

I can still remember the pattering of the heavy raindrops on the bronze vessels that hung over the slaves' shoulders . . . and the rustling of the leaves under our feet . . . and, above all, the treetops . . . the eternal murmuring of the treetops in that wild deserted forest . . . That sound almost drove me crazy."

So much talking appeared to have tired Serbulus. He suddenly lost his hold on the horse and slid to the ground. Obdjørn bent over him.

"What is it?"

"I shall never hear that sound again," Serbulus moaned. "I can't go on. When I'm dead you can turn back and make your way home . . . I've something here you can take with you to repay you for your help."

Serbulus thrust his hand into his tunic and tried to free the little bag that contained the piece of amber. But Odbjørn did not give him time.

"Rubbish!" he cried. "I came away to gain wealth and power in the city on the seven hills—and you've been good enough to show me the way!"

Odbjørn seemed to gain new strength at the thought that they had got as far as the German forest. With great difficulty he managed to lift the Roman up onto the horse, and when he had secured him firmly he seized the horse's mane.

"Come on!" he cried.

And Graywind broke into a trot, dragging him along toward the dark forest and the range of blue-black hills that covered the horizon like threatening storm clouds.

He had expected the German forest to rise up suddenly and without warning in front of him like a green wall, impenetrably dark between its massive tree trunks. But the way to the forest wilderness lay over vast stretches of scrub and bog, many miles across, and as he endeavored to keep his footing on the uncertain tufts of grass and had as much as he could do to make his way across the treacherous swamps, the forest gradually grew up around him. Scratched and bleeding, he pushed his way through the thorny scrub with no firm ground underfoot.

But it seemed all the time as if the forest were refusing to accept him. His legs grew heavier and heavier until he could hardly move one before the other. He had to stop and gasp for breath before he could gather sufficient strength to trudge on a little farther. The treetops began to meet overhead, but the forest was reluctant to receive him into its green depths. He realized that only too clearly: it was just as if his legs were paralyzed by witchcraft and sorcery. He pressed his hands against the painful muscles in his thighs and struggled on with back bent. Then suddenly he stopped.

In front of him a naked wall of rock rose up among the tree trunks. Odbjørn stared at it with wide-open eyes. It was a strange sight—never before had he seen so large a stone. He took a step nearer and passed his hand over the surface of the red rock. He found the stone was so soft that he could break pieces off it.

He happened at that moment to look back over his shoulder, and saw the way he had come lying far below him. Was it so strange after all that his legs had grown weary when he had climbed half-way up into the sky! Fascinated, Odbjørn gazed down into the valley.

So Serbulus had been right, then, when he told him about mountains. Full of wonder, he began once more to climb up the montain slope. Suddenly he heard a bump and a groan behind him. The Roman had slipped off the horse and lay moaning on the ground. As Odbjørn knelt down by his side he lost consciousness again. Odbjørn took hold of him and shook him until he awoke.

"Serbulus!" he cried. "I've seen mountains now, Serbulus!"

The Roman opened one eye under his short black fringe of hair. The eye regarded Odbjørn scornfully.

"Mountains!" he snorted. "A few hills, perhaps— nothing more! Ah, you should see real mountains!" And he suddenly started whimpering. "I shall never see them again!" he lamented. "The white mountains about the green lakes—like emeralds set in fine silverwork! The noble jewels of my beautiful country!—I shall die of hunger before I see them again!"

Odbjørn took pity on him and set about searching for food. Round about he found beechnuts and acorns, but Serbulus grumbled that the beechnuts were too small to satisfy and the others, the acorns, were too bitter to swallow. All the same, he made short work of both. Odbjørn gained renewed strength from that wretched meal, but the Roman seemed to grow weaker than ever, and when Odbjørn rose to depart Serbulus fainted again.

Odbjørn would otherwise have considered that it was now his turn to ride, but as there was nothing else for it he struggled to get the unconscious Serbulus up onto the horse. Perhaps he pushed a little too hard. Whatever it was, the Roman mounted the horse with such impetus that he slid right over his back and fell down on the opposite side. He woke with a roar before he even hit the ground.

"Watch what you're doing, you slave!" he yelled.

The blood rushed to Odbjørn's cheeks, and whipping his sword out of its sheath, he slipped under Graywind's belly.

"Did you say 'slave'?" he shouted as he raised his sword.

"No, no, Odbjørn! I was dreaming . . . I dreamed I was being carried through the streets of Capua in my litter, and all at once one of the slaves dropped his pole. I fell out of the litter and hit the pavement, and then I woke . . ."

"You'd better mind what you're saying—even when you're asleep!" cried Odbjørn, his gray eyes smouldering with anger. After some hesitation he thrust his sword back into its sheath.

Serbulus got up and brushed the leaves off his tunic. He fumbled for an ivory comb and began tidying the front of his hair. Then all at once the comb stopped, and Serbulus opened his eyes wide. They looked right through Odbjørn with a glassy, sightless stare.

"What's the matter?" cried Odbjørn, as a cold shiver went down his spine. "What are you staring at?" He took hold of the Roman by the front of his tunic and shook him.

"Listen!" whispered Serbulus hoarsely. "Listen to the buccina!"

"The buccina?" Odbjørn wrinkled his brows.

"The buccina's the horn that's sounded when the Roman army advances to attack," the Roman whispered, "or when a soldier must suffer death for cowardice."

He had been standing with his eyes closed. He now opened them and seized Odbjørn by the arm.

"We're saved!" he cried. "The Romans are close at hand . . . Listen!"

Odbjørn listened, and above the rustling of the treetops he heard a sound that he knew and couldn't mistake.

"Maybe you're right!" he laughed. "I don't know that horn you talk of, but to me it sounds like a horse neighing!"

"It's the buccina!" Serbulus shouted, as he began to stagger forward between the tree trunks. Odbjørn and Graywind had difficulty in keeping up with him. Fearing to see the red tunic disappear, he did not stop to mount the horse, and was now rushing in and out among the trees with the horse behind him. Suddenly he fell. At that instant he heard a loud cry close by, and as he rose to his feet he saw Serbulus standing stiff and motionless in a grassy glade among the trees.

9

White Stallions in a Sacred Grove

"Save me from delusion and double-sight!" gasped Odbjørn, clutching Serbulus by the arm. "Am I seeing right? Is it one I'm looking at, or are there several of them? And are they all white?"

"Yes, yes . . . There are many of them, and they're all white," the Roman whispered hoarsely.

At the farther end of the sloping meadow a wall of red rock rose vertically, throwing a dark shadow across the glade which was fenced in on all sides by the trees of the forest. In the middle of the glade grazed a herd of white stallions—and it was the sight of them that made Odbjørn stare open-mouthed, for you couldn't tell one of the horses from another.

"Perhaps the horses belong to a squadron of Roman cavalry," suggested Serbulus.

Odbjørn burst into loud laughter.

"Not on your life, Serbulus! . . . You made me believe a buccina can neigh like a horse, I grant you that! But you're not having me this time! Those horses over there have never been ridden in their lives! Just you watch!"

He clapped his hands. A sharp ring re-echoed from the rock face, and the impact of it passed through the white stallions like a shock. They struck the ground with their hoofs, and stood for a moment tense and rigid, their ears twitching.

"You see? But every horse can be broken in!" Odbjørn laughed, and the gleam of his white teeth matched the sparkle in his eye.

"What are you going to do?" Serbulus cried.

"What am I going to do? I'm going to get us the horse we're short!" he shouted. He wheeled Graywind around. His heels thudded like drumsticks against the horse's flanks, and they thundered across the glade, leaving a banner of neighing and ringing laughter to fly behind them.

And now look! . . . If it hadn't been that laughing on an empty stomach proved very painful, Serbulus would undoubtedly have admitted that he had never enjoyed himself better on the benches of the Circus Maximus than he did that day—there in the wilds of the German forest.

Graywind came bounding riderless out of the herd of horses, and at the same time Serbulus saw Odbjørn leap astride a white stallion whose back arched like a bow. The horses scattered like fragments of splintered glass, and Odbjørn and the stallion were left alone together. But before long, it seemed, these two would part company as well. Now rearing, now lashing out with his hind legs, the stallion jerked Odbjørn from neck to cropper and back again, this way and that, with his arms outspread like flapping wings.

"Now . . . now!" groaned Serbulus, clutching at the empty air as though he would grab Odbjørn as he hung swaying over the stallion's unruly back.

"Yes . . . yes . . . now!" Serbulus gasped with excitement and hammered the tree trunk with his clenched fists. "Out of the way!" he shouted to himself as he slipped behind the tree. The thunder of hoofs shook the ground beneath him. A heavy snorting swept past and was gone. As he cautiously poked his head out he saw Odbjørn getting up off the ground. A little later he vaulted onto Graywind's back and resumed the chase.

Three times he tried, and each time he flew from the stallion's back like a stone from a catapult. In the end he came limping over to Serbulus. His face was streaked with dirt, he had a cut across the temple and his lip was bleeding where he had bitten it. A naked shoulder showed through a rent in his cloak.

"It seems hunger has robbed me of my strength," he said. "Let's find shelter for the night. I'll have another go in the morning."

"You may as well spare your strength," grinned Serbulus. "After what I've just seen, I'd prefer to trust to my own legs!"

"I'm not taming horses for you!" Odbjørn growled. "Tomorrow we ride away from here with you on Graywind and me on the stallion."

"You can arrange that with the stallion tomorrow," said Serbulus. "But let's find shelter for the night now." He pointed up the rock face toward a dark shadow among the crags. "There's bound to be somewhere up there where we can find shelter from the night dew and the cold."

He was right. The shadow turned out to be the entrance to a dark cave. They made themselves a soft bed of grass and withered leaves just inside the opening. Neither of them felt any particular desire to penetrate farther into the darkness of the cave, and when they had put away a meal of beech mast and acorns they prepared to lie down to rest.

"The way it's blowing, there must be an opening at the other end, too," muttered Serbulus.

Odbjørn sat down and, as he wiped the dirt off his face with a handful of grass, wondered at Serbulus. Before the Roman went to bed he would undress completely, keeping on nothing but a white shirtlike undergarment. No matter how cold it was, he would fold his clothes carefully and lay them aside, and then during the night he would lie shivering with a pile of clothing within reach!

"It's like going to bed in the middle of a triumphal arch," he grunted, struggling with his tunic as it flapped like a flag in the draught. As he lay down a swarm of withered leaves swirled out of the cave. "If I'm lying in the meadow in the morning, then I've been blown out!" he muttered, and a moment later fell asleep.

Odbjørn sat gazing out over the forest glade where Graywind was grazing among the white stallions. He looked up over the treetops, searching for the moon in the graying sky. But it was still too light. The flaming red sun, hidden behind the mountain wall, slowly withdrew its shimmering, dust-laden rays from the forest. Black shadows crept out from behind trees and bushes, patching together the darkness of night.

What was that? . . . Odbjørn jumped back with a start.

Something over where the shadow of the rock drove the point of its wedge into the fringe of the forest—a repulsive, painted face hovering above the shadow in a gleam of glowing sunlight . . . The changing light gave its coarse features a lifelike quality, and its wide mouth seemed to open in a voiceless shout.

"Serbulus!" He crept over to the Roman and shook him till he woke. Serbulus turned over.

"Reef the sails!" he shouted, still in his dream.

"Serbulus!"

"Yes, what is it?"

"Look over there!" whispered Odbjørn, pointing. What was it? The face of the god had vanished now. "It's gone," he stammered. "The shadow's hidden it—there's an image of a god standing over there at the edge of the forest!"

"Well, let it stand there, then," mumbled Serbulus, yawning.

"We've got into a sacred grove," said Odbjørn, anxious to keep Serbulus awake. But the Roman lay down again, consigning sacred groves and holy places to the devil.

"I once fell asleep on the marble floor of the Temple of Jupiter, and, apart from the fact that I was confoundedly cold, nothing came of it! Go to sleep now," he said, yawning so heartily that his jaws creaked.

The Roman's cool levelheadedness infected Odbjørn, but it was nevertheless a long time before he fell asleep, for that night the moon rose full and silvery-bright over the black forest. A month had passed, and a new one had begun. Odbjørn untied one of the knots in his leather thong, and as he sat fingering it the wind blew over the forest and carried his thoughts northward. He fell asleep with his back propped against the cold stone of the rocky cave.

He suddenly jumped up with a start. A gray gleam of dawn was filtering through the mouth of the cave. His forehead was icy cold and damp with sweat. He had been dreaming that he had offered Graywind as a sacrifice to the god Tyr. In his dream he had done what he had failed to do before—he had thrust his sword into the horse's neck— and the horse had neighed and struck out with his hind legs and splintered the image of the god. The noise woke him.

"Something or other's happened to Graywind," he thought, unable to free himself from the horror of his dream.

He went over to Serbulus and woke him. The Roman turned over wide awake.

"What's the matter now?"

"I don't know, but . . ." Odbjørn bent down ready to

crawl out of the cave, but stopped abruptly. "There . . . Look there!" he gasped, backing away.

Outside stood a dozen warriors, silent and sinister, staring at Odbjørn and the Roman. Beneath their horned helmets their faces were furrowed with scars and slashes, expressionless masks of stone. The men were dressed in earth-brown tunics and trousers tightly bound around the ankles with leather thongs, and some wore a short blue cape fastened around the neck. In front of the warriors a little bent-backed fellow stood lurking in the shadows. He stared at them with his small piercing eyes, and his lips were drawn back from his teeth in a broad grin. As he came closer, limping and stealing sideways toward the mouth of the cave, Serbulus started back and gripped Odbjørn's arm. The little fellow, with his odd swaying gait, stopped short, standing close and watchful.

"Come along!" cried Serbulus as he dragged Odbjørn after him.

In the dark recesses of the cave they bumped into something. It was a wagon. They edged past the wheels, stumbled over the pole and groped their way along the wall of rock. They stopped to listen and heard the sound of limping footsteps. Serbulus was out of breath and panting heavily.

"Odbjørn!" he called. "Odbjørn! Come on, hurry up!" And putting his hands out in front of him, Odbjørn broke into a run.

Ahead of them the darkness grew less intense. In a moment they would be out of the cave and in daylight again.

"This way . . . this way!" gasped Serbulus. He cleared a rise in the ground and edged his way through a narrow cleft in the rock. As he did so Odbjørn heard him give a shout. Odbjørn followed, wriggling through the cleft, and staggered a couple of steps forward . . .

They were in a grotto, hemmed in by sheer walls of rock,

and high above their heads the blue eye of heaven gazed down upon them through an opening in the rocks.

Serbulus, pale and trembling, leaned his back against the rock.

"We're hemmed in," he moaned. "We're finished!"

From the cleft in the rock came the sound of limping footsteps. They stopped, and then, stealthily and hesitantly, the sound returned.

10

Captives of the Cherusci

They had been taken some way down the mountain slope and brought to a village that lay in a clearing in the forest—fifty or sixty mud huts around a dozen large halls, all built on the steep slope of the mountainside.

"Like a flock of gray sheep around a dozen or so great oxen," thought Odbjørn, as, with hands bound behind his back and a rope about his neck, he was led down into the village.

The innumerable posts everywhere driven into the ground to support walls and gables made the huts look like animals with their legs braced against the mountainside to stop them from sliding down into the valley. He and Serbulus were dragged through the narrow alleyways that ran in and out among these wooden buttresses and climbed upward over countless steps hewn out of the red rock. They reached a great hall where, their hands and feet lashed together, they were thrown into a corner. A little later a couple of thralls fed them with hot soup and great hunks of tender pork.

At the other end of the hall, between the pillars that flanked the high seat, sat a great white-bearded warrior. He had been sitting there all day, and all day there had been a constant stream of warriors in and out of the hall. They had talked in low excited voices to the old man. Much to his surprise, Odbjørn discovered that he could understand a good deal of the language used by the Cherusci, but only when they were talking loudly did their voices reach him. What he most frequently heard was the name of Arminius.

"When Arminius comes . . . Arminius is on the way . . ."

They were waiting for someone called Arminius. And they had been waiting a long time and had begun to grow impatient. Something was going on here . . . something that had nothing to do with him and Serbulus. The narrow alleys had been swarming with warriors, and in the forest he had heard a buzzing murmur of voices. Horses stood tethered to the trees in large groups, and in the village square he had seen women cooking food in great bronze cauldrons which they stirred with poles the height of a man.

Night had fallen and flaming torches had been stuck in the beams of the hall. Over at the long table the warriors were seated shoulder to shoulder. They sat and waited. They sat turning their heavy earthenware tankards between their hands, and from time to time there came a heavy sigh of impatience.

One of them began to sing, and the others joined in, in a rumbling chorus of deep voices. One moment it sounded like a swarm of wasps buzzing over the tabletop, to rise the next like the roaring of breakers underneath the roof-beams. Then all at once the song broke off. From far, far away came the murmur of voices. Outside, the warriors were lying among the trees on the mountain slopes and singing. It was as though the chieftains' voices still lived, as though the song had fled into the forest and was stealing around between the tree trunks.

Odbjørn turned his head with a start. A warrior had banged his tankard down on the table and jumped up, his eyes gleaming in the red firelight.

"Here we are, singing lays and ballads as a good omen for the outcome of battle, but who says there's going to be a battle? Why doesn't he come?"

"I know . . . I know why Arminius doesn't come!" shouted a voice from the bottom of the table. "He's summoned us here and bidden us gather all our warriors on the mountain, and in the meantime . . ."

"Mind what you're saying, Bardrik!" The one with the white beard had jumped up.

"It's your son I'm speaking of, Segimer—your son Arminius! I ask you whether he's not called upon us to meet here for the very purpose of emptying the land of its warriors, so that he can at his leisure lead the Romans on a plundering expedition!"

"I told you to mind your words, Bardrik!"

The old man stepped over the bench, but a warrior stood up and barred his way.

"Let's not pick quarrels! Hard words have been spoken about your son, Segimer. But yesterday word was brought to Bardrik that his land had been ravaged by the Romans."

"They stole all the hides and skins they could find and carried women and children off as slaves!" shouted Bardrik from the end of the table. "A lad and three old men who offered resistance were condemned to death!"

"That's how it is!" said the warrior who stood in front of Segimer. "While we're sitting about here the Roman army's scouring the countryside and plundering without opposition! And your son Arminius is leading them! We all know he's taken service with Rome and has fought against Rome's enemies!"

"Only until Drusus penetrated our borders!" cried Segimer.

"Who'll guarantee we can trust him?" one of them called out.

"Who'll guarantee he isn't trying to gain power over all our lands?"

Odbjørn saw the old man pass his hand wearily over his eyes.

"I trust Arminius," he said. "At this very moment three Roman legions are roaming the country from the Rhine to the Elbe. They're demanding tribute for the Emperor in Rome. They give judgment according to their own laws, and make free men slaves. Everyone knows the Roman army numbers twenty thousand men, and you know, too, that individually you can do nothing!"

The old man was silent a moment.

"Do you know the marshes out there?" he cried, pointing through the doorway into the darkness. "Do you know them?" he shouted. "That's where Arminius is leading the Romans! He'll leave them there and come over to us. And there in the marshes he'll crush them! At one stroke he'll free the land from the Roman yoke! Mark my word!"

Segimer sat down heavily.

"On your word I'll give Arminius till daybreak!" cried Bardrik. "Then I take my warriors with me and return home!"

"So shall I!" they shouted.

"Then it's time to go now!" a voice called out.

The men turned around. And there between the doorposts they saw the dawn breaking in a dappled gray sky. Bardrik rose and walked across the hall. He stopped in front of the high seat.

"Don't take it amiss, Segimer. I'm leaving now!"

Segimer sat with bowed head, staring into the flames of the hearth fire. There was a clattering around the table as the warriors rose one after another.

And then Odbjørn heard a strange sound. He was the

first to hear it because he was lying with his head close to the wall: a murmur of voices that came from somewhere down by the foot of the mountain. The sound came nearer and nearer, rolling up over the mountainside like a tidal wave to break over the village in a thundering roar.

Segimer had jumped up.

"Listen . . . !" he shouted. "Listen . . . !"

The men stood still and listened.

From outside came the sound of rhythmic shouting—over and over again. The mountain re-echoed with a noise of thunder. Segimer clapped his hands to his ears and shook his head. They saw him throw his head back and roar with laughter.

Then without warning a man was standing in the door-way. He shouted something, but his voice was drowned in the noise. Bardrik kicked the door shut and gave him a chance to make himself heard.

"He's coming . . . He's on his way up the mountain . . . !" The man was gasping for breath and leaning against the door post. "Arminius is on the way!" he panted.

From outside came the rhythmic clash of sword against shield, and then all at once the noise was drowned in the shouting of thousands of voices. It sounded as if a heavy sea had broken against the walls of the hall.

At that moment the door was flung open . . . In the door-way stood a young warrior, his fair hair falling from his horned helmet to his shoulders. His breast was covered in a byrnie of scaled armor, and over his broad shoulders hung a green cloak. But it was his sword that held Odbjørn's eyes—the long sword he wore belted about his waist. Any other man would have been forced to hang that sword around his neck to keep it from trailing on the ground. He looked a giant to Odbjørn.

There was a deathly silence in the hall. The young warrior took a step forward and raised his hand in greeting.

"The hour has come!" he cried, striding over the bench, and as he unfastened his cloak and let it fall from his shoulders their eyes avoided his scrutiny. "What's the matter? . . . Have I invited too many guests to the feast?" he mocked. "Is it fear that takes the color from your cheeks?"

Bardrik detached himself from the others and stepped toward him.

"It was my intention to desert you, Arminius. Just before you arrived!"

"Quiet!" Segimer shouted. "No one was going to desert, but we began to grow weary of waiting so long."

"That I can well understand," Arminius nodded. "But Varus was feeling the cold and wanted to go into winter quarters by the Rhine, so I had to lead him around and around until the stars were playing leapfrog in the sky and he no longer knew the difference between east and west!"

The men shouted with laughter.

"Now he's shut in between the river and the mountains," Arminius cried, "with the marshes at his back!"

"And when you'd left him there . . . ?" Segimer asked with a smirk of satisfaction, his eyes traveling from his son to the warriors.

"Then I took our warriors and came away. But Segestes refused to leave. He stayed with the Romans."

They nodded gloomily.

"Segestes will fight on their side then?" someone asked in a somber voice.

"He'll have to share their fate," replied Arminius.

"And . . . and Flavus . . . ?" Segimer hadn't the courage to look up.

"At this moment my brother Flavus is looking for a place for our men to sleep," Arminius laughed. "The rest of you have pretty well filled the mountainside!"

"We've gathered together nearly ten thousand men," said Segimer proudly.

There was a hoarse whisper behind Odbjørn. He turned and saw the Roman gazing at him with his dark eyes.

"Did you hear that?" he whispered. "They're thinking of attacking the Romans!"

Arminius turned around. "Who are those two?" he asked as he stood up.

"Two strangers," answered Segimer. "One of them's a Roman. They came from the north and broke into the sacred glade. They were trying to break one of the wild stallions."

"Which one of them did that?"

"The young one," Segimer replied.

Odbjørn looked up and met the Cheruscan's eyes. Green and hot, they seemed to burn deep into his own, and reminded Odbjørn of the sparks that fly from molten bog iron. Tall as a giant, he stood with legs astride gazing down at him and seemed to Odbjørn to be supporting the roof beams across the back of his neck. Arminius turned away and spoke briefly with Serbulus in the Roman tongue. Then he went back to the table.

"The Roman's a merchant," Odbjørn heard him say. "He and the lad come from somewhere up north in the land of the Cimbri. Hang them on the tree of sacrifice and let's get them out of the way!"

Odbjørn felt as if his bonds were tightening and slowly strangling him.

11

Arminius Makes an Offer

He woke and sat up. The gray light of dawn had penetrated the shutter, revealing the outline of slats and bars.
On the other side of the wall he heard the sound of heavy
steps approaching.

"Serbulus . . . They're coming!" he whispered. The
Roman grunted in his sleep and stretched till his bonds
creaked. But he did not wake.

Odbjørn watched the shadows glide across the shutter
like black bird's wings. The bolt was drawn back and the
shutter quietly opened. The daylight blinded him, but
between the fumbling hands that were loosening the
leather thongs from his arms and legs he caught sight of a
pair of cross-gartered legs standing astride in front of the
opening.

"Get up and follow me!" said a voice.

The benches around the long table stood empty and
Arminius told him to take a seat. A thrall came in and
placed tankards and a bronze vessel on the table. He poured
a yellowish fermented drink into the tankards and disappeared.

"Drink up!" said Arminius. "And that you may not find

your drink bitter, I'll tell you at once that I've decided to let you go free—on one condition!" he added.

"On condition I take the Roman with me," said Odbjørn, taking a pull at his beer. "And my horse," he added. "I mustn't forget him either!"

"I'm the one who makes conditions here!" Arminius shouted. "And don't forget it!"

The blood mounted to his cheeks, but suddenly he laughed. "Good!" he said. "You shall take them with you! The friendship you've shown for the Roman and your horse is something I'd like to have myself," he continued.

Odbjørn looked up in surprise. But he found no hint of mockery in the greenish eyes that seemed to glow and burn beneath their bushy brows.

"If you set any store by my friendship, you can have it!" he said.

"And if I put your friendship to the proof?"

The smile on Arminius's face had vanished. Odbjørn gazed into his hard eyes and felt as if he were looking down from a dizzy height into a blue-green pool.

"If I put your friendship to the proof?" said a far-off voice.

"Do it," he said.

"They may sear your flesh with red-hot irons to make you talk. And if you remain silent they will kill you," said the voice.

"You can rely upon me!" he answered.

"Good!" Arminius smiled and wrinkles appeared around his eyes. "Listen carefully then. And if you change your mind afterward, you can go in peace.

"For a long time I led a company of men to fight for the Romans," he began. "But the odd thing about peoples and nations is that they get on best with one another if their lands are far apart. If they're separated by the sea they're brothers for life! A great river will sometimes do as well.

But if there's nothing but ditches and hedges between them, then they'll be eternally at war! If it weren't so, we could turn all our swords into plowshares. The Romans have now penetrated across the Rhine and established themselves in the lands that belong to us. Three days ago I took my company with me and left them, after I'd shut them up in the fastness of the forest. I reckoned that Varus would at once be on the move again. But the Romans are now reported to be raising ramparts and erecting palisades as if they were preparing a permanent camp for the winter."

Arminius jumped up and strode over to the hearth, where he stood, chin in hand, staring into the flames.

"The chieftains of the Cherusci are beginning to grow impatient. They don't think there's anything to be gained by further waiting. Soon they'll be off, one after another, taking their men with them. And when they've all gone Varus will be free to leave camp and continue his plundering. These same chieftains who are now clearing off will later be dragged behind Varus's chariot in triumph through the streets of Rome, and the women and children of the Germans will be sold as slaves on the Field of Mars."

Arminius suddenly turned towards him.

"I must know what the Romans intend to do! When they're going to break camp, and what direction they'll choose to follow. Have you courage enough to penetrate the Roman camp?"

"Me?" cried Odbjørn.

"Yes, you . . . and the Roman, Serbulus."

"Serbulus?"

"Yes, it's just because we have him that the plan may succeed. You can tell them you helped him to escape. They may believe you—they may not!"

Arminius made a gesture with his hand as if tightening a noose around his neck.

"If you succeed in returning with the information I need, you won't go unrewarded."

"A man gains greater glory by facing the enemy with his sword than by slinking behind his back!" said Odbjørn.

"This demands greater courage and shrewdness than open battle," Arminius replied. "And if you do what I ask of you, you shall later have the opportunity of leading a band of men to fight against the Romans."

He could not believe his own ears.

"Will you let me lead a war band?"

Arminius nodded. "A war band, and whatever else you want, you shall have, if you can find out for me what the Romans intend to do."

Odbjørn jumped up—and sat down again heavily. His heart was beating fast. Arminius was going to give him a band of followers! He had reached his goal—and the second month had not yet come to an end.

"Do you think . . . Do you think I could get my men to go with me to the land of the Cimbri?" he stammered.

"The men of these parts are readily persuaded by boldness," Arminius replied. "And there are many here eager to try their luck in strange lands." He looked at him questioningly, and Odbjørn began to tell his story. He told him of the spring sacrifice: he told him how he and Thorkim were to meet again to measure their prowess one against the other, and how Hugwa was to give his daughter to the one with the greater following. It was for that reason he had left home with the Roman merchant—to win wealth and power in foreign lands.

"Power's a rare thing!" Arminius laughed. "But power and wealth won't win you men's hearts, unless it be this old graybeard Hugwa's!"

"He who has power has everything!" said Odbjørn, setting his jaw.

"So we say! And here's the power you set out to win.

Tomorrow you'll be either a Roman slave or a chieftain of
the Cherusci! Have you a mind to enter the Roman camp?
Yes or no?"

"Yes, I'll go . . . But there's one thing you're forgetting,
Arminius!"

"And that is?"

"Serbulus will betray us to his countrymen as soon as
we're in their camp."

"You're mistaken. By that time Serbulus will be as dumb
as an ox!"

"What do you mean?"

"We shall cut out his tongue!"

The tankard tumbled to the ground as Odbjørn sprang
up.

"No one who lays a hand upon Serbulus shall count on
my help!" he said.

Arminius stepped up close to him.

"Do you realize that as far as Serbulus is concerned—and
all other Romans, too—we're nothing but barbarians," he
whispered. Odbjørn felt his hot breath on his face. "Barbarians are no better than animals, to be whipped and
branded and sold into slavery! At this very moment slave
drivers' whips are leaving weals across the backs of barbarians under the broiling sun of Campania—in the dark
hulls of galleys—in . . ."

"It makes no difference," said Odbjørn. "I gave him my
word that as long as I could lift a hand I would protect him
against harm!"

Arminius gave a deep sigh and strolled across the hall.

"Volkai!" he shouted. "Volkai!"

A thrall appeared from the door that led into the store-
room.

"Find Buekil, and tell him to come at once!" Arminius
called out.

He was not very big. But he was thin and bony, and his gauntness made him seem taller than he really was. He tripped over the doorstep and entered Segimer's hall head-first, and Odbjørn saw there were bits of straw sticking in his black tousled hair. The fellow got up, pulling such a face that his snub nose was the only distinguishable feature in a mass of wrinkles—like the bung in a shriveled wineskin.

"That's Buekil!" grinned Arminius. "He's as dark as a Roman, but unfortunately he doesn't speak their language."

The fellow poked a finger into his ear and prodded vigorously, like a dog shaking itself. He drew a deep breath, sighed, and, with arms hanging loosely, sauntered along by the wall, carefully studying the boards as if he were looking for a knothole he could slip through.

Odbjørn looked at Arminius questioningly.

"Is he a thrall?" he asked.

Buekil jerked his head around and glared at him. Then he drew his arm under his nose from elbow to fingertip and turned his back on him with a contemptuous sniff. Arminius chuckled with suppressed laughter.

"No, he's thrall to none and master of none," he grinned. "He came wandering through the forest from the west one day and settled down among us. The women call him 'Sun of Gaul,' and spoil him so that he shan't take himself off again. When he's not lazing in the sunshine, he makes beautiful pots for them, more beautiful than . . . Buekil!" he shouted.

The fellow was on his way out of the hall. He stopped with a loose swing of his long arms, came back and threw himself down on the bench.

"It'll be a sad day when he disappears! That day will cast a gloom over this place," Arminius said. He stood kneading between his hands a lump of clay the thrall Volkai had brought him. "You watch now and see what'll happen!" he said with a grin that revealed his strong white teeth. "Buekil!" he called.

Over on the bench Buekil turned his head slowly around and caught sight of the lump of clay. He brought his feet to the floor and sat up. Odbjørn saw his eyes gazing intently at Arminius's hands, as he sat there chewing his lower lip without once taking his eyes away. And when Arminius threw him the lump of clay he jumped up and caught it in mid-air.

"Now look and see what he'll do!" said Arminius.

Odbjørn stepped across to the table and looked over Buekil's shoulder. The fellow's long supple fingers darted backward and forward over the clay, pressing and squeezing. He smoothed it, he marked and scratched it with his fingernails.

Odbjørn was astounded. There in that gray clay was Graywind to the life: Graywind, rearing up with distended nostrils and flowing mane, no bigger than his clenched fist!

He put his hand out to take the clay figure, but before he could pick it up Buekil had set his thumb upon it and flattened it.

"What did you do that for?" Odbjørn cried indignantly.

"No good . . ." Buekil shrugged his narrow shoulders and threw out his hands. "Didn't smell like a horse!"

"Smell? But it was just like looking at Graywind!"

"It didn't smell right," Buekil repeated obstinately. "And you didn't hear it neigh, either!" He banged his fist down on the lump of clay and got up.

Odbjørn turned with open mouth and looked at Arminius for an explanation. The Cheruscan's heavy body was shaking with laughter.

"He means it wasn't lifelike enough," he laughed. "It's like that every time! Buekil!" he shouted.

The fellow was on his way out of the hall again. He

pulled himself up on the threshold and turned slowly round.

"Come over here and listen to me! Tomorrow you're going with Odbjørn."

Buekil poked a finger into his ear and prodded. With his head on one side, he looked Odbjørn up and down with his black eyes.

"Where to?" he asked.

"You're going with him to the Roman camp."

He stopped poking his ear.

"I am?"

"Yes . . . You're to change clothes with the Roman, Serbulus, and pretend you are a Roman merchant who's been held prisoner for many years here in the forest. Torture and . . ."

Buekil turned smartly on his heel and made off, but the thrall, Volkai, standing ready behind him, grabbed him in time.

"Torture and imprisonment have left you dumb," Arminius continued. "Do you understand?"

Buekil swallowed hard and nodded, his black eyes unfathomable pools of fear.

12

In the Roman Camp

Arminius had told them to follow the river. The Romans had pitched their camp where the river forked at the foot of the mountains.

Odbjørn continually had to stop short to hurry Buekil along. As they advanced he lagged farther and farther behind, and Odbjørn would turn back angrily and shake him by the shoulders. And when he had stopped shaking him Buekil's teeth would continue to chatter.

"They've got iron bracelets which they'll screw tight into our arms and legs to make us talk!" he would whisper, looking at Odbjørn with eyes wild with fear.

From somewhere within the forest came a shattering crash. They stood still for a long time and listened. Above their heads the branches of the swaying trees creaked, and all around them heavy raindrops fell pattering to the ground like stealthy footsteps among the withered leaves.

"Come on," said Odbjørn, letting go of Buekil and continuing on his way between the trees. As he turned around he saw Buekil hobbling along painfully.

"What's the trouble now?"

"I can't go any farther," moaned Buekil, his red cloak flapping round him as he collapsed. "Remember, I've been sitting bent and cramped for three or four years in a hole in the ground!"

Odbjørn was over him like a whirlwind.

"Will you get up!" he shouted.

"My legs won't let me!" Buekil wailed.

"You're a fine fellow to send with me!" Odbjørn sat down.

"Did . . . did . . . did I by . . . by any chance ask to come?" Buekil stammered.

"What did you say?"

"I said, 'Did . . . did . . . I . . .' "

"If you're practicing losing your voice," grinned Odbjørn, "you needn't bother! Before the evening's out you'll be hanging dumb and stiff from a tree if you go on behaving like that!"

"They don't do much of that," said Buekil. "Hanging folk, I mean. They usually nail them to a post and then . . ."

He broke off suddenly.

Above the rustling of the treetops came the blaring notes of a horn like the hoarse baying of hounds over their heads, and Buekil ducked as if he expected something to fall and strike him.

"Look there!" Odbjørn pointed eagerly ahead toward a clearing in the trees. Something was moving there.

"It's the Roman camp!" Buekil said through his chattering teeth.

The horn brayed again, and the wind seemed to tear its message to shreds and blow them away over the treetops. Odbjørn nudged him.

"Come on!" he whispered.

They crawled to the edge of the forest and crept under some bushes. On the flat open ground in front of them they could see the rampart of newly thrown-up earth, its brown ridge stretching along the edge of the forest.

"It's square," said Buekil. "A Roman camp's always square. All the sides are the same length."

Odbjørn was overcome by the size of the camp. On top of the ramparts square wooden towers had been erected, and every now and then in their dark interiors he caught a glimpse of a soldier on guard. Arminius had said there were twenty thousand Romans. Had he said that the Roman army numbered as many men as there were trees in the German forests, Odbjørn would have grasped his meaning better. He was so taken up with the watchtowers that he had only just noticed the clods that came flying up from the ground a little way in front of the rampart.

"They're digging a trench," Buekil whispered. "Can you see those treetrunks they've pointed at one end? They'll set them point upwards in the trench when they've finished it —the idea being that when the Cherusci charge to assault the ramparts they'll tumble in and be impaled. The camp's got four gates," he continued in a low voice, "one in each side—just so that you know, in case you have to get out. If they bar one, you can always try one of the others!" he laughed.

"Meanwhile, let's go through the nearest," Odbjørn suggested.

They crept out of the bushes and stood up.

"Tyr be with me!" Odbjørn whispered.

"Don't know him, but if he's more powerful than the Romans' Jupiter, you can remember me to him as well!" murmured Buekil.

"Be quiet, and lean on me! And remember, you mustn't let a sound cross your lips from now on—not until we're out of the camp again!"

As they stumbled across the clearing toward the camp gate, Buekil, supported by Odbjørn, staggered unsteadily, as if at any moment his legs would give way under him. Beneath lowered lids, Odbjørn kept his eyes fixed on the two

Roman soldiers standing by the gateway. They reached the trench and lurched across a narrow gangplank. Odbjørn was just able to make out the faces beneath the polished helmets, when he suddenly felt Buekil's body stiffen. Before he could stop him, Buekil had ducked down and snatched up a lump of clay from the excavated earth.

"Drop it!" Odbjørn hissed, knocking the clay out of his hand. "Are you mad? Do you want an arrow through your body already?"

One of the Roman sentries lowered his spear and stepped toward them.

"Halt!" he shouted. "Who are you, and what do you want?"

Odbjørn stopped and took Buekil by the arm.

"I've fled from the Cherusci," he said, "and I've brought a Roman with me."

"Let the Roman speak for himself, slave!"

"He's dumb!" Odbjørn snarled.

The soldier's eyes glanced suspiciously from Odbjørn to Buekil.

"Take them to Varus!" he said without taking his eyes off them. Two of the guards fell in behind Odbjørn and Buekil.

"Come on! Forward!"

Odbjørn felt the point of a spear between his shoulder-blades. He took hold of Buekil and stumbled through the gateway into the camp.

Thousands of earth-brown tents had shot up behind the ramparts like gigantic molehills, but they were not scattered haphazardly, the way molehills dot a green meadow. The tents were pitched in dead straight lines with roadways in between; and as Odbjørn was taken farther and farther into this labyrinth of roads, he discovered that the tents were divided into blocks of fifty. In the open spaces between the tents workshops had been set up, a regular market with benches and stalls—and there were stables, too, crowded with steaming horses, and with mules that Odbjørn now saw for the first time. From somewhere behind a glowing forge came the rhythmic blows of a sledge-hammer, answered from a distance by the hollow sound of a carpenter's ax. In a matter of a few days the Romans had established a town behind the protection of high ramparts. But the town had shot up in the middle of a march, and thousands of tramping feet had turned the camp roads into a filthy mire.

They passed a group of soldiers huddled together around a campfire, their bare knees hidden under blankets and skins. Some were polishing leather straps and weapons; others sat warming their hands over the fire and staring listlessly into the flames. Odbjørn thought to himself that if Arminius failed to drive them out of the forests they would be forced to clothe their legs in trousers like other folk. And he tried to picture to himself how warm it must be in the Romans' own country if you could go about with your legs bare under a knee-length skirt.

Then a blow across his left shoulder with the shaft of a spear turned him to the right. He now caught a glimpse of the rampart, and along the crest of the mound he noticed what looked at first glance like gigantic insects—heavily-armored beetles and spindle-legged spiders. He remembered what Serbulus had told him about catapults and stone-throwers that could fling arrows and heavy stones for hundreds of yards. And he thought that if Arminius should succeed in . . .

He got no farther, for at that moment the shaft of a spear struck him across the chest.

"Halt there!" The guard was holding his spear across their bodies. "Fetch the centurion of the guard!" he shouted.

The other soldier disappeared into a large tent before which a forest of standards had been planted—poles bearing the copper hands of the cohorts and the golden eagles of the legions set in wreaths of glittering metal leaves.

The centurion edged past the standards and came toward them.

"Marcus Lembo, this fellow here came staggering out of the forest with a Roman."

A sharp flurry of wind swept blustering and unexpected down the camp road and the soldier had to raise his voice.

"He says the Roman's dumb and that he set him free from the barbarians!" he shouted.

The centurion pushed the soldier to one side with his staff, and walked once around Odbjørn and Buekil. His eyes were overshadowed by the visor of his helmet, and his cheeks and chin were covered by its plated chain. The black horsetail on the crest of his helmet flicked Odbjørn across the face.

The wind had blown up suddenly, and it swept whining in and out of the roadways, whipping the canvas of the tents. The centurion stepped back and stood for a long time regarding them in silence. Then he turned and beckoned them with his staff to follow him. He led them around the back of the tent with the standards in front of it to another that was considerably bigger than the rest—as big as Hugwa's hall, Odbjørn reckoned.

The centurion exchanged a couple of words with the soldier on guard before the tent. They thrust the canvas flap to one side, and he and Buekil stepped into a kind of anteroom. In the darkness along the billowing sides of the tent, soldiers were standing drawn up in ranks, silent and immovable like pillars of stone. From inside the tent they could hear a deep murmur of voices, broken every now and then as one was raised in high-pitched excitement . . .

The inside of the tent was lit by oil lamps hanging from

the roof poles by chains, and the lamps swung to and fro as the wind beat upon the canvas.

At a table in the middle of the room sat the Roman governor of Germany, Publius Varus, and behind him and the four officers who stood leaning over the table Odbjørn caught sight of a stretched skin on which was painted a she-wolf suckling two babies.

Varus drew himself slowly up. He seemed to find difficulty in keeping his heavy head with its fat pock-marked cheeks erect upon his shoulders. He appeared unable to manage it, and remained sitting with his head drooping, scowling at them from under his bushy eyebrows. Deep within his small yellowish eyes, Odbjørn, to his surprise, caught a hint of fear and alarm.

"Have the barbarians tortured you?" he asked in a voice that came with a husky melancholy from the folds of his thick neck.

Buekil shifted uneasily and looked helplessly at Odbjørn.

"Answer then!" Varus raised his voice in irritation.

"He's dumb," Odbjørn said. "The Cherusci have tortured and tormented him. I found him lying in a pit."

"Who are you?"

"I'm a Cimbrian, and I came down from the north through the land of the Cherusci and found the Roman merchant here shut up in a hole in the ground," Odbjørn lied.

The governor made an involuntary movement and shook his head sympathetically.

"You, too. What were you doing in these cursed forests?" he sighed. "And what am I doing here?" he cried suddenly. "Why should I be sent here where everything is cold and damp to the touch, where the trees drip with moisture and the earth stinks of decay!" He had stood up, and red blotches showed on the skin of his forehead. "Just listen!" he cried.

Odbjørn listened to the wind whistling through the tree-tops with the sound of a heavy sea breaking over the Roman camp.

"In Syria," Varus muttered, "in Syria there was sunlight and golden sand—sand as far as the eye could reach, but here . . ." He fell back heavily into his chair. "Here traitors lurk behind every rotten tree trunk . . . How do I know whether . . . ! Have they been searched for weapons?" he cried suddenly.

"They carry no weapons," the centurion answered.

"Take a look and see whether he wears the trader's mark about his neck!"

The centurion thrust a hand inside Buekil's tunic, snapped a chain and handed Varus a tin disc.

" 'Marcus Serbulus, Capua,' " he read. "Marcus Serbulus . . . But the disc might have been stolen! They might have killed Serbulus and stolen his clothes. Perhaps Arminius is behind this! Has he reported back, the traitor?"

"We've heard nothing of Arminius since he left the camp," said a voice.

Varus sat for a long time with his head bowed, scratching his dry blotchy forehead with his fingernails.

"Let the Cheruscan Segestes and his daughter come in . . ."

As the hangings were pulled aside Odbjørn was taken by surprise. He rubbed his eyes, and when he opened them again he saw it was not she after all. But the young girl who had stepped into the tent was very like Groa, only taller and more powerfully built. Her long hair, bound with leather thongs, had the same golden luster, her eyes the same blue as Groa's.

She came in with a grayhaired, thickset warrior dressed in the manner of the Cherusci. As he bowed to Varus with an ingratiating smile on his lips, Odbjørn heard the jingle of his ring-mailed byrnie.

"Have you news of Arminius?" Varus asked.

Segestes shook his head regretfully.

"I warned you, Varus. I told you Arminius was leading you astray and taking you farther and farther away from the Rhine."

"Yes, yes. You warned me. Not for my sake, but because you hate Arminius—because he has greater power over the Cherusci than you have!" Varus pulled a wry face.

"That's what you say, Varus. But believe me, it's only for your good that I now warn you against leaving this camp," Segestes answered with a smirk.

"Am I to lie here in this mudhole instead of going into winter quarters behind the Rhine? . . . I don't know . . . Perhaps . . . But that's for me to decide, not you, Segestes!"

The governor thumped the table with his chubby be-ringed hand, and Segestes bowed low. The wind outside shook the walls of the tent.

"There's something else . . ." Varus pointed to Buekil. "Have you ever heard tell that your fellow-tribesmen were holding a Roman merchant prisoner?"

"Can't he speak for himself?"

"He's dumb!" Varus snapped. "Answer, if you please!"

"I know nothing of it. See if the rack will cure his dumbness!" he laughed.

"One doesn't stretch a Roman on the rack!" Varus answered.

"Can't he write either?" Segestes' voice sent a cold shiver down Odbjørn's spine.

"Write?" gaped Varus. "Write? That's true, Segestes! If he's a Roman he can write his own name!"

"Write," thought Odbjørn. Writing—those queer signs and marks on the bottom of the bronze pots. Hugwa had once turned his green glass drinking-vessel upside-down and shown him the signs which told where the glass had been made. But Buekil couldn't write—neither his own name nor Serbulus's either! He was certain of that.

"Marcus Lembo," Varus called, "fetch wax tablets!"

Odbjørn's eyes wandered round the tent. The canvas was stretched down tightly all around the bottom. A spear would get him before he could squeeze himself out under the wall of the tent. How could he warn Buekil?

He suddenly noticed Segestes' daughter looking at him intently—as if she had already guessed the truth. He dropped his eyes, staring down at his leather-bound feet, at the knotted thong—he would never untie those knots now.

At that moment the centurion returned with the wax tablets under his arm.

"That's right," Varus grunted. "Now write your name, and add whether this fellow's telling the truth."

Hesitantly Buekil took the tablets and stylus the centurion handed him. He looked questioningly at Odbjørn, but Odbjørn turned his head away. "In a minute I'll give a shout and bolt through the tent flap. If only Buekil can find some way of getting rid of those tablets in time!" he thought.

"Get on and write!" shouted Varus. "Ah, good! At last . . ."

Odbjørn was startled to see Buekil writing. Buekil had opened the tablets and was scratching away at the wax with his stylus. He poked a finger into his ear and gave it a good shake. The stylus slipped out of his hand and fell to the ground. But he did not pick it up. He . . . Odbjørn's eyes opened wide.

"The fool!" he exclaimed to himself. "The damn fool!" There he was scraping the wax clean off the tablets! And then his fingers moved dexterously and with catlike agility over the lump of yellow wax . . .

Odbjørn measured with his eye the distance to the tent flap, ready to make his exit.

"What's that he's doing?" cried Varus, leaning across the table with an angry snort. "What is it? What in the name of the divine Augustus . . . ?"

Varus was quivering all over, his heavy body shaking with mirth before the laughter escaped from his throat.

"The she-wolf of Rome!" he chuckled, throwing his head back in a paroxysm of laughter. "Pass me the wolf, Roman!" he grinned, as he held out his hand for the tablets on which the golden-yellow wolf was standing. But before he could reach it Buekil placed his thumb firmly on the figure and squashed it flat.

"What do you mean by that?" The laughter died away in the governor's heavy body. "What's the idea, Serbulus?"

"You're mistaken, Varus." It was the voice of Segestes.

"What do you mean?"

"You asked me before if I'd ever heard of a Roman who was held prisoner by the Cherusci, and I answered no. But I have heard of a Gaul who lives with Segimer, Arminius's father, and who has a great reputation for his ability to fashion images in clay!"

"What are you driving at? Is this . . . is this the man?" Varus exclaimed. "Stop him!" he shouted. "He's making off!"

The centurion thrust out his foot. Odbjørn tripped and fell. A pair of heavy knees landed on his shoulders and his arms were twisted behind his back.

"I've failed Arminius!" he thought.

At that moment a searing pain shot through his head and he sank into unconsciousness.

13

Thusnelda

Hail and scurries of rain beat a tattoo on the canvas, and the wind thudded against the tent, shaking down the damp dust over his face. The wet ground had soaked his clothes, and as he shivered with the cold his slender chains rattled.

When he had come to again, he heard Varus ordering him to be strung up on a post before the ramparts so that the traitor Arminius might be aware of his fate. He was now lying in the cold and the dark, waiting for them to come and nail his hands and feet to the post.

It seemed strange that peace never fell over the camp's swarming mound of men. There was a constant low murmur of restlessness—a distant muttering of muffled voices in the night behind the tent walls, a humming in the air as if a cauldron were boiling far away in the darkness.

And then, without warning, the cauldron boiled over, the lid flew off and the water poured, spluttering and hissing, over the burning logs. That, at any rate, was how it seemed to Odbjørn's fancy—the muffled shouts, the beat of tramping feet and horses' hoofs, the hoarse braying of a mule punctuating the noisy confusion. Odbjørn turned over, his heart beating wildly in his breast.

"They're coming now," he moaned. "They're coming to fetch me."

In the distance he heard the rumbling of heavily creaking wagons, approaching out of the darkness. Odbjørn pulled himself together as a shadow slid over the wall of the tent—someone or other rushing past: running feet splashing through the muddy slush and disappearing.

The wagons were coming nearer now. He lay listening to the creak of wheels and the squelch of hoofs in the sticky mire. The first wagon lumbered past and continued on its way. It was followed by a long line of wagons rumbling along the roadway.

Then all at once the wagons pulled up, one after another, and the shrill grating stopped. One of the wagons had drawn up right outside the tent. He heard the drivers talking together, and then he saw a helmeted head appear through the opening of the tent. The head disappeared again and the voices died away. But the wagon was left standing outside. The wheels creaked, and the horse's muzzle pushed and snorted against the canvas. At any moment they would be back again to fetch him out of the tent and fling him into the wagon.

Odbjørn sank back and covered his eyes with a chained arm. Swifter than lightning, his thoughts sped through the dark, through the forest and away over the plains—back to Hugwa's dwelling place, to the farm-chieftain's daughter. Groa seemed to have come to him. He heard the whisper of her voice, he felt her cool hand stroking his arm comfortingly.

He started. He flung out his arm and shrank back. "Who's that?"

"Don't be afraid. And above all, keep quiet!" whispered a voice. "I'm Segestes' daughter."

He could just see the outline of the young woman's figure as she knelt on the ground behind him. In spite of the darkness he recognized the girl he had seen in the governor's tent.

"Do you understand the speech of the Cherusci?" she asked in a low voice.

Odbjørn nodded and his chains rattled.

"Listen carefully then," she whispered. "Tonight the Romans are laying a roadway of tree trunks across the marsh. That's why the camp roads are full of carts and wagons. At the moment tools are being handed out to the drivers. When they've got them they'll be back to fetch you."

She was silent a moment.

"You know Varus has condemned you to death?"

"Yes," he said.

"But you may be able to save your life. When I've freed you from your chains you must try to slip out to the wagon without being seen. Cling tight underneath it and hang on till you're outside the gate. Don't try to escape through the camp. You'll never do it." She stopped abruptly.

They heard voices outside and the sound of footsteps approaching the tent.

"It's too late. Get away quickly," he whispered hoarsely. She did not move, but her hand gripped his arm tightly.

As one of the Romans appeared from behind the wagon his shadow swept across the canvas. They sat still, listening to their voices.

"Why is it always us he gives the rottenest jobs to?"

"Who?"

"The centurion, of course," growled the voice. "Why has it got to be us? Why couldn't one of the first wagons take the fellow and string him up? As it is, we'll get left behind, and we'll have to drive into the forest alone!"

The clatter of tools on the bottom of the wagon drowned the grumbling voice.

"That's all right! By that time the forest'll be full of

soldiers. You wouldn't care about being the first wagon, either, to . . ."

The voices died away and disappeared.

She pulled an awl out of her skirt and set about picking the rivets out of the iron rings. A moment later he was free of his chains.

"Do what I tell you now. And if you manage to get away to Arminius, tell him that tonight the Romans are bridging the stream that runs into the Weser. Tomorrow at daybreak they're leaving camp and making for the south. If he hurries, he'll be in time to attack them as they're marching through the swamps. Tell him Segestes' daughter has half her father's men on her side. Say she'll turn them against the Romans as soon as Arminius attacks. Now off with you, Cimbrian!"

"What about Buekil?"

"I can't do anything for him—but I think he's doing what he can to help himself," she whispered. "He's in Varus's tent at the moment, making a bust of the governor. Varus won't have him put to death till it's finished. I think he'll make the job last a long time!"

"When he's finished he'll flatten Varus's face out as he always does," grinned Odbjørn, "and then . . ."

"No, he won't be able to. Varus has placed two legionaries at his side. They're to seize his hands as soon as he's finished. But hurry up now before they come back!"

Odbjørn lifted up the canvas of the tent. He was just about to slip out into the dark when she seized him by the arm and drew him back.

"You're forgetting the most important thing of all," she whispered into his ear.

"What's that?"

"That you must give Arminius Thusnelda's love. That's what you're forgetting!"

She breathed so heavily into his ear that he was startled. He turned around, but Segestes' daughter had vanished.

As he crept out of the tent the wagon horse shied, throwing its head back and trying to rear away.

"Stand still!" growled a voice.

Odbjørn slipped behind the wagon wheel, and from the other side of the tents came the sound of heavy running footsteps. He crawled underneath the wagon and groped his way over the bottom, and just as the driver's legs appeared out of the darkness he felt the pole under his hands. In no time at all he drew his legs up and thrust his toes over the back axle.

"What did I tell you, Gaius! Even the horse knows the fellow's going to die! Look how he's backed away from the tent!"

Odbjørn recognized the grumbling voice he had heard earlier.

"Well, what about it, old man, so long as he don't back away from you! Just take it quietly, Urbanus . . . No, don't take it quietly. Here comes your friend Pontus!"

The running footsteps drew close and stopped abruptly.

"What are you waiting for? Get the fellow into the wagon! We're off now!" The centurion stepped over to the tent and flung aside the canvas flap. "Good, you've done it. We can get off then."

"What have we done?" cried Urbanus. "We haven't done anything . . . We . . ." The driver gave a yell. "He's gone, Pontus! I peeped in a moment ago and he was still there then! I . . ."

Odbjørn heard a crack and the driver groaned with pain.

"Wait here till I can get a word with Varus!"

The centurion disappeared at the double.

"The swine!" muttered Urbanus. "Always has to lay about him with that staff of his! Can I help it if the prisoner got away?"

Odbjørn turned his head and saw that the Romans stood leaning against the edge of the wagon. He lowered his body until his back was resting on the ground. If he stretched out an arm he could touch the drivers' sandals. The centurion Pontus returned, and Odbjørn pulled himself up by his arms and clung close to the bottom of the wagon.

"We're to set off at once!" shouted Pontus. Varus has sent patrols out to grab him. The wagons'll be searched at the gate!"

Pontus seemed to have got a load off his mind; he appeared to be in high spirits and his voice had a confident ring.

"I was hoping Varus had knocked your head off," muttered Urbanus.

"What's that you said?"

"Me? I didn't say anything!"

"Follow on behind then, when the wagons get started!" shouted Pontus.

Odbjørn heard the drivers clamber into the wagon, and shortly afterward it set off, jolting and creaking along the camp roads. The shaking of the wagon pulled Odbjørn's arm muscles with a stabbing pain and his strength began to give out. In the end he let his back drag along the ground with his shoulders plowing through the mire. Odbjørn uttered a silent prayer to Tyr. He swore that when he returned home he would have a new image of the god set up before the temple door if only Tyr would see to it that anyone catching sight of him should take him for an old stack —or perhaps a mangy Roman cur running along underneath the wagon.

The wagons were halted before the gate. Odbjørn's wagon was the last of the line, and jolted forward bit by bit as those in front were searched and allowed to leave the camp. Over by the gateway he could hear raised voices and the clatter of arms.

"Come along! . . . Next!" a voice shouted.

He clenched his teeth and heaved himself up close to the pole. The wagon jerked forward and halted. The glare of flaming torches reddened the wet mud and drove the shadows deeper into the ruts. The guards thrust their spear-shafts into the wagon and poked about among the tools. He could not hold on any longer—his trembling fingers were beginning to slip.

"Is this the last of the wagons?" asked the guard.

"We're the last, and don't keep us too long. We don't want to be too far behind the others!"

Odbjørn's fingernails scraped the pole and his arms gave way. His body sank slowly down to the ground.

"Have you seen anything of the condemned Cheruscan?"

"It was us that should have had him with us," Urbanus said grumpily.

One of the guards got down on his knee to take a look underneath the wagon. But he jumped up again with a shout and threw himself against the rampart.

"Stop!" he yelled. "Stop, over there!"

A body of horsemen had galloped up alongside the wagon. A dozen or so hoofs splashing in the mire sent a spray of mud and filth over Odbjørn, who was surrounded on all side by the stamping and curvetting of horses' legs.

"No one's allowed to leave the camp!" cried the guard. "Those are Varus's orders!"

"Not even I?"

Odbjørn recognized Thusnelda's voice.

"No, not even you! Only Romans on official business outside the ramparts are permitted to leave the camp!"

"If you make so bold as to detain me and my men, you shall pay dearly for it!" Thusnelda cried indignantly. "What's your legion—and your century?"

"Those are Varus's own orders! There's a Cheruscan

who's made off. He should have been put to death, and so . . ."

"Answer me! I asked you your name and your century!"

"When am I going to get leave to drive off?" Urbanus shouted impatiently.

"All right, drive off!" yelled the guard. "Who's stopping you? Hurry it up!"

The wagon set off with a jerk and rolled out through the ramparts. In the distance, above the creaking of the wheels, Odbjørn heard Thusnelda's angry voice and the Roman answering in desperation.

"Varus made the decision himself. I can't go against his orders! Varus himself . . ."

It was the second time that night that the traitor Segestes' daughter had saved his life. He sent her a silent word of gratitude as he clung underneath the wagon, letting himself drag along the ground which seemed to take a peculiarly fiendish delight in bumping and jolting him. As the wagon trundled off the planks that bridged the trench, the swivel-bolster above the front axle jarred and nipped his fingers. He let out a half-suppressed yell.

The wagon stopped.

"What was that? What was it, Gaius?"

"I didn't hear anything."

"But I did," Urbanus muttered. "It sounded like some-one gasping." Urbanus shook himself and spat three times over the side of the wagon. Then he gave the horse a crack with the whip and the wagon set off again.

"What's it all in aid of?" he grumbled. "One day we dig ramparts and trenches as if we were going into winter-quarters, and then, before we know where we are, we're off again! D'you think old Varus knows what he's up to?"

Gaius did not answer.

"By Jupiter, what are we doing here anyway? What's the good of a country where it's always raining and blowing?

You mark my words, it's too close to the ends of the world —too close to the everlasting night! Just you notice how short the days are!"

"It's only this time of the year the days are short, Urbanus. You know that as well as I do! In the summer they're longer than ours."

"Anyway, why couldn't we have stayed behind the Rhine? Haven't we got enough already?"

"I don't know. But they say the Emperor Augustus wants to advance to the Visurgis to make the Empire's boundaries shorter. I don't know, I'm sure. You leave it to the high-ups. Augustus knows what he's doing!"

Urbanus seemed doubtful.

"Maybe, but Varus don't, anyway! Hi, give me some more rug—you're pulling it all over to your side! Listen to that . . . ! Listen to it whining and howling in that cursed forest!"

As the wagon trundled in among the trees Odbjørn let go of the pole.

"What's up now?" Urbanus tightened the reins and drew up. "Did you notice anything that time, Gaius?"

"Yeah," admitted the other. "I think it was a tree stump."

"Tree stump yourself!" Urbanus snapped. He climbed down to the ground and walked once around the wagon.

"Look over there!" Gaius whispered. "There's something dark lying in the track!"

"Where?" Urbanus screwed up his eyes. He drew his sword and went slowly and hesitantly toward the dark object. And at that instant the object vanished in a whirl of crackling leaves. Urbanus jumped back and knocked into Gaius.

"Did you see that?" he gasped.

"He's sitting over there behind that bush," whispered

Gaius. "Bend your bow and send an arrow into the undergrowth. Quickly now!"

Odbjørn was off at a bound in among the trees. An arrow whistled past under his chin. It grazed his throat and he felt a warm trickle of blood inside his tunic. He heard the drivers' shouts ring out, and the trees around him were suddenly alive with creakings and crashings. Branches cracked sharply and the dried leaves on the ground rustled like hissing foam.

"Over there! Get him . . . Let go, you fool, that's me! . . . There! . . . There he is!" The shouting and yelling resounded through the darkness above the soughing of the treetops.

Odbjørn crashed on through the undergrowth, stumbling and catching his hands on thorns and sharp twigs. Then he was on his feet again, dashing in and out among the trees. He left the trees behind him and plunged into scrub and reed. The ground gave under him. The muddy swamp took hold of his feet and let them go again with a hollow squelch. He threw himself forward, dragging himself along through reeds and tufts of grass out into the river. He felt the current take hold of him and carry him along.

14

The Golden Rostrum

Arminius had sent for his brother Flavus.

"Wait a bit," Odbjørn said. "There's something I must say to you!"

But Arminius was busy. Arminius had been chalking on the planks of the trestle table. He had drawn rivers and mountains—there lay the Roman camp, and there the tributary ran into the Weser.

The tribal chieftains came and went. This one was to lead his men across the Weser and attack northward along the river. The horse were to sweep around to the west and attack toward the east. The Romans' road to the west must be blocked, but at the same time they must stop them from making for the high ridges.

"You, Gothar, you'll attack from the mountain!"

At this point his brother Flavus stepped into the hall.

"Flavus, what about the Angrivari? Their horse, I mean?"

"They're riding along with the Cherusci."

"Split them up again, and let Odbjørn lead their attack. Take him with you, Flavus."

Arminius waved them away and turned to the chieftains again. But Odbjørn stepped over to the table.

"Arminius!" he cried. "Arminius, you're forgetting the Roman. You forget I promised to take Serbulus back to his countrymen."

Arminius looked at him questioningly.

"Ah, Serbulus . . . Always that damned Roman merchant!" he had shouted, banging the chalk down on the table and crushing it in the middle of the Roman camp. "You've nothing against attacking Roman soldiers, but when it comes to that one Roman . . ."

"I gave my word to that one Roman," he answered.

And so it had ended with Arminius giving him leave to set off toward the west with Serbulus that very night.

"Ride southward until you come to the River Lupia. The Romans have made a road along its bank. If you follow it you'll hit the Rhine and the Roman colony of Vetera. Deliver your Roman safely and then come back so that I can keep my promise to you."

That day in the sacred glade, when Odbjørn had tried to tame one of the white stallions, Graywind had injured a leg. And so he now borrowed two horses from the Cherusci and bade Widuhudar the priest take good care of Graywind as long as he was away. The bent-backed little fellow limped into the stall where Graywind stood and stroked his injured leg. And he swore to Odbjørn that the leg would be whole again when he returned in a few days' time.

Odbjørn and Serbulus had ridden westward for three whole days, and on the morning of the fourth day they came to the Rhine.

The broad river flowed smooth and unruffled through flat countryside, winding like the gleaming track of a snail from the misty blue hills to the south. On the opposite bank of the river lay the Roman camp of Vetera with its crenelated walls and square stone towers. Outside the walls a town of gray stone houses had sprung up like a swarm of toadstools round an old tree stump.

They caught sight of a wooden tower and a broad landing stage down by the riverbank. Serbulus clambered up the tower and from the gallery railing hung out a red cloth on the end of a pole. A moment later they saw a broad-beamed barge put out from Vetera in their direction.

Odbjørn had not yet told Serbulus that it was his intention to return to the Cherusci, but the time had now come to take his leave.

"Serbulus, in a few moments you'll be among your own countrymen. Have I fulfilled the promise I gave you?"

"Yes, indeed you have," the Roman nodded.

"Then our ways part," said Odbjørn as he held out his hand. "I'm going back to Arminius."

"Are you turning back now that it's my turn to repay you? What about the city on the seven hills?" Serbulus cried. "Didn't you set out to gain wealth and power?"

"I've no need to go any farther," Odbjørn answered. "I've found all the power I need."

"I've . . . I've a promise to keep, too," Serbulus muttered. Under his tunic he could feel the lump of amber pressing lightly against his chest.

"You owe me nothing," Odbjørn said. "If I hadn't come with you, I shouldn't have met Arminius. I'm in your debt!"

Serbulus drew a heavy breath, and the piece of amber seemed to weigh him down like a stone. He put his hand to his forehead and wiped away the cold sweat.

"It doesn't matter," he said. He thrust a hand into his tunic and would have flung the amber far out into the river, but at that moment the barge grated against the landing stage and startled the horses. And when Serbulus slipped his hand out of his tunic it was empty.

"Odbjørn," he cried, "let me show you around Vetera.

The city on the seven hills you won't be able to see, but at least let me show you something of a Roman town, and let me give you something to eat."

"If you want to cross, you'll have to come now!" shouted the skipper.

"Listen," whispered Serbulus. His face was pale, and he avoided Odbjørn's eyes. "You can spend the night in Vetera, and you can begin your journey back first thing in the morning. Come over with me."

"All right, then, if it means so much to you!" Odbjørn laughed.

The skipper pushed off from the shore and the boatmen paddled the rocking barge out into midstream.

"You may come to like Vetera so well you'll not be able to tear yourself away again," said Serbulus, his mouth twisted in a wry grin.

They tethered their horses to the boathouse and left them in pledge for the fare which Serbulus promised to pay later in the day. The skipper stood scratching his beard and glowering after them. They were both dressed like barbarians, though one of them had spoken good Latin like a proper Roman. He shook his head and sent a stream of spit spurting out of the corner of his mouth. Then he shambled over to the boathouse and settled down to glare at the horses.

"Many of the Roman legionaries have married Gaulish girls," said Serbulus. "They've got permission to build houses and settle down outside the walls, and so, bit by bit, the town's grown up."

He was silent a moment as he edged his way forward through the crowd.

"Not exactly marble," he grunted, nodding toward the square-built blocks of houses—they were built of flat dark-gray stones set one on top of the other without any kind of mortar—"but it is stone, not wooden boards such as the huts where you come from are made of, where the wind whistles through the knotholes and cracks."

Serbulus turned around, and there, to his surprise, was an old Gaul trudging along by his side with a sack on his back. He had been walking along talking to the old fellow. The Gaul looked at him from under the sack with a smirk and a grin. Serbulus gave the old chap a push and forced his way back through the throng of people. And there was Odbjørn standing in the middle of the roadway, gazing down at the paving and passing his foot backward and forward in astonishment over the flat squared stones. A cobbler was sitting by the wall of a house nailing strips of white wood onto the thick sole of a boot. Odbjørn's wondering eyes went from the cobbler up over the gray walls of the house with its narrow openings high up under the roof.

"Well, well!" Serbulus's patience was severely tried. Time after time the gaping Odbjørn loitered behind, and the Roman had to go back and fetch him.

He was so spellbound by what he saw that when a Roman legionary tugged his long hair, and with a grin offered to show him the way to a man that sheared sheep and sold horsehair to the army for catapults, he stared at the legionary vacantly and openmouthed. And the soldier shook his head sympathetically.

The third time he came to a standstill was under some heavy beams projecting from the façade of a house. Yellow planks were nailed firmly to the beams, and the whole thing looked more like the bow of a ship than anything else—a ship cutting its way across the narrow defile of the street. Under the prow hung a sign which read, "The Golden Rostrum."

Serbulus, his patience gone, retraced his steps.

"A rostrum's a ship's prow," he said, "and 'The Golden Rostrum's' an inn! And in we go!"

As they opened the door they were overwhelmed by the hubbub of a public bar. The walls of the taproom were covered in planks to put one in mind of the cabin on board a galley. But it looked much more like a gigantic wine cask—a cask filled with shouting and yelling, the clatter of weapons and the rattle of tankards, and the blue smoke of cooking. At the bottom of the cask soldiers sprawled across the round tables, throwing dice in a chaos of drinking pots and spilt wine.

"Venus!"

"Rot! You threw the Dog! Look out, you long-haired ram!"

Odbjørn was stumbling over legs and shins. Serbulus took him by the arm and led him over to an empty table.

"Wine!" he called. "A jug of good Falernian! Two jugs, while we're about it!"

And so Odbjørn drank Falernian wine from a transparent drinking cup exactly like the one Hugwa the farmer kept on his shelf at home. The wine sparkled like sunbeams in the glass. It was tart at first, but afterward it tasted sweeter. It made the tips of his fingers tingle and his cheeks glow.

Wine was a strange drink, he thought. And you could see through glass. When you lifted it up you could look through time and space and see your heart's desire. He was standing on the swaying deck of a galley, and in the golden gleam of the wine Groa's face rose up before him.

"You like being here?" bawled Serbulus.

"I'm longing to be off—to where I am now!" Odbjørn said, and laughed at his own nonsense.

Yes, wine is a strange drink. Sometimes it makes people forget what they have no wish to remember. But Serbulus now, he drank three jugs of Falernian and yet found no peace of mind. He turned and twisted on his bench, and at last he stood up.

"Wait for me," he said. "I'll be back when I've seen

about some fodder for the horses. But stay where you are at the table . . . here by the pillar."

Odbjørn nodded.

"Then I can find you again," Serbulus said as he patted the pillar. He laughed nervously. Then he turned and disappeared.

Time passed and Serbulus did not come back. Once Odbjørn went outside to look for him, and he noticed that there were not nearly so many people about in the street. At the same time he heard the bray of the buccina behind the ramparts of the Roman fortress, and when he stepped inside again, the Roman soldiers were on the point of breaking up. "The Golden Rostrum" was gradually emptying.

He returned to his seat and settled down to wait. A group of soldiers stood up behind him. A helmet fell off the table, hit a chair and rolled rattling across the floor. Suddenly he heard a hoarse voice whisper in an undertone behind his back, "Hurry up and get out of here!"

He turned around. Behind him stood two Roman soldiers. One of them had put his foot up on a chair and was busily fastening his leg armor. The other was standing with his back turned, waiting for his comrade. Which of them had wanted to warn him? And why?

Odbjørn turned his head slowly and looked around the room. Over in the doorway stood two sinister-looking fellows dressed in leather jerkins and long brown cloaks. They had been watching him, and they now edged their way in between the tables and sat down not far off.

One of them, a fair-haired man with a lean bony face, ordered sausages and wine. The other, pock-marked and dirty-looking, with arms as thick as hams, sat motionless, staring straight in front of him. His arms lay stretched out across the table, and around his right forearm he wore a broad iron-studded leather strap.

The fair-haired man sat chewing sausages with toothless gums. When he had disposed of a sausage in four or five noisy gulps, he would raise his head and stare at Odbjørn while he sucked his gums. Then he would bend over the dish and push the next sausage into his mouth. The moment Odbjørn rose to go he stopped in the middle of a bite.

By the door Odbjørn turned around. The two men had got up and were coming toward him . . .

It had grown dark while he was waiting for Serbulus, and the street now disappeared into the night like a black deserted ravine between the bare stone walls of the houses. Just as he was about to break into a run a dark shadow glided out from the wall. He was startled, but then he saw that it was only a bent old man who had been supporting the weight of his sack against the wall. The old man turned a wrinkled face toward him, grinning and leering.

At the same time he heard heavy footsteps in the entrance to the inn. In a flash, Odbjørn saw the old man throw his sack down in front of the step, and he heard someone trip over it with a curse. Then he heard nothing but the whistling of the wind in his ears, and he ran on into a white mist which made him slacken his speed for fear of knocking his shoulders against the walls. The damp clammy mist was coming from the river.

"The river," he thought. He must find his way down to the Rhine.

He stopped and listened. Close behind him he heard heavy clattering steps. Then there was silence.

"They heard me stop," he thought. "And now . . . now they're creeping quietly up behind me in the mist."

He spun around, and realized to his dismay that he had lost his sense of direction. Which way had he come from? Where did the river lie?

He suddenly made out a dark streak in the mist, a narrow

opening between the houses. He slipped into the alley and groped his way along the wall. Whenever he held his breath he thought he heard the sounds of stealthy footsteps, and the moment he caught sight of a dark recess in the gray expanse of wall he quietly drew his sword and pressed his back into the narrow passage.

As he did so he was seized from behind. A pair of hard muscular arms fastened themselves about his chest, and he was held in a vicelike grip with his arms pinned to his side. A steel-clad arm pressed upward under his chin and left him gasping for breath.

A shadow slipped out of the darkness.

"Lay off! You'll choke him like that!" lisped a voice. "What do you think Æmilius will say if we bring him a long-haired corpse!"

The grip relaxed. Odbjørn, panting heavily, felt the damp night air rush into his throat.

He was lying in a large dark room, and around him in the darkness he could hear the deep breathing of sleeping men. Now and then, as a man turned in his sleep, a chain rattled. The darkness was alive, full of heavy breathing and the mumbling of men drunk with sleep.

Some way off a door stood ajar, and through it the wavering glare of torchlight reached him, together with the sound of voices. One of the voices had an odd cackling note, which every now and again broke into a thin high-pitched squeak, like a hacked sword drawn from a rusty sheath.

"Did you say 'Cimbrian'?" The rusty voice rose high. "Cimbrian?" it piped.

"Yes. At any rate, I came across him in the Cimbrian peninsula."

Odbjørn recognized Serbulus's deep tones.

"How old do you think he is?"

"Round about eighteen. Perhaps nineteen, Æmilius—perhaps nineteen. I don't suppose he knows himself."

"Good. I'll put eighteen."

They were silent a moment. Then in the darkness he heard the slave dealer's cracked voice again.

"Has the lad any special gifts?"

"He's good with horses," Serbulus answered.

"Anyone can ride and manage a horse!" Æmilius snapped.

"But some are better at it than others, and he's one of the best I've ever seen."

"Well, well! I'll give you twelve hundred sesterces for him."

"Twelve hundred?" cried Serbulus. "He's big and strong!"

"Twelve hundred's a lot!" Æmilius squeaked. "A good deal too much—and all because Augustus has stopped waging war! Prices have risen like nobody's business! What do you suppose a black Ethopian will fetch?"

"That's as may be," grumbled Serbulus, "but you're offering me no more for him than the price of a skinny Cappadocian!"

"Ah, don't you run away with the idea that Cappadocians are cheap either!"

"Give me fifteen hundred sesterces!" Serbulus entreated.

"Twelve hundred or you can keep him!"

Odbjørn heard a pile of money overturn and rattle across the floor. A couple of coins hit the door and spun jingling to the ground.

"Take 'em or leave 'em!" Æmilius screamed.

There was a sudden silence, the door opened and Odbjørn saw a smoking torch coming toward him through the darkness. The red flare halted above his head, and when he had grown accustomed to the light and slowly opened his eyes he saw Serbulus bending over him. The torch drove black shadows into the Roman's eye sockets, and so Odbjørn could not see his eyes, but he noticed that his cheeks were pale.

"I've sold you," whispered Serbulus. "You're a slave now."

Odbjørn nodded.

"You're the stronger and you can do what you will. That's what you've taught me," he said. "That's how it has to be. Perhaps if we ever meet again I shall be the stronger."

His eyes were cold and empty. There was no hatred in them, but Serbulus saw they were no longer in a fit state to distinguish between good and evil. The realization sent a cold shudder through him, and he looked away. He turned to go but stopped short.

"Here," he said. Something heavy rolled across the floor and hit Odbjørn, and when he picked it up he saw it was a piece of amber.

"I got it from the one they call Thorkim," Serbulus said. "In return, I was to see to it that you never came back. I've fulfilled my promise to him now, but the amber burns my fingers and I'll have no more of it! Take it . . . If no one takes it from you, you can sell it in Rome. Good luck," he whispered, and as he spoke he sounded as if he were begging the slave for an answer.

But as Odbjørn only stared at him, he turned away and hurriedly left the prison cell. The door slammed heavily behind him and cut off the torchlight.

That night the moon rose full and bright, sprinkling sparkles of silver on the waves of the Rhine. And that night it was just two months since Odbjørn had left Hugwa's dwelling in company with the Roman Serbulus.

15

In the Salt Mines

Vetera was in a frenzy. Day and night the scattered remnants of Varus's legions emerged from the forest. Worn out and stained with blood, they dragged themselves as far as the Rhine. Ruined weapons, splintered shields, battered cooking vessels and broken standards of broken cohorts lay scattered over the riverbank. On the top of a rise stood an abandoned catapult, looking like a gigantic grasshopper with enormous thighs. Down by the water's edge the standard of one of the legions stood planted in the mud, the golden eagle glittering in the sun with wings outspread as though it were about to fly across the Rhine to seek safety behind the massive ramparts of Vetera. Filthy, ragged and bloody, all that remained of Varus's legions lay along the riverbank like crawling vermin. Most of them had been left in the forest, Varus among them. Varus had thrown himself upon his sword when the hour of defeat overtook him . . .

A centurion was telling the story as, with a bloodstained rag wound around his forehead, he sat on the rail of the barge and talked away about their defeat, describing how Varus had taken his own life when Arminius's wild hordes had surrounded them.

"The men were followed by their women, who drove up in the wagons, beating the leather hoods with their hands, howling and screeching and taunting those who didn't spring quickly enough to the attack," gasped the centurion, out of breath.

Odbjørn was standing chained to the barge, pulling an oar as he listened to the centurion's stumbling talk. He smiled to himself. And the other barge slaves around him gloated over the Roman defeat as they let their oars glide steadily through the water.

"Keep your mouth shut, centurion!" growled one of the legionaries. "Save it for the commander!"

And suddenly the centurion stopped talking. He doubled up, slid over the rail and disappeared into the river. They searched for him with their oars, but the current had carried him away and they were unable to find him. And so he never told the commander all that had happened in the gloomy depths of the forest.

Day and night the barges sailed backward and forward across the river to bring back the wounded.

The slave dealer, Æmilius, had placed his slaves at the disposal of the Roman commander in Vetera—and he was well-paid for his services. And when it was all over he made another deal with the commander, taking off his hands at a cheap rate the hundreds of prisoners that the beaten Romans had, in spite of everything, managed to drag along with them. Varus had gone, and there was, therefore, no question of a triumphal procession through the streets of Rome. Æmilius promised in return that he and his slave drivers would disappear southward before long, taking the crowd of slaves with them so that they should not be a drain on Vetera's corn reserves.

A fortnight after Serbulus had sold Odbjørn, Æmilius had his slaves chained together. For no other reason than to accustom them right from the start to respect and obedience, the slave drivers wielded their whips and with their lashes drove the long columns, chained and rattling, out of Vetera. The slave dealer had driven on ahead in his carriage to arrange accommodation for his slaves as they progressed on their journey.

Day after day the convoy of slaves crept southward. Like a hundred-legged monster, the chained column wound its way along the banks of the Rhine. Stretches of road paved with flat squared stones alternated with stretches that were surfaced with round sections of tree trunks. Their aching feet now beat upon hard stone, now sank into soft, fine dust.

From time to time they passed through small Roman colonies that had grown up around the square watchtowers, built at regular intervals along the river as a protection against the wild barbarians.

The river, and with it the boundary, ran in between softly curving ranges of hills, and where, here and there, a wall of rock rose bare and perpendicular above the river valley it looked like a stack of flat gray stones or a roofed mountain knoll.

As Odbjørn trudged along he wondered what had happened to Buekil and whether he had managed to escape from the Romans. He discovered that he missed him. The fellow undoubtedly lacked seriousness and strength of purpose, but then you could grow melancholy from too much seriousness. He began to understand why Arminius valued him so highly.

Three days after their departure from Vetera they reached the Roman colony of Confluentes—the town where the rivers met. They spent the night behind the ramparts of the fort, where the Roman commander had, for the one night, put the camp's prison cells at Æmilius's disposal.

Early the next morning they were shipped across the

Rhine at the point where the River Moselle flows broad and full into the main stream.

Day and night they trudged eastward along a road that followed an earthwork surmounted by a palisade of pointed tree trunks. As they passed one square watchtower after another, road and rampart wound endlessly up and down over hill and dale, and disappeared like a thin thread on the horizon. And Odbjørn began to realize that the Roman Empire was mightier than Serbulus had managed to convey to him.

Then one day the earthwork came to an end, but where it stopped it was succeeded by a stone wall that seemed, in the evening twilight, to peter out in the darkness. But when it was light again they saw it stretching endlessly into the red glow of the morning sun.

One morning they turned off from the boundary wall and made their way southward, and from that time until they reached the Alps the slaves were given nothing to eat: Æmilius's stocks of provisions had given out.

Two of the slaves died of starvation on the way, and a rumor was whispered along the line of rattling chains that Æmilius had hired the rest of them out to the mountain folk. Before they could continue their journey over the mountains he would have to let them earn their keep by laboring in the salt-bearing mountains of the Celts.

The rumor was right. For a month and ten days Æmilius's slaves worked in the Celts' salt mines in the mountains. Forty days turned into one long night. In the morning, before it was yet light, the slave drivers drove them into the eternal darkness of the salt mountain, and they did not emerge again until night had fallen over the mountains and hidden the salt treasure-chamber under its black coverlet.

But Odbjørn stored away in his memory one of the most

beautiful sights he had ever seen. They had clambered along a narrow path hewn out of the sheer mountain wall. On one side boulders and outcrops of stone rubbed their shoulders; on the other the scarred precipitous rock face disappeared into the clear giddy depths of a mountain lake.

All day they had followed the path along the lake, whose blue surface was like a polished mirror, and then it suddenly vanished behind a wall of rock, and they found themselves in a mountain-folk's village that seemed to lie clinging to the mountain slope, its huts and houses reflected in the water that washed about their feet.

From there they climbed up into the mountains, higher and higher. Sweat beaded their foreheads and dripped from their noses, and the thin mountain air felt like cool icicles in their burning throats. When they turned around they saw the lake lying far, far below them like a patch of woad-dyed cloth on a crumpled earth-brown cloak. Beyond the rock walls of the salt mountain a snow-clad peak rose into the clear blue sky.

High on the face of the mountain they caught sight of the black round openings of the mine shafts . . .

It was one of the elders of the mountain folk, old Masvatka with the shaggy beard, who led the slaves into the mountain. The Roman guards felt no great urge to scramble down the narrow mine shafts with those half-wild barbarians. And it was Masvatka who taught them how to handle the bronze picks as they lay on their stomachs in the low-roofed galleries. A bundle of tapers was handed out to each man every morning and the old man showed them how to hold the lit tapers between their teeth so that they should have as much light as possible to work by. To begin with, the slaves were chained to one another, but when Masvatka insisted that he was deafened by the rattling of the chains the Romans loosed them. And so the long night began, and it seemed it would never have an end.

Often, as Odbjørn lay in the dank passages of the mine, its walls running with water, and threw lumps of salt over his shoulder into the funnel-shaped leather bag on his back, his thoughts would travel far away to the Cimbrian coast. Then he would stop a moment and reflect that one day perhaps Hugwa would taste the very lump of salt he now held in his hand.

One evening as the slave driver Furius was ticking off the slaves as they came out of the mine shaft he found one missing. Cracking his whip, he lined them up and checked them again, but it made no difference—one of the slaves was still missing.

He glanced sideways at Æmilius, bent over his wax tablets, sniffed and wiped his nose on his arm. Then he got down to it again, counting and re-counting. Æmilius came over and snatched the wax tablets from him—a missing slave meant a loss.

"Who's missing?" he snarled.

Who's missing! Did the old dotard think that he, Furius, knew all those beasts by name? Yes, he remembered one— the chap they'd caught that night in Vetera.

"Perhaps he's the one—the Cimbrian . . ." Furius stammered.

"I'm here," said Odbjørn.

Meanwhile old Masvatka had opened the gate to the mineshaft.

"Listen!" he whispered, stepping back.

"Be quiet!"

They could now hear a strange sound inside the mountain—a sound of banging far away in the darkness—and a cold shudder ran down their spines.

"Out with him!" shouted Æmilius. "Fetch him out!"

Furius stepped hastily out of the way and left Odbjørn standing nearest to Æmilius.

"In after him!" screamed the slave dealer, giving him a push toward the mine shaft.

Odbjørn thrust a taper into the fire. The old Celt handed him a fresh bundle and followed him in. Even Æmilius could not restrain his curiosity.

Two or three times Odbjørn missed the way in the labyrinth of narrow galleries. The noise of banging died away, and as he turned back, squeezing past the slave dealer and the Celt, the old man laid a wrinkled clawlike hand on his arm.

"Perhaps he's not the one you're after!" he whispered.

"Who else is it?" Odbjørn laughed uncertainly.

Who else then?

"It sometimes happens that we hear sighs and groans down here at nighttime. Take care what you're doing!" the old man whispered through his chattering teeth. "Something's going on in the mountain—something we don't know about!" As he listened to the man's cracked voice Odbjørn could feel his hot breath on his face, but he laughed and pulled himself away.

The noise grew in volume as the blows rang out louder and louder. Then all at once the gallery was filled with a booming clang, and away in the darkness a gleam of torchlight trickled into the passage, black shadows flickering like bats in and out of the light.

A little farther on the passage turned off. The old man crept up to Odbjørn.

"All the upper galleries come to an end there in a large chamber," he whispered, "and from it a shaft descends to the salt-workings lower down in the mountain."

Odbjørn nodded and stole up to the opening in the wall of the shaft. He leaned forward carefully and peered through the hole.

Inside the lofty chamber he caught sight of a black silhouette in a flare of reddish torchlight. A man was hacking away at the salt face, and as he drove his pick into the rock his cloak flew out behind him like black wings.

Above his head a gigantic face stood out from the wall of the cavern. The salt crystals glittered in the glare of the flames, and the face glowed with warmth and life. Time after time the bronze pick struck the wall, smoothing the face with its blows, rounding it off and cutting furrows into the salt.

Odbjørn gasped. That black tousled hair? Hadn't he seen that hair before somewhere—full of straw and bits of chaff? Shouldn't he recognize that thin body and those long loose limbs that made the fellow look like a long-legged foal?

And now . . . The fellow had dropped his bronze pick. He had poked his finger into his ear and was giving it a good shake.

"Buekil!" shouted Odbjørn, as he jumped down into the cavern.

Buekil!

"Wait a bit," said Buekil. "Just wait a minute!"

He glanced briefly at Odbjørn and pushed him aside as if he were in the way and making a nuisance of himself. Odbjørn stared open-mouthed at Buekil as he stepped back and gazed intently at the face in the salt rock.

"Look," he said eagerly, "when I hold the torch here the nose is right, but it doesn't look like him! And when the light falls from this side, then it's him all right, but the nose . . . The nose is the most difficult bit," he groaned.

"Buekil," cried Odbjørn, "don't you recognize me at all?"

Buekil turned around and looked at him in surprise.

"Why shouldn't I recognize you? After all, it's your fault

I can't get Varus's ugly mug out of my head! But perhaps it wasn't you that dragged me along to the Roman camp?"

"Yes, of course it was!" Odbjørn nodded.

"Good. Do you realize I spent all that night trying to model Varus's fat face, and when I'd done it I was to die? Well, every time I'd nearly finished I nipped his nose off and started on it all over again! But do you know what that means?" Buekil whispered hoarsely. "Do you understand what it means to make noses a whole night through? I can't stop now, I tell you! I've hundreds and hundreds of noses running around in my head!"

At that moment they caught sight of Æmilius. The slave dealer stood open-mouthed, staring in wonder at the rock-hewn head, at Varus's face that Buekil had conjured out of the salt with his bronze pick. He scratched his bald crown and screwed up his eyes. He stood there with his mouth wide open, stroking his bare head. And suddenly a broad grin spread over Æmilius's narrow, hawklike face.

16

Ordeal in the Alps

Odbjørn expected no good from the slave dealer's crafty grin, and his misgivings proved well-founded.

The next day Æmilius took Buekil along with him and sold him to Petronia, a Roman lady who lived on an estate somewhere in the mointains. Petronia, who ran a salt mine and was part-owner of a quicksilver mine as far away as Baetica, was exceedingly rich in both goods and slaves. And since she esteemed sculpture and fine pottery very highly, she paid Æmilius well for Buekil the Gaul—so well that the money would cover the slaves' keep on their way to Rome.

Work in the salt mines was stopped that very day, and the day after, they began the journey southward over the Alps. The track wound upward through dark forests of fir, and high over their heads the wind howled and whined in the tangle of fir needles. Above the trees rose the snow-clad mountains, their high battlemented peaks obscured in a frosty mist. From the valley below, the precipitous mountain range had looked like jagged white fangs rising above the green belt of fir. But now the mountains had vanished, hidden in a howling snowstorm, and at their backs seethed the fir trees, a wind-swept forest on the edge of the abyss of the sky. As the snowstorm struck them they staggered forward, ever forward and upward into the roaring emptiness of the sky. Below them the wind raged through the gorges like a howling wolf pack. The crack of the slave drivers' whips echoed through the swirling snow, and the chains jingled like muted bells.

Ever onward—in among the mountain crags, over barren levels of rock and smooth snowfields where their feet sank deep into the cold whiteness. The Alpine winter had stolen a march on Æmilius and was barring the way to Rome. But Æmilius was not going to let himself be deterred. . . .

A gray wall of rock, the snow swirling around and spiraling up over it, towered in front of them. Suddenly the heavily falling snow was filled with shouting voices, and a red cloak was whipping in the snowstorm like splashing blood. The tribune from the mountain fort had come to warn Æmilius, with a hand laid on the slave dealer's shoulder so that he should not lose sight of him.

"The pass is blocked with snow!" he cried. "You won't get through. Turn back before it's too late!"

The wind snatched the words out of their mouths . . . "Avalanche!" roared the wind . . . "Certain death . . ."

"On!" yelled Æmilius . . . "Forward!"

Ahead, the slave market in Rome was calling. The many delays were emptying the leather bag beneath his cloak—he had no time for waiting.

"On with you!"

But the slave drivers stood hesitating, shivering with cold and fear. Æmilius snatched the whip of the one who stood nearest and clouted him with the handle.

"On!" he bawled. "Get on!"

The whips cracked over the slaves' backs, the slave drivers laying on hard as though whipping their own fears out of their bodies.

"Stop!" Æmilius pushed forward and seized the foremost slave by the shoulder. "Stand still! . . . Stay where you are!"

The rattling of the chains died away. Somewhere in the ravines a sudden squall of wind roared against the rock face.

"Look there!" Æmilius pointed backward. "Can't you see anything? Are you blind?"

Against the white snowfield they could just see the outline of a dark object moving forward, coming nearer and nearer. It grew slowly larger, became a black figure staggering toward them over the white waste of snow. From time to time the figure vanished in the snowstorm to reappear a moment later, each time bigger, each time nearer. Perhaps a legionary from the mountain fortress, they thought.

At last he reached them, stumbling into their midst. He stopped and stood there, silent and unsteady, his face hidden beneath his hat. Æmilius had stepped backward, but he now sprang forward again and snatched the stranger's hat off. They heard a hoarse half-suppressed cry, and then they saw him dancing round and round the lonely mountain wanderer.

"Odbjørn!" a voice called. "Odbjørn!"

"Here . . . I'm here!" Odbjørn shouted.

The stranger tottered toward him. Æmilius followed, clapping him on the shoulder, digging him in the back. He was beside himself with delight, his hoarse shouts of laughter penetrating the noise of the wind.

"Buekil! It's Buekil!" Odbjørn seized him by the shoulder and shook him. "Is it really you?"

"Were you expecting someone else?" Buekil grinned.

So Buekil had come back!

"Like a faithful dog to his master!" Æmilius said with a smirk as he slapped his shoulder.

"Away . . . Away with you!" he cried, as one of the slave drivers came up dragging an iron chain with him. "Take it away!" cried Æmilius. "He won't be chained! You can see for yourself he follows me like a dog! The fellow's worth his weight in gold!" The slave dealer put his hand inside his cloak and lovingly caressed the leather bag which held the many thousand sesterces that the Roman lady Petronia had paid him for Buekil, the sculptor-slave. "Worth twice his weight!" he muttered.

The chained column of slaves was set in motion. They were now close to the pass over the mountains, and Æmilius had the slaves divided and chained together in small groups of a dozen or so, so that if one of the slaves stumbled and fell he would drag at the most only a dozen others into the depths below.

The Roman military road that climbed in a zigzag up over the almost sheer mountain range was snowed under. They went sideways, at arm's length from one another, their chests pressed against the wall of rock.

"How did you find us?" Odbjørn called out.

Buekil told him all that had happened to him since they had parted on the salt mountain. He shouted into the face of the rock and the wind swept some of his words away; but from what he heard, Odbjørn understood that when Buekil arrived at Petronia's villa he was set to making a pot to show his skill. Æmilius meanwhile had disappeared into the atrium with Petronia, and then Buekil saw him leave the villa and start on his way downward through the valley.

"So I thought he'd forgotten me!" Buekil yelled. "Now if I'd been his knapsack I'd have stayed where I was; but as I wasn't, I got up and went after him!"

A piercing scream rose suddenly above the howling of the wind.

Æmilius came by crawling on his hands and knees and

poked his head out over the precipice. On the mountain path below lay a swarthy slave driver.

Three of the slaves had slipped over the edge and were hanging by their chains over the dizzy precipice. The swarthy fellow had taken hold of the chain, and behind him five or six slaves were straining their backs against the mountain wall and trying to twist their hands out of the iron grip of the chain.

"Hold on!" yelled Æmilius.

The slave driver did not let go, but as his heavy body sank deeper and deeper into the snow he was dragged half-sideways toward the edge of the precipice.

"Take hold of him . . . Do you hear? Hold . . ."

Æmilius stopped short. The slave driver's body had vanished. Like an anchor dropped overboard and dragging the anchor chain after it, the slave driver's heavy body swept the chained slaves with him over the edge of the precipice. Like a rattling cable, their screams of fear rose above the wind. Then all was still.

Æmilius got up and clung to the mountainside.

"On!" he yelled.

For two whole days they labored on over the high-pitched roof of the world. Blinded by the stinging pin-pricks of the snowstorm, deafened by the fury of the wind, they groped their way along by furrowed mountain walls and giddy precipices. And the iron links of their chains chafed frost-sores on their arms.

But gradually the wind fell. Their legs felt light, and time after time their feet slipped from under them—they were now going downhill. The snow crunched underfoot, and all around them the air was full of swarming snow-flakes drifting softly and silently to the ground. Somewhere far away, beyond snow and mountains and sky, a wolf howled, and still farther away a branch cracked, but the snow stifled the sound of it. The stillness was full of silent footfalls and the throb of blood behind aching eardrums.

The snow slowly retreated and winter with it. In the course of a single day they seemed to journey through spring into the warm sunshine of summer.

But Odbjørn wandered from the gentle warmth of summer into the scorching desert heat of fever. His tunic was soaked with sweat, his cheeks were burning hot, and his teeth chattered with cold. He plodded on in a coma of shimmering red mist. But he had someone to talk to him, to support him, to hold him up—someone who poured water into his mouth and covered him with his own tunic —and that was Buekil. Buekil took on many different forms: sometimes he seemed to shrink, to recede into the distance until he was no bigger than a finger, and then the next moment he would grow to the size of a giant.

The fever conjured up strange visions in the red mist. Odbjørn wandered over a stony wilderness of grayish-white boulders and along white mountain walls reflected in glittering green lakes. The limestone mountains crept away behind him, and in front lay a golden green landscape, with pinetrees, flat-topped and somber like huge toadstools, growing around him, and tall, slender cypresses flanking the dusty highroad.

What he saw were not the visions of a fevered mind, for one fine day when the fever had subsided a strange new world lay spread before his wondering eyes; a riot of color in the sparkling sunlight, with the delicate green of the vine-covered hills alternating with the gray foliage of the olive groves, huddled like flocks of sheep on the ocher-colored slopes.

The darkness of the night was soft black velvet powdered with sparkling stars like the twinkling embers of a dying fire.

Odbjørn lay staring up into the glittering night sky.

Among the black pillars of the cypresses, the moon hung full and silver-bright. At home in Hugwa's dwelling they would now be celebrating the coming of summer, and at the next spring sacrifice the farmer would give his daughter's hand to the one who kept tryst at the folk-meet with the greater following—to him who had won the greater honor in foreign lands. There were now only twelve months to the spring sacrifice, and he was farther from wealth and power than ever before. True, he had been poor and unknown when he departed, but slave-born he was not.

He covered his eyes with his fettered hands, and he was glad there were mountains and rivers and broad plains between him and Groa so that she could not see the stars of Italy twinkling and sparkling in the tears on his cheeks.

Early one evening they reached the Sabatine Lake. Here Æmilius called a halt and ordered the slaves to be driven down to the thick banks of reeds along the water's edge so that they could wash the dust of travel off their bodies before they were offered for sale in the slave market.

The next day, when they reached the top of the range of hills to the south of the lake, they caught a glimpse of the city on the seven hills, a labyrinth of streets and alleys between slender columns and huge buildings of sparkling marble, and farther off, as far as the eye could reach, the gloomy barracks of lodginghouses. There in the stony desert of the city, the threads of power were woven together, a spider's web covering the mighty Roman Empire.

The long journey had come to an end. . . .

17

The Roman Slave Market

He stood on a turntable, his feet whitewashed to show that this was the first time he was to be sold as a slave, his name and age written on a board hung about his neck. Æmilius put a foot on the table and turned Odbjørn around so that he could be inspected from all sides. And as the table was set in motion the Campus Martius turned before Odbjørn's wondering gaze.

The road that had led them into Rome, the Via Flaminia, disappeared, its gray paving running straight as an arrow, behind the towering, round, stone colossus where the Emperor Augustus would one day be laid to rest. Then followed the bowl-shaped sundial with its slender pillar throwing the black shadow of time across its marble walls.

The slave dealer turned the turbid yellow waters of the Tiber before his wondering eyes just as a heavily-laden passenger boat was mooring alongside the quay in front of the stone bridge. Odbjørn caught a glimpse of the passengers swarming up the stone steps that led from the riverside quay. Then Æmilius turned the domed roof of the Pantheon and the colonnades of the Circus Flaminius before him. And there, high above the glittering rooftops, he saw a spray of water descending from the open channel of an aqueduct, which, raised on thousands of stone piers like so many long legs, brought water down from the hills. Æmilius continued turning him around amid the murmuring sea of people in the slave market.

A horseman of the imperial household galloped past, the black horsehair plume on his helmet waving over a swirl of brightly colored garments. And Odbjørn did not notice the fingers prying over his body, nor did he hear Æmilius's grating voice rising above the buzz of the chattering crowd. A little way off a couple of lads lay on the pavement throwing dice. Three men dressed in togas were walking around among the chained slaves. They were buying for the fleet, choosing galley slaves for the Roman warships. Æmilius kept his eye on them. Æmilius's eyes were everywhere. You had to keep your wits about you in a slave market, and Æmilius had six turntables going. He beckoned to a slave driver to stay near the buyers. Then he turned back to the business in hand.

"Honored citizens, men of Rome! Look at this powerful lad! Not a Gaul . . . not a German . . . What then? He comes from the land of the Cimbrians on the uttermost edge of the world! From a somber misty coast by the German sea. In short, a rarity on the Roman market!"

Æmilius coughed and started in again.

"Odbjørn . . . Cimbrian . . . eighteen. Odbjørn knows about as much as a horse—knows much about horses, I mean!"

Æmilius roared with laughter. You had to make your little joke!

"Stand up straight!" he snapped, cutting Odbjørn across the chest with his whip. "Odbjørn!" he yelled. But he suddenly stopped short and went storming over to one of the other turntables.

Odbjørn was left standing by himself, stiff and motionless. If he moved, the boards would creak under his whitewashed feet, and then people would turn and stare up at him with eyes as cold and indifferent as if they were glancing at a mangy cur.

Below him an old man came trudging by. A stool was hanging from the back of his thin sunburnt neck, and the tools of a street barber rattled beneath his grayish-white tunic. The old man disappeared into the throng and his place was taken by a litter. Odbjørn could scarcely believe his own eyes, for the litter was borne along by four slaves as black as the Italian night. On the white silk cushions inside the litter reclined a young high-born Roman lady dressed in a thin tunic of yellow silk. Her hair was raven black, her lips painted red and her eyelids shadowed blue. Her dark eyes glanced at Odbjørn over the edge of her palm-leaf fan. Then the litter and its black slaves vanished into the sea of people.

A cavalry squadron of the Praetorian Guard galloped northward along the Via Flaminia, helmets and breastplates gleaming in the sun. A veil of sparkling water drops hung between the stone piers of the aqueduct.

Odbjørn started. Æmilius had come back to the turntable and struck the board on Odbjørn's chest with his stick. Over by the sundial Æmilius had caught sight of the manager of the Reds—the Red Charioteers of the Circus Maximus.

"Domini Vatia!" he yelled.

The rider turned his horse around and came toward them. Vatia was short and stocky, and a ring of black hair hung limply like rotten thatch around his bald crown. The heat was too much for Vatia, and the sweat that streaked his chubby cheeks glistened like snail tracks. He was dressed in a sleeveless tunic and a red cloak which he had thrown back to cool his bare arms. Round one swelling upper arm he wore an ivory bracelet. It was much too tight for him—in fact, he looked as if everything had gradually become too small for him.

Odbjørn noticed that people turned and stared inquisitively at the manager of the Red Stables. They moved back respectfully from the turntable, and Æmilius had turned into a cringing dog crawling under Vatia's stirrups.

"I was very glad to hear Nikalos beat Diocles by three lengths in the last race," he said with a fawning smirk.

"Nikalos is the best we've got," Vatia grunted, his voice appearing to come from somewhere near the saddle. "We can manage the Blues and the Whites every time, but . . ."

"And the Greens, too! Definitely, my dear Vatia," Æmilius fawned. "When I return home next time, I shall hear that Domini Vatia has led the Red Charioteers to victory over the Greens!"

"Nikalos is good," nodded Vatia, "but Metellus Rutilius is better . . ." He suddenly fell silent and glanced uneasily out of the corner of his eye at the listening throng around him. "Enough of that!" he muttered. "See if you can't get me a good charioteer that we can bring up in the right way!"

"That'll be difficult, Vatia. But take a look here . . . I've got a first-class stable slave here at any rate, a fellow who understands horses. Sixteen hundred sesterces and he's yours!"

"Hm, so he understands horses . . ."

A suppressed gurgling sound shook Vatia's heavy body. He slipped a handkerchief out of his tunic and wiped the sweat off his brow. Then he rode up to the turntable as though to take a good look at Odbjørn.

Suddenly he tugged the reins hard, and with a vigorous shake of the head the horse struck Odbjørn and sent him tumbling off the turntable. He fell backward and hit the marble pavement with a dull thud.

A roar of laughter rose around him.

He got up red in the face, but just as he was climbing back onto the turntable Vatia jerked the bridle. The horse's muzzle struck Odbjørn over the ear and knocked him down again. Vatia spluttered with suppressed laughter.

"I think the fellow's scared of horses," he hiccoughed. The thunderous roar of laughter tickled his vanity, and Odbjørn had scarcely mounted the turntable before, with a flick of the rein, he knocked him down again.

"Get up!" snarled Æmilius, giving Odbjørn a slash across the neck with his stick. He cursed Serbulus who had led him to believe that the lad understood horses. And he went on laying about him as though it were Serbulus he was striking. "Up with you!" he fumed. "Come on, get up!"

Odbjørn clenched his teeth. He felt as if a white flash were penetrating his brain every time the stick struck him. He got up slowly. But suddenly an uncontrollable fit of rage flared up inside him, and as quick as lightning he sprang onto the turntable, seized the horse by the muzzle and clamped his fingers around the distended nostrils. The horse whinnied and shook his head vigorously to free himself from the stifling grip. Vatia felt the animal tremble under him.

"Let go!" he shouted.

"Let go!" yelled Æmilius, as he continued to belabor Odbjørn with his stick. But Odbjørn clenched his teeth and hung on.

The horse's forelegs crumpled under him and he sent Odbjørn flying off the turntable, but he did not let go, and just as the animal, with a hoarse rattle in the throat, sank to the ground, Vatia sprang out of the saddle.

Odbjørn released the muzzle and placed a foot on the horse's neck. In a flash he unbuckled the girth and flung away the saddle.

"What's got into him?" roared Vatia. Æmilius darted forward with his stick but sprang back in astonishment.

The horse had jumped up, and astride his back sat Odbjørn wheeling him around with tightened rein in sweeping circles that sent people running for their lives. Then, with sparks flying from his hoofs, the horse pounded across the Campus Martius. The sound died away and returned. Like a roll of thunder Odbjørn galloped in and out among the terrified knots of people scattering like chaff before the wind.

"Look . . . Look at the slave!"

A wave of excitement roared through the sea of people, and broke in a breathless silence as they all seemed to gasp at once.

Now he stood upright on the horse's hindquarters, hopping like a magpie. Now he threw himself forward on his stomach and disappeared from view. Now look! . . . There he was under the horse's belly, among the galloping legs . . . A swell of applause rose and ebbed away. And as he sprang off the horse and landed with a bang on the turntable a storm of enthusiasm broke around him.

"How much?" shouted Vatia's rumbling voice.

"Three thousand sesterces!" yelled the slave dealer.

"Didn't you say sixteen hundred before?"

"That was his price then! He'll cost you three thousand five hundred now!"

"Three thousand, you said!"

"Four thousand's what I meant!"

"All right, I'll take him," cried Vatia.

The excitement was dying away in a buzzing murmur of voices over the Campus Martius.

"He's yours for four thousand!" Æmilius called out. "And what about a couple of sturdy Cheruscans at the same time?"

"All right, then. Pick two out for me, Æmilius. I'll send a wagon along for all three of them."

As Odbjørn was clambering into the cart he saw Buekil standing on the turntable. His face was smeared white, as the custom was with slaves from Gaul.

"Look! Watch what happens!" Æmilius rattled away. "Honorable citizens, you see here a lump of clay—a shapeless lump of clay in my hand that in the slave's hand will turn into . . . into a . . . what shall we say? A bear!" he cried as he threw the clay to Buekil. "A bear. Watch carefully now . . . Look, now it's coming . . . swaying along and growling, like those in the dark forests of Germany, or like the brown bear you've seen in the arena . . . Did you see it?"

Buekil had flattened out the bear with a blow of his hand.

"A squirrel! . . . Look at it climbing up between his fingers, holding its bushy tail over its back. . . . Where does the gift for modeling and the power of creating come from? No one knows! But here, citizens of Rome, here you can acquire a master of the art for the paltry sum of six thousand sesterces . . . A hyena, honored citizens! Just look . . ."

But nothing happened. Buekil was pulling faces and playing ball with the lump of clay.

"A hyena!" Æmilius snarled . . . "All right, a lion then! . . . Do you hear? A lion," he prattled, "a lion from the deserts of Ethiopia with a mane and whiskers. In one second it will be prowling along on its belly over the slave's hand. Come on!" he hissed between his teeth as he fetched Buekil a rap with his stick. Buekil sniffed and wiped his nose along his arm, from his elbow to the tip of his finger. The audience howled with laughter.

Then the light suddenly dawned on Æmilius.

"Aha!" he cried. "The Gaul doesn't know the beasts of

the desert! But once he's seen them they'll come tumbling out of the clay one after another! Let's finish off with something he knows instead. A stag, for example . . . a stag with spreading antlers." Flicking his fingers, Æmilius raised his hands upwards and outwards from his bald head to indicate a pair of invisible antlers. "A stag!" he whispered.

But Buekil had had enough of it by this time. He slapped the lump of clay down on Æmilius's bald pate and wiped his hands clean. A hoarse roar of laughter greeted this gesture. Æmilius scraped the clay off his head and raised his stick.

"Stop!" The sharp voice sounded like the crack of a whip.

A distinguished Roman, dressed in the white, purple-striped toga of a senator, advanced toward the slave dealer. The man's high rank acted like a gust of wind blowing before him to sweep the common people from his path.

"A blow from your stick, should it prove unlucky, might cripple his fingers for life!" the senator said as he stopped in front of Æmilius.

"Greetings, Lucius Galba!" Æmilius raised his hand and bowed his head respectfully.

"What's your price for this Gaul?" Lucius Galba passed a hand over the gray hair that fringed his forehead and down over his tired eyes. "The price?" he asked.

Odbjørn started as the cart was set in motion.

"Buekil!" he called. "Buekil!"

The Gaul looked up and caught sight of him.

"The Circus Maximus!" Odbjørn shouted, pointing to himself. "Circus Maximus!"

Buekil nodded, put his thumb in his ear and waved his fingers.

The cart jolted over the paving blocks of the narrow streets into the jostling life of the city.

Over to their right lay the Capitol. Up on the hill beyond the broad flight of marble steps glittered the bronze
roof of the Temple of Jupiter. Behind its columns and
white temple walls he caught a brief glimpse of the Forum,
its open squares gleaming in sunlight and thronged with
people ceaselessly crossing and recrossing its smooth
marble slabs, its statues motionless and bathed in golden
light behind a mist of fine spray from its fountains.

The cart rumbled along the Via Sacra, the Sacred Way,
and then they suddenly found themselves in the turmoil of
the streets. Behind a colonnade Odbjørn saw people pushing and shoving in front of a long marble counter. A
couple of dark-haired Roman girls were pouring wine
from the winejars on the counter into the jugs that were
stretched out toward them. There were barber's shops,
booksellers and the booths of money-changers. An uproar of
shouting and screaming assailed them from the farther side
of the columns.

Odbjørn stared fascinated at the ever-changing sea of
people. There were faces black as shadows and brown as
the leaves of autumn. He saw men clad in the strange uni-
forms of foreign soldiery, Negroes with their black bodies
naked above their white loincloths, Germans in their
brown cloaks. And he thought that all the peoples of the
world must have arranged to meet one another here in the
city on the seven hills.

It was well past the hour when the streets of Rome had
to be cleared of carts and wagons. The driver urged his
mule forward and they drove a long way around through
narrow alleys that lay between the scabby gray walls of
barracklike blocks of flats. From the poor quarter they
turned back toward the Patrician Way, and a little later
the cart was rolling along by the Palatine Hill, with the
massive walls of the imperial palace abutting on its south-
ern slopes.

Over there in the valley lay the Circus Maximus, long and narrow like a ship. And Odbjørn thought that if a hundred halls the size of Hugwa's were placed one behind the other they would still not be as big. . . . But as they drew nearer he saw that Hugwa's hall would go into any one of the rounded archways that led beneath the towering masonry into the interior of the building. And there were many times a hundred archways around it—more than he could count.

18

Stable Slave to a Charioteer

And so Odbjørn became stable slave to the charioteer Nikalos.

He learned to know the hard brutal world of the racing drivers. He followed their life-and-death struggle as they galloped madly round the arena to the thunderous shouts of applause from the hundreds of thousands of spectators who lined the rows of benches.

He soon realized that Rome's four companies of charioteers fought one another with all the means at their disposal—outside the arena as well as within. They often tried to entice the most skilful drivers from their rivals with promises of vast sums of money. And if that failed . . . well, a horse could suddenly collapse in his stall, the victim of a mysterious poisoner. A wheel might fall to pieces during a race. Perhaps a charioteer would vanish without trace, never to return.

When a charioteer went to sleep it was well for him to shut only one eye at a time—and the stable slave who slept with the horses was well advised to keep both his eyes open.

Odbjørn did not go to such lengths, but his ears were always on the alert, even in sleep. If one of Nikalos's horses stamped, or the shake of a head rattled a chain, he was awake at once, and then he would lie for a long time staring into the dark and listening for creeping footsteps. Even a snort in the manger was sufficient to drive sleep away.

Nikalos came in one night and found Odbjørn lying on a beam immediately above the horses. One could tell from the charioteer's face that he wondered how anyone could go to sleep on a beam without falling down among the animals. But since it could be done it was a good place to choose. Nikalos was satisfied, but he said nothing.

During the first month that Odbjørn spent as a slave in the Red Stables, he did not, in fact, hear Nikalos's voice at all. The charioteer would enter the stable silently at odd moments and survey Odbjørn's work. Every time he found the horses well groomed and well cared for, and every time he inspected the litter the straw was clean and dry. Nikalos found nothing to comment on. Then one day he spoke to him for the first time.

Nikalos was a tall broad-shouldered Macedonian with corn-colored hair as curly as a Negro's. A patch of white skin, as big as the fingers of one hand, covered one side of his broad chin. He had once had a fall and torn the skin off.

"And where the sand of the arena kisses your cheek your beard won't grow again," he explained to Odbjørn.

Nikalos was the Reds' best charioteer, and so Odbjørn was proud of serving in his stable. As time went by he learned to know the others, too. One of the best was Diocles of the Blues. He was lame as the result of a fall, but once he had the reins around his waist he drove even faster than Antonius Tubero of the Whites. But the fastest of them all was Metellus Rutilius of the Greens—faster than Nikalos, faster than Thallus, Gordius, Sporpus and all the rest of them.

Metellus Rutilius had over nine hundred victories to his credit. He had conferred on nine horses the distinction of being called "hundred-horses" by bringing them first past the finish post a hundred times. Metellus, a dark thickset man, always arrived at the races in a litter. Malicious tongues asserted that his dark-skinned Libyan slaves had to lift him out of the litter and put him in his racing chariot, so lazy, so arrogant and overbearing had he become. He did not talk to the other charioteers, and unless everything was exactly to his liking he would simply refuse to start.

It was clear to everyone in Rome that if anybody were to wrest the reins of victory from Metellus it would have to be Nikalos the Macedonian. Time after time he had clung close to the heels of Metellus and kept pace with him right up to the finish—but never any farther. Just before the finish post the tails of the Roman's horses had always swished past the Macedonian's head-trappings and waved good-by.

That was how the talk went in Rome—in market and wineshop, street and alleyway. The great race of the year was drawing close. At the festival of the Saturnalia the battle would be between the Reds and the Greens, between Nikalos and Metellus. That the two other companies could seriously compete, no one thought for a moment. It was on Metellus or Nikalos that men laid their money.

There was still some time to go before the festival, but in a month's time the trial race would be run, and of the eight teams taking part only the four best would be selected to run in the Saturnalia itself. Even in the trial Metellus and Nikalos would be taking one another's measure.

Every day Nikalos trained his horses in the Circus Maximus. The crack of the whip and the beating of hoofs echoed backward and forward down the length of the auditorium, until it seemed as if hundreds of invisible horses were clattering round between the empty rows of seats.

The race track lay like a ravine between the sheer mountainsides of the auditorium, and when the Circus Maximus was filled with a howling, shouting mob the spectators on the top rows looked like nothing so much as waving grasses on a hillside.

The spina, a broad low wall, ran down the middle of the course like a backbone, and on it stood a water clock which Odbjørn watched carefully as Nikalos drove around the track. From time to time Nikalos would climb, panting and running with sweat, onto the spina and take a look at the clock, and then he would shake his head doubtfully and try again. Nikalos was dissatisfied with his leader—it was too slow swinging the rest of the team around the ends of the spina—and he would grind his teeth and lay his whip across the animal's hindquarters until it reared in its traces.

Odbjørn stood on the spina and fell into a reverie. All the strange new things he had seen had sometimes led him to forget that time was passing quickly and the spring sacrifice drawing closer and closer. But now the dripping of water in the water clock sounded like stealthy footsteps —as if time were creeping quietly past. Odbjørn had learned the Roman names for the months of the year, and he no longer had any need to count knots. As he was standing there on the spina, they had reached the month the Romans had named after the Emperor Augustus. In December they would celebrate the Saturnalia, and in the month that took its name from Mars, the God of War, the spring sacrifice would be held on the meetingplace by Hugwa's dwelling. In seven months he would have to be home. He was suddenly startled out of his thoughts.

"Are you asleep?" cried Nikalos, giving him a push. "You can take the reins now. And try to keep the leader as close in to the spina as possible!"

As he spoke, Nikalos handed him his belt with his knife in it—the knife every charioteer had to carry, for if his chariot overturned and he were dragged along behind the horses he had to be able to cut through the reins. Nikalos had, little by little, taught Odbjørn to drive the quadriga, the four-horsed racing chariot of the circus. To begin with, he had let him stand beside him in the chariot while he showed him how to change direction quickly and brush past his opponent, how to give the leader its head, how to take the sharp turns at the ends of the spina. In short, he had taught Odbjørn the whole art of the charioteer. And then one day he fastened the reins about Odbjørn's waist and jumped off the chariot, for he thought he would be better able to see how the horses performed individually if someone else were driving. Odbjørn set off with a jerk. The little two-wheeled chariot skidded around the metae, the three conical pillars that marked the ends of the spina, and as it shot forward down the long straight track the heavy sweating horses gathered speed.

"Faster!" Nikalos shouted from the spina. "Use your whip! Do you hear? Now! Give the leader his head! . . ."

Odbjørn had traveled far in his search for wealth and power, and he often thought he had gone astray. But as he stood with the reins about his waist, he realized that fate had led him to the one place in the world where the scramble for fortune's favors ended in a savage, ruthless struggle. The Circus Maximus presented a true picture of life. On the metaled surface of the race track the charioteers strove for dear life to bring their horses first past the winning post. And on the rows of benches the spectators shouted like ten thousand Hugwas to applaud the one fortune smiled upon.

"Stop!" shouted Nikalos. "It's no good," he said. "I shall never beat Metellus with that horse!"

The next day Nikalos and Odbjørn rode to the horse market in Ostia.

There in the port of Rome at the mouth of the Tiber,

the Egyptian corn-ships lay moored one behind the other. In front of the quay rose a wall of ship's timbers, but between stern and bowsprit Odbjørn caught a glimpse of open blue sea. The quayside was a swarming anthill of slaves laboring with sacks of corn and trundling casks of wine from ship to warehouse.

Close to the mouth of the river lay a shipyard right at the end of a mole. The dull thudding of hammers seemed to nail Odbjørn to the spot. On a slipway sloping down into the water, the naked ribs of a ship rose from the keel timbers like the skeleton of a sea monster, but in his mind's eye Odbjørn could see the ship as she would look when the ribs were covered with a golden-colored skin of oak planks.

"That's Lurco Nauclerus's shipyard," Nikalos explained. "And that's a liburna with two banks of oars that he's building—a bireme. But come along now—I've a lot to do!"

When Mango Plancius the horse dealer caught sight of Nikalos he clapped his plump hands together with a resounding smack.

"Here he comes! What did I say? Here comes Nikalos after a new leader for his team!"

"Where did you find out that I . . ."

"Nikalos, all Rome's talking about that ox you use as a leader!" Mango cried. "But when I hear people talking, I say, 'Wait and see,' say I! 'One of these fine days Nikalos'll come and get the horse he needs!' "

"You've got something you can offer me?"

"I've got a savage beast from Arcadia," Plancius cried. "Just arrived from overseas. But don't ask me how I got him in there!" He pointed to a paddock where a black stallion stood twitching his ears. "You can take him as he stands for three thousand sesterces. I shall be thankful to

see the back of the beast! But don't tell me afterwards that
I didn't warn you! If you can break him in he'll bring you
to victory, but otherwise . . ."

Without interrupting his flow of conversation, Mango
Plancius took cover behind a stable door while Nikalos and
Odbjørn made ready to catch the stallion. Odbjørn tied a
noose in a rope and tried throwing it over the fence so that
the noose fell over the stallion's head. Just as he had
managed to do it, the stallion struck the ground with his
hoofs, arched his neck and broke through the fence.

"I don't mind if he butts like a goat so long as he runs
better than one!" grinned Nikalos, and on the spur of the
moment he named him Capellus—the goat.

They rode back along the Via Ostensia, one on each side
of the road with the stallion between them. They had fastened a rope around his neck and they had their work cut
out to keep a tight hold on the spirited animal prancing
around in the middle of the road.

"Nikalos!"

"Well?"

"What does it cost to have a liburna built?" Odbjørn
shouted under the rearing chest. "A liburna with two
banks of oars?" he yelled.

Nikalos tried to work it out while the stallion made the
most persistent efforts to wrench his arm out of its socket.

"Three hundred thousand sesterces," he gasped. "Then
there'd be sixty galley slaves for about ninety thousand . . .
I reckon about four hundred thousand."

"What do you get if you win a race?" Odbjørn called out

"Fifty—sometimes sixty—thousand sesterces. More or
less. But what's it all about? Are you thinking of building a
ship?"

"I . . . I want to be a charioteer!" Odbjørn shouted over
Capellus's arched neck.

19

Buekil Earns Money

"So that's what you want . . ."

Domini Vatia had made short work of an excellent roast grouse—Phrygian grouse was Vatia's favorite dish, especially when it was washed down with a bottle of sweet golden wine from the valley of the Aulon. Vatia's broad jowl was shiny with grease. He was satisfied and well content. Nikalos had got hold of the perfect leading-horse—Capellus, the goat, he called him. He wriggled his massive body with satisfaction—within two months the goat's name would be on everyone's lips. Vatia streched, turned over among the cushions, and put his hand out for a morsel of cheesecake. He opened his wide jaws and dropped the cheesecake into his capacious mouth.

Then his thoughts turned to the slave standing on the other side of the table. Long-haired like a woman. All the same, he had a good appearance—upright, tall, broad-shouldered. By holy Epona, goddess of horses, what makes these barbarians grow and shoot up like that in that dark misty land of theirs?

"That's what you want, is it? You wear a slave's badge about your neck, and yet you're thinking of becoming a racing driver!"

A slave entered and began clearing the table. Vatia

wiped the grease from the corners of his mouth and dried his fingers in the slave's hair.

"Well, so you want to be a charioteer! Perhaps you're counting on the Red Stables to provide you with four horses and . . ."

"I'll buy the horses myself," Odbjørn replied.

"What with?" Vatia grunted.

"I thought I could sell this."

"What is it? Let me look . . . Ah, yes, a piece of amber."

Domini Vatia held the amber up to the light, and inside the yellow stone he saw a spider and a gnat, petrified at the very moment the spider's long legs were reaching out to seize the gnat. Lifelike. Very lifelike. That piece of amber was worth two or three teams of horses! Strictly speaking, it belonged to him—everything a slave possessed belonged to his master. But it came to the same thing in the end, thought Vatia. If the lad bought horses with the money, the horses would still belong to the Red Stables. And perhaps in a couple of years or so the fellow might develop into a good charioteer.

"I'll give you eight thousand sesterces for it," he said. "Buy your horses with the money. But don't neglect your work in the stables!"

Odbjørn did not neglect his work. In the middle of the night he climbed down from his roof beam, lit an oil lamp on the stable wall, and set about grooming the horses and cleaning out the stables. He had arranged for Buekil to slip out of Senator Galba's house and come along to the stables, and, sure enough, when the stable door creaked, there he was. Odbjørn let him take over the job of guarding Nikalos's horses, and rode through the dead of the night to Ostia. And before the she-wolf in her cage on the Capitol had risen to her feet and stretched herself, he was back with three roans.

"Three roans from Cyrene," Odbjørn explained, as he showed them proudly to Nikalos when he came along to the stable the same morning.

"This one's spent a good many years under the desert sun," Nikalos said. "It looks a bit faded." The charioteer passed his hand over their lean flanks. True, they were all three thin. Their ribs protruded noticeably beneath their coats, but . . . "And this one's blind in the right eye," Nikalos continued.

That he knew. He had noticed it before he left Ostia. He had also noticed the insincerity of the horse dealer's smile as he sang the roans' praises. But for all that, both the horse dealer and Nikalos were making a mistake. There was nothing wrong with the horses when it came to running!

"They run as if they had a leathermaker after them!" Nikalos admitted the first time he saw Odbjørn trying the roans out.

Nikalos laughed at them no more, but he was the only one who didn't laugh. The rest of the charioteers were always finding some excuse for going to the stables, where they never grew tired of watching Odbjørn and his horses.

Nikalos dug out a dusty old chariot for Odbjørn over in one of the cart sheds. It was a type which had not been in use in the arena for the past ten or twelve years. It was a bit too big and a bit too heavy. But Odbjørn replaced the pole and swingle-trees and removed the heavy bronze plates from the inside of the chariot to make it lighter— so much lighter that Nikalos shook his head anxiously.

"Mind what you're doing!" he warned him. "Remember that chariot'll take the corners sharply!"

One night as Odbjørn lay greasing the hubs of his chariot with tallow he heard the stable door open, and when he turned around he saw Buekil creeping in. Buekil sank down in the straw with a heavy sigh. His face and neck were covered in angry-looking weals, and a cut of the whip had drawn blood from a gash across his lips.

"Who's been flogging you?" Odbjørn cried indignantly.

"Two of Galba's slaves."

"But why?"

"Well, you see . . ." Buekil poked a finger into his ear and looked like a dog scratching for fleas. "You see Lucius Galba's got a daughter called Clodia. And Clodia's got a head . . . and I must say, a very beautiful one. And Galba has a son . . ."

"And he's got a head, too?" Odbjørn hazarded.

Buekil nodded. "Yes, that's right. And Galba has a wife . . ."

"That's enough!" cried Odbjørn.

"That's what I thought as well, but they want two each," Buekil sighed. "I began with Clodia. The gods made that face of hers—it's impossible to copy it!" Buekil cupped his restless hands about the flame of the oil lamp as though he were modeling some invisible form. "It's impossible," he sighed, as he let his hands fall.

"And when you'd finished you destroyed it because you weren't satisfied." Odbjørn shook his head. "You could be rich," he said, "if only you didn't . . ."

Buekil stretched himself in the straw.

"Lucius Galba says the same thing. I could sell my clay animals on the market, he says. And I could keep the money myself. He'd give me my freedom and pay the five per cent tax to the State himself."

"Then why don't you do it? Why do you destroy your clay animals as soon as you've made them?"

"Because I can't make them come right, Odbjørn . . . Because something's missing, something you can't see."

"No, and other people can't see it either, so you don't have to worry!" Odbjørn replied.

Buekil was silent, and for a long time neither of them

spoke. Chains rattled in the stalls and a horse snorted in the manger, raising a cloud of chaff.

"Odbjørn!"

"Yes?"

"If you win enough money to buy a ship . . . will you take me with you?"

"Of course I'll take you with me! The only question is —when will Vatia let me start racing? None of 'em believe I can manage a quadriga in the arena—none, except Nikalos perhaps." Odbjørn was silent a moment. He lay with his chin resting in his hands and stared into the flame of the lamp. "And then I want a good leader, too," he said.

"When will you get one?"

"Hm, when!" Odbjørn got up and strolled the length of the stalls. Buekil followed him. "Some time when it's too late!" he said, scratching one of the roans at the base of the tail. "That Mango Plancius in Ostia, he let me have these for six thousand. But he's asking three for a good leader— and I've only two thousand left."

"So you're a thousand sesterces short?"

"Just a thousand," Odbjørn nodded. "What did you say?"

"Me?" asked Buekil with a start. "I was only counting."

"Counting?"

"Yes, to a thousand," said Buekil. "A thousand little round shiny silver coins."

On his way home Buekil ran through the dark empty alleyways behind the Capitol. His footsteps, clattering on the stone pavements, re-echoed from the gray walls of the houses and broke the silence with their noise.

"Forty, fifty, sixty," he muttered.

He continued on his way along by the Palatine Hill, with its massive palaces hanging above his head like pale mists in the darkness. He trotted past the temple of Castor and

Pollux, and when he reached the round temple of the Vestal Virgins he put an arm out and ran once around the building, touching the columns one by one with his hand.

"Two hundred . . . ten . . . twenty . . . thirty . . ."

He ran through the triumphal arch into the Forum, where the smooth marble pavements, like huge dice, lay bathed in moonlight.

"Sixty, seventy, eighty," he gasped, as he hopped on one foot over the stone flags. All around the square, temples and basilicas lay as dark as the grave between their white columns.

He came to a sudden halt before an equestrian statue. He stood still for a minute and peered all around him. Then he climbed up onto the pedestal, set a foot on the horse's foreleg, and swung himself up onto its back. He let his fingers glide over the horseman's hair and down over the bronze muscles of the cheeks. His fingertips followed the lines of the nose and ran gently over the Cupid's bow of the lips. He took a deep breath and slid down to the ground. He stood there for a long time gazing raptly at the face of the statue, which the moonlight had furrowed with shadows and made wonderfully lifelike.

Then he set off running across the square and disappeared into the dark streets behind the Forum.

"A thousand!" he whispered, as he crept stealthily into the entrance to the house. In a recess in the wall the porter lay sleeping on his bench. Buekil listened to his heavy breathing as he slipped through the passage into the atrium. The moonlight fell through the square opening in the roof and hung like a transparent veil over the stone basin in the floor. A drop fell and hit the gleaming, mirror-like surface of the water with a tinkling sound. He crept across the marble floor and slipped out into the colonnade that surrounded Lucius Galba's magnificently laid-out garden. Over there in the darkness lay the slaves' sleeping-quarters.

"A thousand sesterces!" Buekil whispered as he pulled the blanket up over his head.

"A thousand," Buekil mumbled, as he woke and noticed someone standing by his side and shaking him. And when he opened his eyes he saw the household slaves grinning all round him.

"Are you lying there counting the lashes you've had, or those you've got coming to you?" inquired the librarian Phoebus with a laugh.

Buekil jumped up and dressed.

Lucius Galba rose from the table and prepared to enter the atrium where his friends and clients would call upon him, one after another, with their greetings and good wishes for the day. Galba bowed before the household gods in their recess, and as he turned around found that rascal from Gaul standing behind him.

"Well, have you changed your mind?" he asked.

Buekil nodded. He would begin that very day. Lucius clapped him on the shoulder.

"And you will let others pass judgment on your work, and not ruin it yourself as soon as it's finished?"

Buekil poked his finger into his ear.

He inquired cautiously if he might now begin selling his earthenware animals on the market.

"As soon as the bust of Clodia's finished," Galba growled.

And so the model was called in. She was fourteen and her black eyes had an angry glint in them as, with sulky looks and eyes upcast, she sank down into the chair and stretched her long lanky legs out in front of her. Every time he asked her to turn her head toward him, she would pull a face and stick her tongue out—or she would turn

her back upon him, and then he would fly into a temper
and prod her in the back of the neck with his modeling-
tool. Whereupon Clodia would bite Buekil's hand and try
to scratch his eyes out. In between times she would fall
asleep.

Three days passed after this fashion, and then the bust
stood finished on the modeling-table, smiling so gently and
beautifully that Lucius Galba turned away and with his
finger wiped a tear from the corner of his eye.

Then Buekil was sent out for the bronze-founder. On
the way home, as he passed through the street of the pot-
ters, he nipped inside Cotta Gabinius's workshop.

The old man was sitting at his wheel throwing a pot.
He did not hear Buekil come in, but he suddenly saw a
hand slip over his shoulder and pinch a lump of clay off
the jug he was making. The old man jumped to his feet,
seized a tripod and threw it at Buekil, but Buekil ducked
and fled for cover behind the table. Round and round the
table he went, closely followed by Gabinius who was now
flourishing a heavy poker. The old man fell, and as he got
up he cursed the gods who had sent this lout to plague
him. The table toppled over with a crash. Buekil slipped
away in a cloud of dust; and when the dust had settled,
the old man saw the lad standing behind the potter's wheel
with a broad grin on his face. Gabinius raised his poker
and crept towards him.

But what was that he had there? There, on the rim of
the ruined jug . . . Gabinius narrowed his eyes. An ante-
lope—no, a mountain goat, a mountain goat with curved
horns.

The old potter threw his poker down and took the clay
animal carefully between his fingers. Buekil pulled another lump of clay off the jug, and stood there modeling
clay animals one after another. Then he offered Gabinius

half the proceeds, half of everything he earned selling the clay figures, if the old man would fire them in his kiln.

Gabinius nodded without a word. One by one he put the clay figures on the tray. At last the jug had disappeared and the kiln looked like a cage filled with all sorts of little animals. Then Gabinius shut the door of the kiln upon them.

When Buekil slipped into the workshop later in the evening, the old potter opened up the kiln and took the herd of diminutive brown animals out of their cage.

"Just feel how warm they are," Gabinius said. "Just as if they were alive!" he said.

All that night the young man and the old one worked by the light of an oil lamp, and when day dawned the workshop was swarming with brown earthenware beasts.

Buekil set up his trestles in the colonnade of the quayside market down by the Tiber. The old potter had advised him to find a spot in the neighborhood of the Bridge of Fabricius which ran across the Island of Tiberina to the densely populated districts on the Janiculan Hill. A steady stream of people passed to and fro across the bridge, and the riverboats landed their passengers on the steps below. He would do a flourishing trade there, Gabinius promised him.

And he was right. Moreover, Buekil was fortunate enough to find himself seated close to the oddest pair either he or the people of Rome had ever set eyes on. Not ten yards away stood a frail little man, his dried-up, sun-tanned face surmounted by a strange bundle of intertwined strips of cloth. But it was not so much the man as his colossal beast that attracted everybody's attention. It stood like a gray weather-beaten boulder at the top of the steps that led down to the river and rocked backward and forward on legs as massive as tree trunks. Its ears were the size of palm leaves and its nose dangled down between its legs.

Every time a riverboat landed its passengers and people came streaming up the stone steps, the man would give his thick-skinned beast a jab with his goad, and then the beast would lift up its trunk and thrust an iron dish among the thronging crowds. The people would scatter in alarm, and one or two of them perhaps would tumble backward down the marble steps. But before long, when they had recovered from their fright, they would press around out of curiosity and throw coins into the dish.

The proximity of this remarkable pair was a great advantage to Buekil's business. The begging elephant attracted an audience, but, oddly enough, they very quickly lost interest in the gray colossus and they soon discovered far greater pleasure in the tiny earthenware animals on Buekil's stall.

One evening a couple of days later he sat down to his accounts, and figured out that they had to have another six hundred and eighty sesterces before Odbjørn could buy the horse he needed.

The traders had long since shut their stalls up, and behind him the colonnade lay empty and deserted, the ground littered with the filth and refuse of the day's business. He watched the elephant, like a gray boulder swaying and bumping against the stone wall, disappear around the corner of the theatre. He was left alone. At the bottom of the steps a riverboat lay moored, chafing against the quayside with a hollow thumping. Buekil tied his leather bag and was on the point of getting up when a dark shadow glided across the top of his trestle table. He raised his head and looked into a pair of sharp steel-gray eyes. He started and gripped his leather bag tightly. The man was dressed in a coarsely-woven, earth-brown tunic, frayed and worn.

His face was thin and his cheeks cleft by two deep furrows that met under his mouth, and as he bent forward to speak his long grizzled hair fell about his shoulders.

"That stable slave in the Circus Maximus," he whispered in a voice hoarse with excitement. "You know the one I mean?"

Buekil nodded.

"Tell me, is his name Odbjørn?"

"Y-yes . . ." Buekil swallowed and wiped his nose on his arm. "That's his name . . . His name's Odbjørn," he stammered.

Buekil's answer seemed to have relieved the stranger of a gnawing doubt. The hard lines of his ravaged face suddenly softened.

"So it is him," he muttered. "It can't be anybody else."

He straightened his back and, looking straight in front of him, nodded in silence.

20

In the Circus Maximus

It was the night before the great race.

Vatia had guards placed all around the stable buildings of the Red Charioteers, and whenever Nikalos stood still Odbjørn could hear them strolling backward and forward out in the yard. From time to time a shadow would pass over the window shutters, and the sound of hushed voices would penetrate the stable wall.

"You ought to go up and try to get some sleep," Odbjørn said. "Things always look better when you've had a good rest."

Nikalos did not answer. The straw rustled about his feet as he began pacing up and down again.

"Try it on him now!" He had come to a halt by Capellus's stall, and at the sound of his voice the stallion started forward, banging his chest so hard against the manger that the wood creaked with the impact.

"If I were you, Nikalos . . ."

"You heard what I said? Do it then!"

Odbjørn rose and took down some leather straps from the wooden peg on which they were hanging. Nikalos had got a saddler to make a blinker to strap over the stallion's left eye. Odbjørn had advised Nikalos against using it, and he now repeated his warning—for the last time.

"Don't do it. Let him alone, Nikalos. You know how often the beast shies! And when he can't see the wall . . ."

"That's the point—he mustn't see it!" Nikalos stood with his back to Odbjørn as if he were talking to the stallion. The stallion shook his halter and twitched his ears nervously. "You know how scared he is of the wall. If he can't see it, I can take the corners more sharply!"

"Yes, and it'll be the end of you if he crashes into the wall!" Odbjørn answered. "Why not wait until you know him better? Wait till the Saturnalia!"

"Do as I tell you!" Nikalos swung round. "Put that blinker on—do you hear?" he cried.

But it was easier said than done, for as soon as Odbjørn showed signs of wanting to enter the stall the stallion flung himself about from the one partition to the other. His agitation spread rapidly to the other horses, and the stable was in a sudden uproar of neighing and stamping and rattling chains. One of the guards opened the stable door a couple of inches and asked if anything was the matter.

"Clear off!" yelled Nikalos. The guard quickly withdrew his head and cleared off.

Straw and splinters flew about their ears, and then all at once Capellus kicked a board out of his stall.

"Stop!" shouted Nikalos. "Wait till later when we harness him to the chariot!"

He stood staring at the stallion as he raged around the stall foaming at the mouth like a savage beast. The muscles twitched in Nikalos's pale cheeks and his eyes narrowed with spite at the thought that he had not yet succeeded in bringing this wild beast to heel.

"The devil's more awkward than ever!" he muttered.

"Perhaps he realizes you're afraid of him," Odbjørn suggested.

"What did you say?" Nikalos stepped threateningly toward him. "Say that again, slave!" Nikalos, his face white as chalk, narrowed his eyes and compressed his lips. "Say it again! Say I'm afraid!" he snarled.

"Perhaps 'afraid' isn't the right word, Nikalos. But if a high-strung horse notices that a man's nervous, then . . ."

"That's enough!" yelled Nikalos as he struck him across the mouth.

Odbjørn turned pale. His gray eyes suddenly seemed to lose their color. Coldly and contemptuously he looked Nikalos steadily in the eye.

"Where I come from," he said in a low voice, "a man who lays a hand on beast or thrall is despised!"

"Mind your impudence, you dog of a slave!" yelled Nikalos, striking again, and yet again. Odbjørn staggered back a step and leaned his back against the partition. The stallion stamped in the straw and stood tense and watchful.

"Now I know you're afraid," Odbjørn whispered.

Nikalos raised his hand to strike again, but when he saw the blood trickling from the corner of the slave's mouth and leaving a red streak down his chin he let his arm drop, and all the muscles of his tensed body seemed suddenly to relax.

"Forgive me, Odbjørn!" He rubbed his brow with his hand. "You're right. I am afraid! But not of Capellus. And I'm not afraid to die, either, if it should come to that. But I'm dead scared of losing," he whispered hoarsely. "Every time Metellus overtakes me and drives past the winning post to victory he takes all the applause and enthusiasm of the crowd with him. He leaves nothing to spare for the rest of us but insults and shouts of abuse! The mocking yells follow you like the howling of a wolf pack . . . out of the Circus Maximus and right over to the stables. The mockery rings in your ears for days after Metellus has won a race. This time I've got to win! That's why I'm harnessing Capellus to the chariot, though, the gods know,

I'd rather see the beast grazing in Hades on the banks of the Styx! I'm not myself tonight, Odbjørn. Forgive me!"

Nikalos held out his hand, but Odbjørn drew back.

"You'd better get some sleep before the race," he said.

The charioteer turned and went out. Odbjørn heard him stumping up the stairs, and he stood still a moment listening to his restless pacing overhead. Then he wiped the blood off his lips and lay down in the straw.

It wasn't that Nikalos had made his mouth bleed. It was worse than that. He had at the same time destroyed the picture of him that Odbjørn had built up in his own mind. He was now nothing but a wretched charioteer driven frantic by anxiety and chasing after fortune like a donkey after a carrot. Nikalos was no different from all the others . . . and no different from himself, either.

Odbjørn's thoughts came to an end as he heard a rustling in the straw. He sat up, and there in front of him stood Nikalos dressed in the uniform of a Red Charioteer —the red tunic picked out with braid, the dagger in his belt, the closely fitting leather helmet.

"It will soon be light," he said. "Let's harness the horses and drive down."

Odbjørn turned around and saw the dawn hanging like a cobweb in the cracks of the stable door.

"You know Vatia's forbidden you to leave the stables before the race begins."

"Yes, I know, but I must go down all the same. I must drive a couple of times around the course and let that beast work off some of his savage temper!"

As they drove out through the gateway, Odbjørn noticed that lights were burning over in the Greens' stable buildings. Metellus was up early, too. And Nikalos and Metellus were not the only ones. All Rome seemed to be astir, although the first rays of the sun were only just appearing over the Esquiline Hill and filtering through the arches of the aqueducts, whose massive structures looked like so many monstrous long-legged caterpillars winding their way over houses and roofs as though over a blazing bonfire.

But in the district behind the Palatine the darkness of night was a long time dispersing from the narrow well-like streets. Lights were burning behind the window shutters of the houses around them, and as the chariot approached, doors were flung open and red flares of light penetrated the darkness. In a very short time the chariot was encircled by an inquisitive throng and a buzz of voices closed in on them.

"Light a torch!" someone shouted. "It's him!"

"Who?"

"Nikalos of the Reds!"

"Nikalos! . . . Nikalos!" they yelled.

The mounted guards closed around the chariot, and Odbjørn, who was riding alongside Capellus and holding him by the bit, felt the stallion's nervousness in the tugging and jerking of his arm. All at once someone ran right up to the chariot with a torch in his hand. Capellus reared and lifted Odbjørn half out of his saddle.

"Nikalos has got a new horse!" came the shout.

"Where?"

"Here! The leader! . . . Fine big beauty, too!"

One of the guards had galloped up alongside Odbjørn and was laying about him with the shaft of his spear among the indiscreet. Cries and catcalls arose, and people bunched together like a living wall in front of the horses.

"Out of the way, people!" Nikalos shouted. "Make way, or there'll be no racing today!" He cracked his whip and the report re-echoed loudly from the walls of the houses.

"Make way!" someone shouted. "Make way for Nikalos!"

They continued on their way through the narrow streets and finally reached the open square in front of the Circus Maximus. The whole length of the building resounded with noise and the hubbub of voices. Thousands of Romans had spent the night under its arches to make sure of their seats when the doors were opened. The massive double gates swung to behind Nikalos and shut out the noise.

In the arena all was quiet. A dozen or so slaves were busy along the top of the spina making ready for the race. The seven parti-colored spheres, which would be removed one by one to mark the seven laps of the race, were adjusted in their tall cuplike holders, and the seven dolphins were turned into position on their iron cradles. The shouts of the Circus slaves sounded faint and hollow in that vast deserted building, like a distant echo in a mountain valley.

A muffled drumbeat gathered volume, grew to a wild crescendo of madly dancing sound, and died away. Odbjørn stood leaning against the obelisk halfway along the spina and watched Nikalos's four horses come nearer and nearer until they flashed past, galloping away down the length of the track. A little later they appeared on the other side and vanished down the course with the little two-wheeled chariot swaying behind them and the screeching of wheels on the metaled surface dying away in the distance.

Nikalos drew up in front of the obelisk and beckoned Odbjørn to come down.

"Well, don't you think the blinker's helped?" Nikalos's cheeks were glowing, and as he drew the reins tight and fastened them more securely round his waist he laughed loudly and confidently. "Did you see how sharply I took that corner? The creature's no idea he's hugging the wall!"

Nikalos took a deep breath. "Take the yoke off the horses!" he puffed.

"The yoke?" Odbjørn gasped. "Don't do that! For heaven's sake, don't drive without a yoke! You'll have the horses scattering like chaff before the wind!"

"You're right! They'll be as light as chaff . . . Good . . . That's it! Now fasten Capellus's breast strap firmly to the next horse!"

Odbjørn did as Nikalos told him, but he shook his head, and the mettlesome Capellus tossed his head back and bespattered Odbjørn's cheeks with foam.

"Are you ready? Then I'll take the last lap!"

"No more now, Nikalos! Listen!" Odbjørn nodded toward the end of the arena from where they could just catch the distant sound of neighing and the thumping of hoofs against wood. "The others are taking up their positions in the starting boxes!" he called out.

"One more lap! Let go!" Nikalos cried.

A crack of the whip exploded behind the horses' ears and the chariot leaped forward.

Odbjørn climbed back onto the spina and was startled to see something moving up in the auditorium—something or other that ducked like lightning and vanished among the empty rows of seats. He stood for a moment staring at the spot where he thought he had seen the movement. But it was all empty and deserted up there. It must have been just a shadow—a cloud passing over the sun, perhaps. But the sky was clear, and the edge of the lofty wall gleamed brightly in the morning sun like a golden rim of flame. He shook his head and went and sat down with his back against the obelisk.

The chariot thundered past. Good old Nikalos—he wasn't content with one lap! He'd end up with his horses unable to crawl when the race started.

Odbjørn heard the horses rounding the end of the spina.

Now they were approching at his back with a resounding
tattoo of thundering hoofs growing louder and louder.

He was overcome by a strange feeling of disquiet. There
was something that wasn't as it should be, some foreboding
of death and misfortune—unless it was just the rumbling
of the chariot that was sending cold shivers down his spine.
The quadriga swept past with a clatter like a ton of bricks
falling about his ears. . . .

It was then that he caught sight of the man among the
empty seats of the auditorium. He had risen to his feet
in the gangway that separated the first and second galleries,
immediately above the spot where the track swung around
the terminal pillars that marked the winning post. He was
standing there like a flaming torch in a gleam of sunlight,
his face and his black hair glowing red as copper.

Paralyzed with fear, Odbjørn watched him raise a sling
and take aim—slowly and carefully. The blood seemed to
freeze in Odbjørn's veins. He wanted to call out and warn
Nikalos, but he couldn't . . . the words stuck in his throat.
He jumped up and stumbled forward a couple of steps.

"Nikalos!" he yelled. "Nikalos!"

The charioteer turned his face toward him.

And then it all happened . . .

Just as Nikalos turned around Capellus shied. The stallion brushed against the masonry of the spina. Mad with
terror, he struck the ground with his hoofs and flung himself away from it, his arched back rising high above the
rest of the team. He caught the next horse a blow that
made him stumble and collide with the pole of the chariot.
The chariot was hurled against the spina with a noise of
shattering, splintering wood. Odbjørn saw a wheel roll
across the arena, and through its whirling spokes he saw
the horses galloping down the track with Nikalos twisting
and turning in a cloud of dust as he was dragged along
behind them. He had got his knife out and was trying

to hack through the reins just as the runaway horses galloped around the bend and disappeared.

Odbjørn ran over to the other side of the spina. The horses appeared from behind the metae and came galloping up the course in a wild, thundering rush, their breasts flecked with foam. Behind them they dragged the broken-off stump of the pole which scratched a winding trail along the ground. And over there, close to the ditch that separated the auditorium from the arena, lay Nikalos. And he wasn't moving. . . .

"Nikalos!"

Odbjørn jumped down from the spina and set off at a run across the track. He fell, coming down on his hands in the rough clinkers, but he noticed nothing.

"Nikalos," he whispered, "it was my fault! It was because I called out to you. Forgive me, Nikalos!" He stopped abruptly.

Nikalos lay on his back, his eyes wide open and staring emptily into the blue sky. His fair curly hair was soaked in blood, his tunic was ripped off his shoulder and chest, and he was bleeding from a deep wound under his armpit. The blood had left a gleaming red streak across his chest and was running on to the ground beneath him.

"Nikalos!" He knelt down by the side of the charioteer whom he thought to be dead. "Nikalos!" he whispered. His sobs choked him as they broke from his quivering lips.

Nikalos had turned his head.

"By Jupiter, I believe the lad's blubbering!" he murmured. He smiled, and the lines that appeared in his face mingled with the scratches. He was sufficiently alive to lie there smiling with a broad grin on his face.

"It was my fault, Nikalos. It was because I called you!"

"Don't you believe it, lad. Don't you imagine you can tip Nikalos out of his chariot. No, I saw the stone hit Capellus on the crupper. Metellus obviously thought it

wasn't healthy for Nikalos to drive that beast. Well, perhaps not Metellus, but someone from the Greens."

Nikalos compressed his lips as if he were uttering a
silent cry of pain. "Stop the horses before they injure
themselves," he groaned.

But when Odbjørn rose to his feet he saw that one of
the slaves had already stopped them. At the same time
he caught sight of Vatia running toward them from the
starting boxes with his toga fluttering behind him.

21

The Chariot Race

Through the gap left between the top of the starting gate and the vaulted ceiling, daylight flooded in, a golden segment of sunshine rising above the edge of the doors. In the dazzling light outside they heard the sound of a hundred thousand voices like the mysterious noises of a swelling sea.

Inside the starting box an oppressive silence reigned. From time to time a hollow groan rose from the half-light under the dividing bar where Nikalos had been laid on a couch. Close by, a dozen stable slaves stood holding the horses in check, pressing their shoulders against the quivering bodies and pushing them back toward the wooden wall of the box.

A horse stirred. Capellus emptied his lungs with a heavy snort.

The door leading to the next stall suddenly flew open, and there on the threshold stood the charioteer Scipio.

"How's it going?"

"Get out!" cried Vatia. "Stay by your chariot and be ready to start!"

Scipio disappeared hastily, and Vatia slammed the door behind him. As he turned around, he saw Nannius, servant of Aesculapius, edging into the stall with his wooden box under his arm.

"At last!" he roared. "You've no business to go sneaking around among the spectators, making bets on racedays! It's your job to stay in the stables! Well, now you are here, take a look at Nikalos! He's had a crash and won't be on his feet for a bit. We're through! That dawdler Scipio won't get us into the Saturnalia!" Vatia lamented. "Curio!" he shouted. "Run over to Sabidius and tell him that Nikalos has withdrawn from the race! . . . What? What's that you say?" Vatia stepped over to the couch and bent over Nikalos. "Did you call for me?"

Nikalos's lips were gray and bloodless. "If you withdraw me, I shan't be able to race against Metellus in the Saturnalia," he said painfully.

"I know. I know. But what am I to do? . . . What did you say?" Vatia put his ear close to Nikalos's mouth.

"Let someone else drive for me," Nikalos whispered. "Disguised . . . and under my name."

"No, no, it'd never do!" Vatia had jumped up. "If it were discovered I should be summoned before the tribunal! I should be hurled from the Tarpeian Rock! No, no, it's cheating! I couldn't do it!"

"If whoever drove for me came in among the first four . . . then I'd be able to drive in the Saturnalia later on and beat Metellus," whispered Nikalos.

"No, no, no!" Vatia threw up his hands, turned abruptly away, and paced restlessly up and down the stall. "Anyway, who could do it?" Vatia had come to a halt, his eyes shining and the blood returning to his cheeks. "We haven't got anyone who looks like you," he muttered. "Scipio's driving himself. Sporpus . . . Sporpus is dark. And Gordius has got a snout on him like the handle on a wine jug! They'd all be recognized, every one of them!" Vatia wiped the sweat off his chubby cheeks with a flick of his toga.

"No, those you've mentioned, they're no good, Vatia."

"Who then?"

"The stable slave, Odbjørn," Nikalos whispered.

"Odbjørn? The stable slave?" gasped Vatia. "Do you mean that . . ."

Odbjørn started at the sound of his own name. Vatia turned and stared at him.

"Do you mean that . . . that . . ."

Nikalos compressed his lips and nodded. "He looks like me, and he knows Capellus. Let him drive the stallion with his own roans."

"He's got hair like a slave girl's," Vatia grunted.

"That'll be hidden by the helmet. Just pull one of my tunics over his head, and you'll have to admit that . . ."

Nikalos pressed his head back and groaned with pain. The muscles of his neck were tense and quivering, and the veins stood out knotted and swollen. Silently and unfeelingly, Vatia watched the spasm of pain in Nikalos's body.

"You're right. From the galleries no one'd be able to see that it wasn't you driving! But let's get it straight, Nikalos. Who's to say you'll be able to drive in the Saturnalia, even if this Odbjørn here should manage to get you a place?" He leaned over the couch. "Suppose you should be dying now?" he whispered.

"Better ask the stable doctor." Nikalos showed his teeth in a broad grin.

"Yes, I suppose I'd better. Nannius!" he yelled. "Crawl closer, you slimy snake of Aesculapius, and tell us if he'll live!"

Nannius put his wooden box down and knelt by the side of the couch. He examined the charioteer's body thoroughly with his hands, and Nikalos swore viciously as the doctor lifted up his arm and a stream of blood gushed from the wound. Nannius let go of his arm and laid his ear against his neck.

"By Jupiter, you stink of wine!" Nikalos muttered.

"Hold your tongue!"

"It's like sticking your nose into a wine press," Nikalos continued. "You stink of the wine harvest!"

"Then it's the last harvest you'll live to see!" said Nannius with a snarl. "You'll die, Nikalos."

"I'm dying now, Nannius, but listen . . ."

"Well, what do you think of him?" Vatia called out.

"Tell him I shall live," Nikalos whispered.

"And when you die he'll strike me dead!"

And while they were whispering in one another's ears the stable slave who had been standing by the starting gate and keeping watch through the hatch turned around.

"The entertainers are coming down from the spina!" he called out.

They heard the spectators clapping like a sudden shower of rain passing over the Circus Maximus.

"Quick, Nannius! Is he going to live or die?" Vatia stamped impatiently on the ground.

"There are two thousand sesterces in my traveling chest," Nikalos whispered. "Both the chest and the money are yours if . . ."

As the stable doctor rose slowly to his feet Nikalos held his gaze.

"Well?" Vatia grabbed Nannius by the sleeve. "What's your verdict?"

"He'll survive. And he'll be none the worse for the crash."

"Good. Then we'll let the fellow drive. But remember, from now until the race is over, your name's Nikalos!" he cried as he seized Odbjørn by the arm.

Odbjørn nodded. He looked helplessly at Nikalos, but Nikalos only shut an eye and winked at him.

"Quick about it!" yelled Vatia. "Fetch his chariot and horses! Off with you! And you, Curio! Nip across to

Sabidius and ask him to put the race off for a quarter of an hour by the sun. Tell him Nikalos is changing horses! And listen, you!" He turned to the stable slaves. "If any of you breathes a word of what's been said I'll have his tongue out!"

He seized a corner of his toga and wiped the sweat off his heavy jowl.

The stable slave Curio was standing by the gate keeping a lookout through the hatch.

"The trumpeters are climbing onto the spina!" he whispered hoarsely.

Vatia had turned his back to them. He was standing in a corner with his hand over his eyes, his teeth gnawing his lower lip and drops of sweat scattered over his bald crown like a broken string of bright pearls.

Somewhere over their heads a distinguished senator was seated in his box. At any moment now he would drop a white napkin onto the track, the trumpeters would raise their horns to their mouths, and . . .

Odbjørn had a sinking feeling. His tongue felt like a dry strip of leather in his mouth, but his hands, gripping the reins and the whip, were drenched with sweat. In a moment the doors would fly open, and there beyond the starting gate lay the wealth and power he had left home to win. On the other side of that gate the triumph of victory or the bitter disappointment of defeat awaited him. He stood within sight of the goal of his long journey. Now, or never . . .

Nikalos made a sign to the stable slaves. They took hold of the couch and lifted him up to the chariot.

"Steady now, Odbjørn," he whispered.

Odbjørn nodded in silence and kept his gaze fixed on the black double doors.

"The third place will give you twenty thousand sesterces," whispered Nikalos. "And if you come in third you'll be in line for other races. You'll soon have earned enough for your ship. . . . Slacken the reins," he added, speaking with difficulty. "They'll be too short like that when you want to give the horses their heads. And listen carefully . . . Metellus will hold back until the last lap Reserve your strength for the end . . . Understand? Good. And watch out for Diocles of the Blues. If he tries to cut in in front of you, don't hold back. He'll have to give way."

Nikalos was panting and breathing heavily.

"And Tubero," he whispered. "Keep your eye on Tubero's whip. He's got a nasty habit of wanting to drive other people's chariots as well as his own . . ."

"They're raising their horns now!" cried Curio from the shutter.

The noise outside died away and an expectant silence settled over the auditorium.

"Try to overtake on your left," cried Nikalos. He had supported his elbows on the couch and raised himself up by his arms.

"Now!" yelled Curio, springing to one side, The stable slaves let go of the horses and scuttled out of the way under the booms.

Outside in the arena the horns blared forth. Odbjørn raised his whip . . .

At that very instant the doors flew open and he was submerged in a sudden blinding glare of light.

"Drive!" roared Nikalos. "Drive like mad!" he yelled, and collapsed onto the couch.

Diocles of the Blues took the lead and kept well in to the wall of the spina. He was closely followed by Tubero and Thallus, the two charioteers from the White Company. A little way behind came the rest of the field, bunched together and hidden in a cloud of dust.

The hoofbeats were lost in a thunderous rumble of applause that rolled down from the steep slopes of the auditorium. The noise overwhelmed him; his smarting eyes were blinded by the dust that left him gasping for breath; and he felt just as he had when, long before, he rode Graywind into the breakers and fished Serbulus out of the sea.

A couple of chariots had now slipped behind, and Odbjørn lay hemmed in between Scipio and a chariot from the Green Stables. It wasn't Metellus: he could see that. Metellus must be somewhere farther back. Then it could only be . . .

It was Cassius . . . And Cassius was trying to get in front. He was trying to cut in front of him and Scipio in order to make the inside of the track before they reached the bend.

"Nikalos . . . Nikalos!" The very sky over his head seemed to reverberate with the rhythmic shouting, as with the heavy blows of a sledge-hammer. Nikalos—that was himself. He was driving for Nikalos, and for Vatia and the Red Stables. But first and foremost he was driving for himself, for himself and Groa who was waiting for him to come before the sickle of the spring moon appeared in the sky above the meeting place.

"Nikalos . . . Nikalos!"

Scipio slipped back and Odbjørn drew across to the inside position. On the bend he shook Cassius off, and now lay third, with Tubero and Thallus in front of him. But he remembered what Nikalos had said and held his horses in.

With only three laps to go the position remained the same: Tubero in front—just disappearing behind the metae, the triple pillars at the end of the spina—and then Thallus.

"Drive! Drive!" came a shout.

"Drive!" roared the chorus of voices. "Give them their head!"

"Nikalos! . . . Nikalos! . . . Nikalos!"

Nikalos's name thundered rhythmically over the arena, and then was suddenly blotted out. The words died away, swamped by a deafening noise. Then the noise subsided and out of the ensuing silence another name emerged.

"Come on, Metellus! . . . Come on!"

He heard the swift clattering of hoofs behind him . . . coming nearer and nearer.

"Come on! . . . Come on! . . ." The spectators, howling and shrieking, were beating time with their feet. "Come on! . . . Come on!"

And there was Metellus. Over his right shoulder Odbjørn saw the horses' heads like black shadows slowly gaining on him. It was Metellus, dark, broad, thickset, the best charioteer in Rome, unbeaten and arrogant. As he turned his ponderous head towards Odbjørn his thin lips curled scornfully. He brushed past, silently, arrogantly, without using his whip, as if he were overtaking a market cart. Earsplitting rounds of applause greeted Metellus's feat.

Vatia pulled a face and threw out his arm as if he were tossing something away. He gave up . . . the Saturnalia—everything!

"Take it quietly," whispered Nikalos. "I told the lad to hold back."

"He's holding back all right, I can promise you that!" Vatia grunted with a sour twist to his mouth.

The spectators switched their attention to Thallus.

"Get a move on, Thallus! Metellus is coming! . . . Drive! Drive!"

Shouts and cries of encouragement filled the air as a rhythmic yelling spread along the top rows of seats.

"Thallus! . . . Thallus!" The shouts rained down from the galleries.

But what was going on now?

Metellus was no longer forging ahead. He pulled out to the side, slackened speed, and slipped in behind Nikalos's chariot. What was he up to? Was he mocking the Macedonian? Look out, Metellus, there are only two laps to go!

Metellus had stared at him inquiringly, suspiciously, and Odbjørn had turned his face away. But suppose he had realized that it wasn't Nikalos driving the chariot after all?

He was catching up again. A peal of laughter rang through the arena: Metellus was playing with the mouse! He was driving level with Nikalos now. But what had come over him? He was lashing out at the Macedonian with his whip! The laughter died away in a loud gasp.

Odbjørn screwed up his eyes: the lash of the whip had caught him across the forehead, and he felt as if he had been branded with a white-hot iron. A searing, throbbing pain. He felt it again, but this time the whiplash had caught his leather helmet . . .

"Look," whispered Vatia hoarsely, "he's lost his helmet!"

Vatia had gripped one of the stable slaves by the arm, and he nipped him so hard that the slave turned pale and looked as pale as Vatia himself.

All was quiet in the Circus Maximus—and the heavy ominous silence was filled with the clattering of horses' hoofs. It wasn't Nikalos driving for the Reds—it was a barbarian, a young lad with a long flying mane of hair.

"Fraud!" The yell tore through the silence like a flash of lightning—and then the storm broke. A roar from ten thousand mouths shook the masonry and made the pillars on the spina quake. The incensed mass of people surged to and fro like a foaming sea.

"String him up! Death to Vatia! Fetch him out!"

"Vatia . . . ! Vatia . . . ! Vatia . . . !"

The rhythmic roaring drove Vatia into the depths of the starting box, where he clung to the boom with sweaty, clammy hands. A hoarse whisper rattled in his throat like a choking breath.

And then Vatia was suddenly forgotten. . . . For look at that!

The barbarian was forging ahead! The fellow with the long hair fought his way up alongside Metellus, his hair flying about his shoulders like a horse's mane.

Metellus pelted his horses with his whip as he tried to slip in front before he was shut in behind Thallus's chariot. But he was too late: he had to hold back.

Odbjørn raced past him . . . past Thallus, too, and on the bend he cut in front of Tubero and led the field.

The spectators had risen to their feet.

The barbarian had taken the lead!

"Bubulcus!" they roared. They had baptized him and given him a name. "Herdsman" they called him, for three of his horses were red as oxen.

"Bubulcus . . . ! Bubulcus . . . !"

Vatia let go of the boom and appeared out of the darkness.

"Carry me outside," gasped Nikalos, and the stable slaves bore the couch outside and set it down in front of the starting gate.

At that moment the chariots swung round the bend and sent a shower of stones over him.

"What did I tell you, Vatia? What did I tell you?" Nikalos's voice broke.

Metellus had pulled out. Metellus was gaining.

The spectators had jumped up on the benches, roaring and yelling. They were stamping in time to the thunderous chorus of voices that surged backward and forward from one side of the arena to the other like foaming breakers.

"Bubulcus . . . ! Bubulcus . . . !" And then, like one wave swamping another, a second shout rang out, "Metellus . . . ! Metellus . . . !" The Roman or the barbarian— the spectators had divided themselves into two camps, urging the charioteers on with hoarse shouts.

Odbjørn glanced out of the corner of his eye and saw Metellus's chariot toiling up alongside him. And it was gaining, inch by inch, as they galloped madly along by the spina. Odbjørn slackened his reins and let them flick up and down over the horses' backs.

But Metellus was still gaining on him. The chariots were lying side by side . . . and now Metellus was ahead.

They were nearing the bend again, but neither of them slackened speed. Metellus pressed on in front of him and gained the corner first. Odbjørn was caught in a cloud of dust—dust and gravel and stone-chippings—and as the chariot was on the point of heeling over he threw himself to one side, knocking his hip against the frame, and righted it.

They were out of the bend now and there was only one length to go. Down by the triple pillars at the other end of the course a white cord had been stretched across the track. Metellus lay first, close in to the spina. Odbjørn pulled out to the right.

Now for it!

He could now spare Capellus no longer. He sent his whip sweeping through the air, and the lash cracked with a sharp report behind the stallion's ear. Capellus jerked his head away, but he did not shy. He plunged straight ahead with neck outstretched, leading the team by a short head.

Metellus plied his whip over his horses' backs—furiously, senselessly. He beat them with the shaft, over and over again, the blows falling like pelting rain on the horses' foam-covered flanks.

But it was all to no purpose.

He suddenly raised his whip and lashed out at Capellus. But Odbjørn was on his guard. The two whip lashes met in mid-air and twined together. With a sharp tug Metellus jerked Odbjørn's whip out of his hand.

Odbjørn threw himself forward across the edge of the chariot and his punches rained down on the horses' hindquarters.

"Come on! . . . Come on!" he yelled.

Just beyond the tape he saw Vatia jumping about with arms waving and toga fluttering.

"Drive! . . . Drive!" he bellowed.

Odbjørn's hands were hot and burning as they beat puffs of dust out of the horses' coats.

"Groa!" he whispered. "Groa!"

His chariot was crawling past—crawling like a snail past Metellus's team.

"I'm coming, Groa! I'm on my way! Now . . . in one moment, then . . ."

And then he heard the noise and the shouting fuse together into a thundering roar of applause. He had done it. He had won!

The white cord was broken.

Odbjørn braced his legs against the shield of the chariot and, throwing all his weight backward, drew rein. The chariot came to a halt in front of the starting boxes. He loosened the reins, but Vatia came running up and bellowed into his ear.

"Stay where you are, do you hear! . . . They want to look at you! Drive once around the course or they'll have all the woodwork in splinters!"

"Bu . . . bul . . . cus! Bu . . . bul . . . cus!" They were

yelling themselves hoarse, stamping and roaring. The slaves who attended to the course felt the stonework of the spina shaking under their feet.

"Bu . . . bul . . . cus! Bu . . . bul . . . cus!"

"Come on now!" screamed Vatia.

But Odbjørn pushed him aside and ran over to the couch where Nikalos lay with his eyes shut. The blood in his hair was stiff and black, and his cheeks were as white as the finest white linen.

"Nikalos!" he called.

The Macedonian opened his eyes and his lips moved. He tried to raise an arm. Odbjørn seized his hand and bent over him.

"Did you see Capellus, Nikalos? Did you see how he pulled the roans along?"

"I saw him," Nikalos whispered hoarsely. "He's a good horse. Keep him."

"What do you mean?"

Vatia bawled something or other in his ear. He took hold of him and dragged him back.

"The Emperor's coming!" he shouted. "He's seen you drive! Do you hear?"

But Odbjørn pulled away and threw himself onto the couch.

"What did you mean by giving me the stallion? Answer me! Nikalos!" he called. "Nikalos!"

"He's dead," said Vatia, as he made a sign to a couple of slaves. "Carry him into the stall and bar the gate!"

Vatia laid a hand on Odbjørn's shoulder.

"Get up," he said. "Get up . . . The Emperor Augustus is coming. . . ."

22

The Hooded Man

Since that night, nearly a year before, when a horseman had galloped up the Palatine Hill with the news of Varus's defeat in the rain-drenched forests far to the north, the Emperor Augustus had not shown himself in the Circus Maximus.

All that wretched night the dark halls of the palace had resounded with a hollow echo—the echo of a thousand restless footsteps over the marble floors, broken from time to time by a hoarse cry that rang out between the misty gray columns. The guards had listened, trembling as they heard the voice and the words it uttered far away in the darkness.

"Varus!" cried the voice. "Varus, give me back my legions! Do you hear me, Varus?"

The whole night through they had heard the Emperor calling upon his dead governor, and they had feared for the old man's reason.

But now . . . now he had come down the marble steps from the Palatine and placed the wreath of victory on the Cimbrian's brow, the Cimbrian who had beaten the best charioteer in Rome, Metellus Rutilius—the Cimbrian Odbjørn!

His name was inscribed for all to read on the tablets

announcing the victory, which were posted the next day in the Forum Romanum. His name was on everybody's lips—the Cimbrian who had entered the race as an unknown slave under a false name, but who, nevertheless, had snapped the tape and driven to the top of the dizzy peak of fame.

Gifts poured in from far and near, covering the floor of Nikalos's apartment over the stable, which Odbjørn had now taken over. Costly trinkets, belts of gilded leather, silver-hafted daggers, tunics and togas, piles of cloth—sufficient to start a clothing stall, concluded Buekil, who had now acquired a taste for trading in the market. There were sandals enough for one of the smaller units of the Roman army—and cherry-red shawls he did not know what to do with. And among the gifts he found heavy leather purses crammed full of shining gold and silver coins.

Odbjørn was invited to feasts at the homes of the wealthy. Odbjørn went nobly clad and reclined at table in distinguished houses. He lived a life of wealth and fame. The good fortune he had traveled so far to find was his.

He was fully occupied all day long. His renown laid claim to a great deal of his time—training and racing took up the rest.

But in the excitement of victory he did not forget that the days were slipping past, that there was no time to lose before he took his departure if he were going to reach home in good time.

With the money that poured in from the races he won, he bought back the piece of amber. It had grown valuable in Vatia's safekeeping, and he had to pay double the price for it. But he thought Thorkim ought to have it back as a reminder of his villainy, for it was with that piece of amber that Thorkim had paid the Roman to get him out of the way. It was only right and proper that Thorkim should have back what he had paid.

He ordered a liburna with two banks of oars from Nauklerus, the shipbuilder in Ostia. He bought Buekil's freedom, and asked him to keep an eye on the building of the ship and make sure that Nauklerus got on with the work.

Immediately after his defeat, Metellus had left Rome, traveling, so it was said, to the great stud farms in Sicily, where he picked out the swiftest horses and tried them out all day long on the country roads.

And while Metellus was getting ready for the Saturnalia the Green Stables enrolled charioteers from far and near. Nothing would be left undone in their attempt to wrest the lead from the Reds.

Nothing would be left undone. . . .

Vatia was convinced that the Greens would not hesitate to get Odbjørn out of the way—not openly, but in secret. A wheel might collapse during a race, if the spokes had been sawn half-through beforehand. A stone might fall from a roof and unluckily strike the fellow on the head. Vatia was full of anxious solicitude for Odbjørn's safety. He appointed two imposing-looking slaves to watch over him, but Odbjørn, who soon grew weary of his bodyguard, quickly learned to give them the slip and rid himself of their company.

But a tall stooping figure, clad in an earth-brown cloak, followed him like a shadow night and day, his long gray hair and rugged face hidden beneath the hood of the cloak. By day he followed Odbjørn hidden in the swarming crowds; by night the hooded figure crept along the walls of the houses and slipped from pillar to pillar after the unsuspecting Odbjørn.

One night Buekil awoke and heard stealthy footsteps rustling in the straw. When he sat up he saw the hooded man leaning against the post at the end of the stall and gazing down at him. He recognized him with a start—it was the fellow who had asked after Odbjørn the day he sold his clay animals down by the Tiber.

Buekil had seen nothing of him since, but there he was now, the gruesome-looking scarecrow. His eyes were gray, Buekil remembered, but the light from the oil lamp cast deep shadows across his eyesockets and his eyes were hidden.

The hooded figure pushed himself away from the post and stepped slowly towards him.

"Where's Odbjørn?" His voice had a hollow ring, as though it came from the bottom of a deep well.

Buekil thrust his finger into his ear and poked.

"Do you have difficulty in hearing?"

"No, no, but I've difficulty in answering, because I don't know where he is. I . . . He'll be home soon. Very soon."

"Then I'll wait." The stranger sat down in the straw.

Buekil moved slightly away. A thousand bewildering thoughts passed through his mind. What did he want with Odbjørn? It was true enough that Odbjørn was not at home and it would not be long before he came back. He decided that as soon as he heard Odbjørn's footsteps over-head he would slip up the stairs from the stable and warn him.

The hooded man sat slouched forward as if he were asleep, his long gray wisps of hair falling from under his hat.

"Are you armed?" asked Buekil.

"Why do you ask that?"

"Because if you're armed you're not allowed in to see the charioteer Odbjørn."

"There was a time when he wasn't afraid of meeting folk who carried arms," the stranger said.

Ignoring Buekil's question, he set about pumping him.

Was Odbjørn going north? Was that why he was having a ship built? When was he intending to leave?

"When the Saturnalia's been run," Buekil said, and was immediately annoyed with himself for answering the stranger's question so readily.

"And the Saturnalia will be run in six days' time," the hooded man muttered, nodding quietly to himself. With every nod his hat slipped farther and farther back, revealing his long faded gray hair. "I'd an idea it couldn't be very long. I've been following the progress of the ship from the time she lay on the stocks. She's afloat now and her masts and yards are rigged."

"And the sails are lying ready on deck," Buekil blurted out. He could have bitten his tongue out for saying it. "Tomorrow I'm buying galley slaves." The words slipped out of his mouth, and he regretted that he hadn't taken his tongue seriously in hand. "But Odbjørn said their chains were to be taken off as soon as they were seated on the thwarts."

"That's as it should be," nodded the stranger. "Now you can see whose son he is! Listen," he added, "has he told Vatia that the Saturnalia will be the last race he's going to run for the Red Stables?"

Buekil glanced at him suspiciously. What did he mean by that question?

"No, he . . . he thought it would be best to leave it as long as possible," he replied hesitantly. "He's going to tell him when the galley slaves are bought."

"Yes, it's best that way," the stranger admitted, nodding his head gravely. He'd a regular habit of nodding, thought Buekil. But who was he, anyway? Was he someone Vatia had sent to find out what Odbjørn intended to do with the ship he had lying at Ostia?

"He doesn't think he'll owe Vatia and the Red Stables

any more once the Saturnalia's been run," Buekil cried irritably. "The Red Stables have earned . . ."

He broke off suddenly.

He heard a key turn in the lock. Then the door creaked and footsteps sounded on the floor above. Odbjørn had come home.

Buekil jumped up and made for the stairs, but just as he was about to run up them he heard a banging and thumping over his head—heavy, noisy footsteps and the sound of something falling onto the floor with a dull thud. There was a half-smothered cry, and he was on the point of rushing up the stairs when he felt a hand on his shoulder.

"Careful!" whispered the hooded man, and Buekil saw that his hollow cheeks had turned pale. For the first time he felt drawn to the stranger. He had a strong feeling that something had happened to Odbjørn, but he no longer felt that he, Buekil, was Odbjørn's only friend.

The grayhaired man prodded him, and together they crept up the stairs. Buekil knew where the boards creaked, and he made signs to the other to show him where he could tread without making a noise.

Carefully he set his head against the trap door. Slowly, very slowly, he stretched his neck and raised the wooden flap until a thin hard streak of light suddenly appeared along its edge.

As he looked through the crack he caught his breath and very nearly let the trap door fall with a bang, for there on the floor lay Odbjørn, his hands tied behind his back and his feet lashed to them. A huge broad-shouldered fellow in a blue cloak was busy gagging him. With a hard jab he thrust a rag in between his teeth. The man's knee resting against Odbjørn's shoulder was knotted and broad like an oak log. Several men were standing around Odbjørn staring down at him. Buekil could see only their legs, crisscrossed by the thongs of their sandals and looking like a fence of stout posts round their victim, with here and there the bright point of a sword directed toward him. Buekil counted six men, but there might have been others he could not see. As the man who had been bending over Odbjørn rose to his feet, Buekil caught a glimpse of a coarse-looking face. Then he heard a low irritable voice from somewhere behind the trap door.

"You must make it look as if he's run out. Understand?" The men muttered affirmatively.

"So both he and the ship have got to disappear. And by Jupiter and his gang of gods, if you make any blunders . . . !" He lowered his voice to a hoarse whisper. Buekil could hear that he was ill at ease and anxious to finish the job and get away. "Now listen carefully. His ship's lying alongside the quay to the south of Nauklerus's shipyard. Very near the slipway but more to the south. You're to drop him on board, hack a hole in the ship's bottom and set the sails. And take care to lash the steering oar so that the ship will stand out to sea between the moles and won't sink till she's clear of the harbor."

"And the wind, Laelius?" asked a gruff voice. "I suppose you've turned the wind round the right way?"

"There's no time to be funny! The wind'll blow the way we want it—due west. Now get a move on and pick him up!"

Buekil bent his head and carefully lowered the trap door.

"They're intending to drown him," he whispered breathlessly. "The Greens want to get him out of the way before the Saturnalia! We've got to get hold of Vatia! Do you hear?"

As he turned around he had a shock and a cold shudder ran down his spine—the hooded man had vanished! At that moment he heard the clattering of horses' hoofs down in the stable, followed by the creaking of the stable door. He leapt down the stairs.

"Where are you off to?" he hissed between his teeth.

But the only answer he got was the rumbling of hoofs out in the yard. The sound died away somewhere far off in the maze of dark, silent streets.

And now he knew who the stranger was. He now realized that he must have been in league with the others. He had kept him, Buekil, in conversation while the gang of murderers employed by the Greens were overpowering Odbjørn. A despairing sob welled up in Buekil's throat. He wrenched open the stable door and set off running toward the Circus Maximus.

"Vatia!" he whimpered. "Vatia!"

He wiped his nose on his arm and hurried down the street past the Temple of Hercules. . . .

23

The Sinking Galley

For a long time the guards at the east gate had heard the cart rumbling through the silent streets, and now they saw it lumbering out of the darkness toward the gate. The night was black and moonless, and they failed to notice the horsemen who rode into the shadows behind the Pyramid of Cestius and there drew rein.

The guards advanced, holding the shafts of their spears diagonally across their bodies.

"Does the fool have to wake the whole city with his creaking rattletrap!" one of them cried.

"Those I haven't waked'll be awake now all right, with all the row you're making!" the peasant answered. He sat slouched forward and spoke into the darkness without turning his head.

"Hold your tongue!" The soldier struck at him with the shaft of his spear. "Don't you know you aren't allowed to drive in the city at nighttime!"

"Yes, and only a couple of hours during the day!" muttered the peasant. "All the same, I'd like to see how you'd get on in your waste of brick and mortar if we didn't sometimes drive a load or two of fresh greens through the jaws of your city gate!"

"Keep away from the taverns, and another time see you leave the city at a proper hour!"

The guard went around to the back of the cart and lifted the canvas hood.

"What are you taking back with you?" he asked.

"Straw and empty pockets!" answered the peasant, still without turning his head.

The guard, letting go of the canvas, stepped back startled. Something or other had moved. He thought he had heard a muffled groan coming from the straw.

"Have you got any livestock in your wagon?"

"Livestock?" The peasant kept his back to him and spoke into the darkness.

"Yes, live animals!" The guard set the point of his spear under his chin and made him lift his head up. "There's something moving in the straw!" he said.

"Must be lice rustling the straws," said the peasant. "Not got anything else alive with me!"

He sat hunched up and motionless on his seat. The guard shook off his uneasiness. "Drive on!" he cried. "Clear off!" He stepped aside hastily as the mule suddenly started off without a word from the peasant or a touch of the reins.

The guards stood staring after the cart until it disappeared into the darkness along the road to Ostia. They could hear the wheels rumbling over the stone blocks, and then, as the paved surface came to an end, crunching on the gravel of the highway.

At that moment they heard the clatter of galloping hoofs close behind them, and they just managed to jump for cover behind the wall as a dozen black shadows burst through the gateway and vanished along the highroad.

"Halt!" The centurion of the guard ran forward a couple of steps and shouted at them to stop. The hoofbeats sounded like mocking laughter in the darkness.

The wagon pulled up a little way outside Ostia. The driver exchanged a couple of words with the horsemen, and shortly afterward Odbjørn heard them turn off the road. They returned a little later and, climbing into the back of the wagon, silently seated themselves around him in the darkness. Odbjørn guessed they had reached the large lake in front of the city gate and that the horsemen had left their horses somewhere down on its banks.

The wagon set off again, rumbling through the paved streets, but in a few minutes the noisy echo from the walls of the houses was silenced, and they were driving northward along the coast road toward the harbor of Augustus. As he lay in the bottom of the cart he could hear they had reached the warehouses. He could tell where they were by the noise they were making. Just over there were Seporius's granaries, and behind the three long buildings . . . No, the wagon had turned to the left now and was driving past the tall timber stacks. The scent of fresh pine was in his nostrils. The thwarts in his ship were made of Black Sea pine, he remembered—the finest to be found. Then came Glaucia Seius's stores of building materials. A notice above the warehouse door read, "Fireproof stone from Alba. Numidian marble. Marble from Alexandria." Seius dealt in all kinds of expensive stone.

The wagon left the narrow alleys between the warehouses behind and turned to the right by the shanty known as the harbor-slaves' tavern. For a long time it rolled creaking along by the quayside. Then it pulled up and the men began to move.

"Wait a bit!" The driver's fingers fumbled over the canvas and made a scratching noise like a cat's claws. "Keep still!" he whispered. "I saw something moving over by one of the warehouses."

The men held their breath and listened.

Inside the canvas hood they could hear the wind whistling through the ships' rigging, and as Odbjørn lay listening to the waves lapping against the sides of the ship he reflected that his first voyage in her would also be his last. He felt lonely and afraid and he was chilled to the bone.

"Quick now!" whispered the driver.

The men jumped down from the wagon. Two of them dragged the bound Odbjørn to the ship and slipped him over the rail. He lay and watched them scurrying backward and forward across the deck like busy silent shadows.

The moon slipped out of the ragged clouds like a silver coin from a tattered purse. Large and round and golden white, it sailed the dark sea of the night sky.

"Have you nearly finished?" The driver, who was standing close to Odbjørn, turned and gazed uneasily over the quayside.

"The steering oar's lashed fast," whispered a voice.

"Good. Then take him down below. And you, Lagos, hack a hole in the ship's bottom and get back as quick as you can! Stand by to set sail!" he commanded in a hushed voice.

They had thrown him down onto the lower rowing deck, and one of them had pulled the floor boards aside and hacked away with an ax at the planks below until the water spouted up from the ship's bottom like a gushing fountain. Then they had disappeared up the ladder.

The moonlight fell aslant through the hatchway, and at the bottom of the ladder, where it was reflected in the flooded hold, the water gleamed black as pitch.

He heard the yard sliding up the mast, and as the wind caught the sail the ship heeled over, and he had to twist his body around to stop himself from tumbling off the rowing deck. At the same time he heard the sound of feet running across the deck above like a shower of rain, and then all was silent.

A low gurgling sound rose from the surface of the water over the spot where the hole had been hacked in the ship's bottom. He felt the ship roll and he knew from her motion that she was adrift: she was sailing out into the empty darkness of the sea, and as she did so she was slowly sinking.

The Romans said that Charon the ferryman sailed the dead across the River Styx into the kingdom of the dead. He remembered it now. They said the Romans placed a copper coin in the dead man's mouth so that he could pay Charon to ferry him across. Charon's ship of death would be just as silent as this, and just as dark.

He lay motionless with his eyes shut, while a gleaming trickle of moisture ran down his cheek from his eyelashes to the corner of his mouth. It tasted salt and bitter on his tongue, just as if he, too, had a copper coin in his mouth.

The ship suddenly shivered and began rolling heavily in the sea and he knew that she was standing out of the harbor. He turned his head and saw that the water was about to close over the fourth step of the ladder. The floor board, floating in the gangway between the rowing decks, bumped into a stanchion a hand's breadth below the level of his head.

He shut his eyes and tried to dream himself back home in the hut among the heather-covered hills. If only he were lying in the hayloft now, with the two old men sitting down below in the straw and wrangling amiably with one another, while Tova clattered about with her pots and spits! As Odbjørn lay there he thought of the bondswoman who had been a mother to him, and the thought of her brought a smile to his lips. When he had driven past the winning post in the Circus Maximus, the moment of triumph and victory carried his thoughts to Groa, but now in his fear it was Tova the thrall he called upon.

"Tova," he whispered, and Tova dropped pot and spit and tottered over to the hayloft on her old legs.

But it wasn't the clattering of the spit on the hearth-
stone that he heard—it was water, water washing under
the rowing deck, sucking and lapping, water rising up between the planks and soaking his clothes. He pulled himself up to the stanchion and propped his head up against
it. Cold and tingling, the water crept over his hands and
feet. . . . In a little while . . .

What was that? He heard something moving above his
head. No, he couldn't be mistaken—there it was again, the
shuffle of stealthy footsteps. Suddenly he saw a shadow
glide across the hatchway. The moonlight was blotted out
and he saw a pair of long thin legs groping their way to
the top of the ladder. The feet, shod in rawhide, took a
couple of steps down and then stopped.

Odbjørn tried to call out, but no sound escaped from
his gagged mouth, and to his dismay he saw the feet withdraw . . . step by step. . . .

He twisted and turned, and suddenly he rolled over and
slipped off the edge of the deck. He tried to throw himself
onto the floating floor board, but as he did so the board
slipped away from him and he plunged into the water between the rowing decks.

Old Egyptian skippers often spoke of the eternal corn-
barks—ships you met at sea in the hour before daybreak,
often in fog, more often in gales and high seas. Like phan-
toms they would glide past with no sign of life on board.
Forsaken by their crews hundreds of years before, they
would sail the sea into eternity, and there were those who
maintained that the cargoes of corn behind their rotting
planks had been harvested on the banks of the Nile thousands of years before. They were talked of frequently in
the quayside taverns of Ostia, in "The Rotting Corn-
Bark", "The Dolphin", and all the rest of them.

Like one of those legendary ghostships, Odbjørn's galley glided out of the harbor mouth. But from the ships

of the legend no sound was heard but the whining of the wind in the rigging. And nothing moved—except perhaps an empty wine cask rumbling to and fro across the deck, or a creaking block turning as the ship heeled. Otherwise the decks of those legendary ships were silent and deserted. But on board the Cimbrian's galley . . .

Look . . . aft there where the locker stood. The lid was raised. The cordage in the locker came alive, turning and twisting like a knotted mass of snakes. Suddenly a man's head appeared, and a tall stooping man in an earth-brown tunic stood up and climbed out of the locker.

He moved stealthily away from the bulwark and crept cautiously between the oak stanchions that raised the bridge above the deck. He felt around the stanchions in the darkness, he ran into the bows, flung open the scuttles and clambered down below: he crawled around on his knees, peering under the bunks. A little later he was standing on deck amidships.

"Odbjørn!" he shouted. "Odbjørn!"

The whistling of the wind in his ears was the only answer he got. A wave washed over the rail, as if the sea put out its tongue at him. The ship was settling fast now, and the water was seeping in through the scuppers. At any moment she would go down.

"He must be aboard," he thought. "They've stowed him away somewhere or other." And then it came to him in a flash—"The rowing decks!"

But as soon as he stood with one foot on the ladder he saw that the water had already risen high below deck. If they had thrown him down there he must be drowned already. He drew back his foot in hesitation. And at that very moment he heard a splash in the water between the rowing decks that startled him. He waded down the ladder and was just in time to see a dark shape roll over and disappear between the stanchion and the floor board. He threw himself forward and caught hold of it—just in time.

He had scarcely cut the cords and set Odbjørn free when the sea washed smooth and gleaming over the rail and the ship sank.

Odbjørn was stiff in every limb, but the hooded man pushed him into the frothing water, jumped in after him and caught hold of his tunic. They struggled desperately to get free of the sinking ship. Then quite suddenly they no longer felt the current sucking them down, and as they turned around in amazement they saw the sea smooth and calm behind them.

The ship had vanished, but the stanchions that supported the bridge rose up above the surface of the sea.

They swam back and climbed onto the bridge. The planks were awash, but they had a firm foothold, and Odbjørn was able to stretch himself out at full length and take a good rest. As he gradually recovered, his fear lost its hold upon him, and he slowly realized that his life had been saved. But when he turned around, the sight of the stranger startled him, and his fear returned.

"Who are you?" His chattering teeth caused him to stammer. He sat up and recoiled from the hooded figure.

"Me? I'm Charon the ferryman!" the stranger murmured.

That was the very thought that had passed through his mind. That was just what Charon must look like—Charon who ferried the dead over the Styx. But at that moment he heard a laugh from beneath the hood, a chuckling laugh. He picked up his ears and listened. No, of course it wasn't Charon! The fellow must have heard him whisper the ferryman's name while he was still lightheaded, and now he thought he would have a bit of fun with him by calling himself Charon. But who was he? Odbjørn had heard that laugh before—somewhere a long time ago.

"Wait a bit!" he cried breathlessly. "I know your voice. Speak again . . . say something!"

The stranger cleared his throat.

"I'll tell you what I once said to your father, Torvik. 'Torvik,' I said, 'before the new moon I shall come back to fetch you and your son. That I swear . . .' "

"Ulver!" cried Odbjørn, as he flung the hood off the other's head.

The moonlight cast black shadows across his eyesockets and the deep furrows in his hollow cheeks. But it was Ulver.

"It's you, Ulver!" he laughed, shaking him by the shoulder. Then all at once he became serious. "Why didn't you come back? No, no, I'm not blaming you for anything. Something must have prevented you from keeping your word. Quick! . . . Tell me what happened to you and the rest when you set off after the Roman fleet."

And so Ulver told Odbjørn all that had happened since he took leave of him on the Cimbrian coast. The Roman fleet had closed around them, pinning their boat in between two ships, and there they had lain, as though in the jaws of a sea monster, while the Romans fished them up one by one.

He and three others had been sold to slave dealers in Britain, and there for a year they had toiled in the tin mines, until at last Ulver succeeded in fleeing across the narrow seas to a land called Gaul.

Odbjørn nodded. He had heard of that land.

"And then?" he asked.

Well, for a time he had roamed about until hunger forced him to seek voluntary service with the German auxiliaries that fought alongside the Roman army. And then when his unit was transferred to Rome he had entered the Emperor's German bodyguard, where he had worked his way up through the ranks and ended as centurion.

"Did you ever hear of a German called Arminius?" Odbjørn asked eagerly.

"Don't remind me of him!" growled Ulver. A shadow passed across his face. "He was the cause of all my troubles after that! This Arminius started a rebellion somewhere up in Germany. He slaughtered twenty thousand Romans in the forests."

"Yes, I know about that," Odbjørn nodded. "And so . . . ?"

"So Augustus flew into a temper every time he caught sight of one of us long-haired men, and in the end sacked the whole of his German bodyguard! Since then I've kept body and soul together minding sheep and cobbling sandals. I've even fed the augur's beasts at one of their temples. At last I became a door porter."

Yes, Ulver had turned his hand to practically everything. Torvik and Odbjørn and his broken promise had often been in his mind. Once he had started to journey northward, but when he got as far as the Sabatine Lake it occurred to him that life was all too short for so long a journey. And so he had turned back and found himself a job as helmsman on a barge that carried corn from Ostia to Rome. He had tried that, too.

"But slave I've never been," Ulver concluded.

"That's what I am, though," said Odbjørn despondently. "And it looks as if I shall be one for a long time yet. The ship's sunk now, and I can't see any way of getting home for the spring sacrifice."

"The spring sacrifice?" Ulver turned his head and looked at him inquiringly.

Then Odbjørn told him of the wager that old Hugwa had concluded between him and Thorkim.

"The old man'll give his daughter's hand to the one

who keeps tryst at the meetingplace with the most men."

"We'll manage it!" cried Ulver. "Take courage! I give you my oath that . . ."

He stopped short suddenly.

"Listen!" he whispered, seizing Odbjørn by the arm.

They heard the sound of oars, and they saw a boat appearing out of the darkness a little way off. Perhaps it was the Greens' gang of murderers come back to make sure the galley had gone to the bottom.

Ulver and Odbjørn lay flat on the wet planks so that the men in the boat should not immediately catch sight of them. As they lay there they kept their eyes on the boat, which drew slowly and hesitantly nearer. But when, a moment later, the moon appeared, Odbjørn caught sight of a stocky figure. A man was standing in the stern. Odbjørn could see only the black outline of his well-nourished body, but he recognized him immediately and sprang to his feet.

"Vatia!" he shouted.

"Odbjørn!" The man in the boat flung his short arms skywards as if he would reach for the moon. "Is that you, Odbjørn?" he yelled.

24

Odbjørn Stands Firm

They were seated in the traveling carriage on their way back to Rome, listening to the soothing sound of hoofbeats. The carriage and its precious load were escorted by a score of horsemen from the Red Stables.

Vatia had rescued his best charioteer from drowning. Vatia chattered away, laughing and calling down the vengeance of the gods on the Green Stables and their manager, on Metellus, on everything that was green. He put his hand out in the dark to feel if Odbjørn were still sitting by his side. He sank back reassured into the cushions, only to stiffen a little later and listen to the sounds outside in the night. But there was nothing there to disquiet him. The tripping hoofbeats of the horses fell like rain, a soothing, splashing rain, all round the traveling carriage.

And then they were in Rome, driving under the archway into the Circus Maximus. Vatia was anxious to look at him in the light, to see whether his body and limbs had escaped injury. A message was sent across to the stables that dry clothes must be brought for Odbjørn. But above all . . . "Lights! Lights!" Vatia cried.

The slaves entered dragging lamp standards with them,

and the oil lamps had scarcely stopped swinging from their branches before they were back again with more lamp standards.

"More! More still!" cried Vatia. Then he called for the captain of the stable guard. "Set a watch on all the entrances! And from now until the Saturnalia's run see that six of your men mount guard in the stables—three over the horses and three at Odbjørn's door. Understand?"

The captain raised his hand in salute and disappeared.

"Wine on the table!" Vatia commanded. "The best vintage Falernian!"

He turned to Odbjørn, rubbing his hands together and smiling so broadly that his round cheeks hid his ears.

"And now . . ."

And now Odbjørn seized the opportunity to tell Vatia that the Saturnalia would be the last race he would take part in for the Red Stables.

Vatia stopped rubbing his hands and his smile vanished. Odbjørn, anxious to coax it back again, told Vatia about Groa and the wager between him and Thorkim, the wager that made it necessary for him to get to the meetingplace at home by the spring sacrifice. He told him all this to make him understand that nothing else could be done, but Vatia's face was dark and forbidding like a storm cloud.

When Odbjørn had finished he stepped close up to him.

"Don't forget you're a slave!" he hissed. "I've bought you and paid for you, and don't you forget it!"

"I've money enough to buy my freedom."

"So you may have. But I'm not selling!" Vatia snarled.

And then he suddenly changed his tune. His voice became kindly and persuasive, and he said that if Odbjørn were sensible he could become one of the richest men in Rome, acclaimed and idolized by everyone. The time would come when his statue in bronze would stand in the colonnades alongside those of the famous charioteers of former days. He would be able to buy a place in the country near Baiae, and in the summertime he would be able to leave the oppressive heat of the great city and move into his palace by the sea. And if it was just a sweetheart he wanted—Vatia leered and winked at him—why, all the prettiest girls in Rome would be vying with one another to win his favor!

But Odbjørn was not to be moved. After the Saturnalia he would make his way northward toward the Cimbrian peninsula. It was already high time he started—he would have to be home within three months.

Vatia's attitude changed again. Shouting and swearing, he paced furiously up and down the room, and the lamplight flickered like flashes of lightning among the fluttering shadows on the floor. The slaves hugged the wall in terror or sought shelter from the storm behind the pillars.

Hours passed. Vatia threatened. Vatia begged and prayed. Now he raved with foam at the corners of his mouth and an evil glint in his narrowed eyes, and now he entreated Odbjørn to stay.

But Odbjørn refused to budge.

The night came to an end and the gray light of dawn filtered in through the narrow opening in the wall.

"Up to now I've tried to avoid compulsion," Vatia said, as he came to a halt in front of him. "But from now on until March I'll have you locked up!"

Odbjørn started and glanced quickly at the entrance. The captain of the stable guard was standing there, and when at that moment Vatia raised his hand he called his men into the room.

"Think it over before it's too late!" Vatia shouted.

"If you lock me up, I won't drive in the Saturnalia!" Odbjørn retorted.

"Perhaps you'll drive for all that!" Vatia laughed shortly and ominously. "We shall see . . . Seize him!"

The guards threw themselves at Odbjørn, sweeping him off his feet.

"Look out!" yelled Vatia. "Don't break his arms! That's better! Now drive him over to the stables!"

He drew the captain of the guard aside and whispered a couple of words in his ear. They saw the captain step back and stare incredulously at the manager.

"Do you mean . . . that . . . ?"

"I mean exactly what you heard me say!" Vatia snapped. "And take care no one sees him disappear!"

Although they had blindfolded him with a black cloth, he knew that the wagon had drawn up in the yard in front of the stable buildings, and from the creaking of the stable door and the rustle of straw round their feet it was obvious that they were carrying him along the row of stalls. A moment later they seemed to be stumbling down the cellar steps, and the rank sweet smell of mangolds convinced him that he had guessed right.

He was just beginning to wonder why they had taken the trouble to blindfold him when it suddenly occurred to him that the cellar wasn't as big as this. They should have bumped into the wall some time ago, and yet they were still dragging him along and changing direction every other second.

At one point the ground sloped steeply downward, and two of the guards stumbled, dragging him down with them. They came to a halt there and he heard a bolt being withdrawn. A pair of hard hands seized him by the back of the neck and forced his head down toward his knees. He was pushed into a narrow hole in the wall. They whipped the rag from his eyes and slammed the grille shut.

At first he was blinded by the light from the oil lamps, but as his eyes gradually grew accustomed to it he found himself looking out into a stone-faced passage built in the form of a gigantic pipe. Moisture dripped from the vaulted roof and ran down the musty stone of the concave walls. A thin trickle of water flowed along the stones of the sloping floor and disappeared.

"Stick your nose out between the bars, Odbjørn, and take a look around!" The hollow echo of Vatia's voice rang out in the darkness, and when he pressed his face down toward his knees he could just see the thongs that bound Vatia's sandals to his feet.

"You're down in the sewers of Rome!" he whispered hoarsely. Odbjørn heard him take a deep breath. "The air's not so bad. A little fusty, perhaps, but otherwise all right. The dirt and filth of Rome don't flow this way any more, you see . . . But if there should be a heavy rain, then the water will rise, Odbjørn—right to the roof!"

Vatia put his head back and gazed up at the vaulted stone roof, and as he did so his double chin disappeared into his bull-like neck. "Let's hope we don't have any rain . . . Let's hope so!"

He squatted on his heels, and as he looked Odbjørn full in the eye the smile about his wide mouth vanished.

"You can scream with hunger as much as you like! No one will hear you. Only your own common sense will get you any food! Do you hear?" he whispered. "Answer me! Do you feel like driving in the Saturnalia?"

"Only if you let me leave when the race is over," Odbjørn muttered.

Vatia laughed harshly, and far off in the passages a mocking echo answered.

"And suppose the Romans ask you where I've got to?"

"I shall have sent you away to a safe and secret place. And if you don't turn up for the race it'll be because your enemies have put you out of the way. The Romans will forget you, Odbjørn—and I, too, I shall forget you as well! And one day the rain will come and wash you out into the

Tiber, and your body will be found somewhere along the banks of the river. But no one will remember any longer that it was you who beat Metellus Rutilius in the trial race—a charioteer's quickly forgotten!"

Vatia rose to his feet.

The sound of footsteps died away in the distance, and far off in the labyrinth of passages a door slammed.

And so he was left alone in the darkness. He sat bent double between the massive blocks of stone and listened to the drops of water hitting the stone floor—over and over again. At first they sounded thin and faint, but the sound grew in Odbjørn's ears until it became a heavy relentless pounding on the stones.

It was four days to the Saturnalia . . . then three . . . and then only two.

The drops of water struck the stone floor with a metallic boom like the smiting of a sledge-hammer on the anvil. Time dragged by in the darkness like the slow-passing night of eternity. The pangs of hunger tore at Odbjørn's belly, and his bent body was racked with sharp stabbing pain. His forehead was bathed in a cold sweat, and he felt as if he carried the weight of the sewer's stone vaulting on his shoulders.

Every day Vatia went down to visit him, and the wavering flame of his oil lamp reddened the damp walls like the rising sun.

"Have you come to your senses?" he would ask. "Drive in the race, Odbjørn, and I'll let you out here and now!"

"And when I've driven in the race, can I go?" Odbjørn would mumble.

But every day the answer was the same.

"You must stay in Rome or die!" Vatia would turn his back and walk off down the passage. The darkness would return, closing in behind the uncertain glow of the lamp.

One night in a delirium of hunger his fevered mind conjured up a strange vision. The racing track in the arena was spinning round and round at a bewildering speed. The unsteady ground flashed past under his horses' hoofs, but horses and chariot remained rooted to the spot without gaining an inch.

Suddenly chariot, horses and arena vanished, and he was sitting in a boat, rowing for dear life with a rapid brownish current swirling beneath him and threatening to sweep the boat away if for one moment he rested on his oars.

But when he forced himself to look away from the dizzy current the arena lay in front of him again, and he had to hold tightly to the frame of the chariot as it sprang forward with a jerk. But the track no longer swung round the triple pillars at the end of the spina; it ran straight ahead toward one of the four main gateways of the Circus Maximus, and the horses were galloping furiously along the track without slackening speed. In one moment the quadriga would lie shattered in front of the barred gate, but just as he was expecting to hear the splintering crash he saw the gates slide open and with a rumble of thunder horses and chariot flew through the archway.

Then he awoke and the dream was gone, but the darkness around him was full of strange visions. He saw mountains and rivers and forests. Endless rows of gnarled trees glided past the iron bars, and he heard the soughing of the wind deep in the forest. Then the rustling of the leaves changed suddenly to the beating of surf. He was standing on a heather-covered hill, and there in the distance he caught sight of Hugwa's hall, looking, with its curved roofridge, like a huge ox that had lain down to rest among the heather.

And then he heard a voice.

Somewhere in the darkness a voice was calling him.

"Odbjørn!" called the voice. "Odbjørn!"

It sounded like a cry for help.

"Odbjørn!" The name echoed through the darkness of the underground passages. And the hair rose on his head . . .

For three whole days Buekil searched in vain for Odbjørn. When he inquired among the slaves and stable hands, all they knew was that Odbjørn had been rescued from a sinking ship off Ostia. One or two had seen him, or thought they had seen him, arrive at the Circus Maximus late in the morning.

But when he questioned them his eagerness alarmed them and their eyes shifted uneasily. And when it came to the point, it must have been someone quite different they had seen in the Circus Maximus that morning. He had to remember that the gateway was half in darkness. They had obviously confused him with someone else. No, they knew nothing.

Buekil was able to follow Odbjørn from Ostia until he disappeared without trace in the gateway of the Circus Maximus. But in the half-light of that gateway something had happened that none of them dared tell him about. He was certain they were not as ignorant as they pretended —especially Lurco.

Buekil trotted after the stable guard, to and fro across the forecourt. He could tell from Lurco's face that he knew something or other that might perhaps help him to solve the riddle of Odbjørn's mysterious disappearance.

"I won't say a word, Lurco. I promise . . ."

Lurco stopped so abruptly that Buekil almost stumbled over his own feet.

"Vatia's had him locked up," he whispered. He glanced nervously about him, spun around on his heel and turned his back.

But Buekil went over to the cart shed and stepped under its lean-to roof. He shook all his bright silver sesterces, all the money he had earned selling his clay animals on the market, jingling and rattling onto the floor of the racing chariot.

Lurco could not resist a quick look in his direction, and as Buekil tossed a coin into the air it twinkled like a squirming silver fish. Lurco sauntered slowly over to the cart shed, stopped and stared with envious eyes at the Gaul's accumulation of money. Buekil sat on the pole of the chariot making little piles of silver coins. He rolled one across the floor to Lurco's feet.

"Where did Vatia drag him off to?" he asked.

Lurco picked up the coin and put it into his wallet. "Over to the stables," he whispered.

"Well, we've got so far," Buekil grinned. "Let's see if we can get a bit farther! Catch, Lurco!"

Lurco snatched the coins, one after the other, as they came flying toward him, until at last he was snatching at the empty air. He took a quick look behind him.

"Then Vatia had him hauled down into the cellar," he muttered.

The sesterces came flying toward him again. Lurco stuck the shaft of his spear between his legs and caught the coins in the air.

"Seven, eight, nine, ten . . ." Buekil stopped and took a deep breath. "Hi, Lurco, those cellar stairs have got a devil of a lot of steps! Aren't we nearly at the bottom yet?"

"The cellar leads into the underground sewers," Lurco murmured. He was gazing spellbound at the coins in the bottom of the chariot. He had thrown caution to the winds.

"Into the sewers . . .?" Buekil jumped up. "Lurco!" He seized the guard and shook him. "Lurco, if you tell me as quickly as you can what direction the sewers run in, it's all yours! But you've got to be quick about it, Lurco!"

"Here . . . It should be round about here," Buekil whispered. "Look, here's the grating!"

"Be quiet! There's someone coming!" Ulver hissed as he took him by the arm.

They stood still and listened. They heard footsteps approaching. Then they stopped—and started again. They heard the sound die away somewhere far off in the dark deserted streets.

"But how do you know that it's just here, under this very street, that he's locked in?"

"Old warrior, you've a stout heart, but . . ."

"But what?" Ulver asked.

"But nothing else! Now listen, and we'll go through it all again!" Buekil stuck a finger in his ear and shook it. "If we can trust that chap Lurco, then Odbjørn's been shut away in a sewer that empties into the main drain, the Cloaca Maxima," he said. "Good . . . Well, the Maxima runs in the direction of the Forum Holitorium, but a couple of streets farther on it turns off from River Street and follows the line of Soldier Alley. And at that point where it turns off a smaller sewer runs into it. And that's where Odbjørn's shut in. And that's here! I assure you that it's just as hollow under this street as it is in your . . ."

"In my what?"

"Never mind!" grinned Buekil. "Keep your mouth shut, warrior, and keep your eyes open so that we're not caught napping!"

Buekil took hold of the grating by the bars and raised the cover. They stood still and listened for a moment. Then Buekil lay down on the ground and cupped his hands about his mouth.

"Odbjørn!" he called, and a hollow echo rumbled in the opening to the sewer.

"Not so loud!" Ulver complained. "You'll wake the whole of Rome!"

"If you can call more noiselessly, you do it!" Buekil retorted sharply. "You come and stick your head down here and whisper a shout!"

Buekil called again, and when the sound had died away Ulver bent down beside him. They held their breath and listened.

"Listen!" Buekil whispered hoarsely. "Did you hear that? Odbjørn!" he bawled down the shaft. "Odbjørn! . . . Can you hear me?"

Odbjørn was no longer in doubt. It was Buekil's voice he had heard, calling from somewhere in the darkness.

"Buekil!" he shouted. "Buekil, have they shut you in?"

He held his breath and listened. And then all at once he remembered his dream about the arena and the race track that no longer swung around the pillars but led straight on toward the gateway. And . . . the thought startled him, and in his excitement he knocked his head against the stone. If only Buekil weren't shut in . . . His breath came in quick, heavy gasps.

"Buekil! Have they shut you in?" he shouted. He pressed his head against the bars and listened breathlessly.

Then the answer came, distant and indistinct, like a rumbling echo. His face puckered with desperation, he strained to catch the words. And then, just as he was about to give it up and breathe freely again, he heard two shouted words.

"Sol . . . dier . . . Alley," boomed through the darkness.

There was no mistake about it. Buekil wanted to tell him he was in Soldier Alley behind the Capitol.

"Buekil . . . can . . . you . . . hear me?" He had hardly finished before he heard the darkness bawling, "Yes."

"Yes . . . yes . . . yes!" rang the echo.

"Listen . . . to . . . what . . . I'm . . . saying . . . now!" Odbjørn shouted every word loudly and clearly. "While the Saturnalia's being run, lift the bar from the gate that's nearest the Palatine . . . Tell Ulver . . . and the two Cheruscans . . . Haman and Vodrik . . . tell them they must ride up to the Sabatine Lake to the north of Rome . . . Have you understood?" Odbjørn waited for Buekil to answer and then continued. "You can take the horses from the stable . . . Take a horse for me . . . Wait up by the lake until I come. Buekil . . . can you hear me? . . . Good . . . Don't forget what I've said then . . . Unhook the bar from the gate that's nearest the Palatine . . . Remember, Buekil . . . The gate nearest the Palatine. Did you hear me?" Odbjørn listened but got no reply.

"Buekil!" he shouted.

"Buekil!" rumbled the echo in the pitch-black darkness.

It was now the day before the Saturnalia.

Vatia rattled his bracelet against the iron bars of the grille and woke him up. Vatia's cheeks were sallow, and under his bloodshot eyes lay the shadow of sleepless nights.

"Have you changed your mind?" he whispered, leaning wearily against the bars. He jumped back startled. "Say that again!" he cried.

"I've reconsidered it," whispered the shadow in the hole in the wall. "I'll take part in the race, Vatia."

"That's right . . . That's right, Odbjørn!"

Vatia recovered himself and rubbed his hands together. The fellow could be let out of his hole now. He would have to have something to eat. Vatia tripped over himself in his hurry.

"One moment and you shall be let out! In one moment, Odbjørn!"

He turned to go, but Odbjørn called him back.

"When the race is over . . . what then?"

"I shall be obliged to lock you up again." Vatia wrung his hands regretfully. "But more comfortably. I promise you that. What did you say? For how long? Until it's too late, Odbjørn. Until you won't any longer be able to win your strange wager, even if you do go north."

"That was all I wanted to know," Odbjørn said.

"Well, well!" sighed Vatia. . . . "I'm glad you've come to your senses!"

Odbjørn did not answer. He was wondering if Buekil had understood that he meant the gate nearest the Palatine, and not one of the other three.

25

At the Saturnalia

The Saturnalia had started and Metellus Rutilius was in the lead. Metellus had returned to Rome to beat the barbarian.

"Come on, Metellus!" someone shouted. "Have you driven all the way from Sicily? You look tired out!"

They had lost faith in him. They were mocking him, making a fool of him.

"He's coming! . . . Look out, Metellus! . . . Here he is!"

Metellus started at every shout, and each time a roar of laughter rang forth. Feeling was still against him.

But at the end of the first three laps the Roman was still in the lead. Something was bound to happen now, they had put their money on the barbarian, and they were ready to encourage him.

"Bubulcus . . . ! Bubulcus . . . !"

The shout, growing like a wave of the sea, came crashing down over the terraced benches, and Odbjørn's nickname thundered rhythmically to and fro across the arena. In their enthusiasm, hundreds of thousands of people had scrambled up on the benches and were stamping out the rhythm with their feet.

"Bubulcus . . . ! Bubulcus . . . !" The masonry and the

pillars on the spina shook beneath the rhythmic shouting.

But Odbjørn paid no heed; with four laps behind him and only three to go, he was still lagging behind the rest of the field. No one was going to persuade him to wear out his horses until the moment came to race for freedom. . . . In that race he would win neither gold nor silver nor fame, but if he succeeded he would gain his freedom, and if he failed . . .

The reins in his hands were slippery with sweat. In front of him lay the gateway nearest the Palatine, but he decided to drive another lap before taking the risk. If Buekil had misunderstood him, he would, in a minute or two, lie crushed in front of that gate, amid a chaos of splintered wood, tangled harness and dead horses. But if the bar had been lifted from its sockets, then the double gates would fly open at the touch of his chariot-pole. He glanced down at the pole—he had had it lengthened a couple of yards for this purpose. When Vatia had inquired why he was doing it, he had flown into a temper and told him to mind his own business. If he were going to take part in the race, he would decide for himself how heavy or how light the chariot was to be.

"Oh, well, have it your own way!" Vatia had muttered.

He drove into the bend. There was now but one lap to go, and he was oblivious to the derisive yells of the thousands of spectators. Through the clouds of dust he could just see the gateway at the farther end of the track, and he felt as if a sword blade had been thrust through his midriff.

And now . . . this was his last chance.

He glanced at the yelling crowds that lined the arena, and, whether the gate were barred or not, there was one thing he was certain of—he would never again look upon the Circus Maximus.

He pulled the horses away from the spina into the middle

of the track. He saw Metellus disappear round the pillars
. . . and then Tubero. Then Diocles took the bend and
then . . . then it was his turn.

Out of old habit Capellus began pulling to the left. He
raised his whip, and as he cut him across the muzzle the
stallion shied away from the bend. And now Odbjørn's
lashes rained down over the horses, and the team sprang
madly forward toward the closed gates. In a fury of speed,
the gates rushed headlong to meet them, growing bigger
and bigger . . .

The horses tried to turn aside, but Odbjørn flourished
his whip now to the left of them, now to the right; and
plying his reins, he directed them straight at the gates.
Then as the gateway seemed to collapse on top of him,
Odbjørn's eyes shut tightly.

There was a crash . . . The double gates flew open and
banged against the walls on either side. As they swung back
one of them hit a wheel with the force of a battering ram
and sent the chariot reeling against the opposite wall. The
next moment the chariot shot out of the gateway like a
bolt from a thundercloud.

Not before he reached the Temple of Hercules did
Odbjørn manage to scramble to his feet and grasp the
reins—just in time to swing the horses around the corner
into the street that ran northward around the Palatine.

People jumped for shelter behind columns and walls.
By the basilica the chariot skidded and collided with a market cart loaded with vegetables. As he turned around to
see what damage he had caused, he saw a squad of cavalry
from the city guard appear from behind the Capitol.
When he had driven out on to the Via Flaminia and left
the Field of Mars behind him, he peered around again.
The horsemen had gained on him, but no more than he
reckoned he could hold his own against until he reached

the Sabatine Lake, where Ulver and Buekil would be ready with fresh horses.

As he was about to cross the Tiber, Odbjørn lashed out with his whip to pick up speed before the road began to slope up to the bridge. And then the wheel gave way. Odbjørn heard the sound of splintering and just managed to grasp the edge of the chariot in time. The chariot was dragged behind the horses, swinging from side to side. In one moment the horses would be galloping across the narrow bridge, and the chariot would be shattered against the stone balustrade. He clambered over the edge of the chariot and balanced himself on the pole, and as the horses galloped across the bridge with the chariot trailing behind them he threw himself onto Capellus's back. Oddly enough, the chariot escaped being thrown against the balustrade, but it reduced their speed, and when he looked around he saw to his consternation that the horsemen had reached the end of the bridge.

They were coming nearer and nearer. He caught the glint of a spearhead, and took cover by throwing himself half-off the stallion's back. The spear flashed past like a black streak between the heads of the horses. He fumbled for his knife, and as he began to cut away the traces a horse's head appeared behind the stallion's back. He lashed out with his whip and caught it across the muzzle. The horse dropped behind and disappeared. Then the last thong that held Capellus to the chariot parted and the stallion sprang forward.

When he turned his head he saw the roans careering from one side of the road to the other and holding up the city guard. Odbjørn dug his heels into the stallion's flanks, and shortly afterward, from the top of a rise, he caught sight of Ulver and Buekil and the two Cheruscans. As he flashed past, he shouted to them to follow him, and when they caught up with him he changed horses at the gallop.

"Let's shake them off!" he yelled.

His homeward journey had begun as a flight. He was neither wealthy nor powerful. Ulver and Buekil and the Cheruscans, Vodrik and Haman, were all the followers he had gathered about him in foreign lands.

26

Toward the Rhine

Where the Saar and Moselle meet lay the town of Augusta Treverorum, or Treveri, as it was called after the district. The town was new, recently founded by the Emperor Augustus, with a splendid and magnificent future before it. It was already the headquarters of the Roman army north of the Alps. From it the military roads spread outwards like a spider's web spanning the occupied country with its threads. From Treveri, at the center of the network, orders went out to the units of the army stationed throughout the mighty land of Gaul.

One night in the thirty-ninth year of Augustus three men sat in the cabin of a ship down by the harbor. It was the beginning of the month the Romans called Mars after their god of war. Spring had not yet reached Treveri, and it was still so cold that as they spoke together their breath rose from their mouths like wisps of white wool— as if their very words were clothed against the cold.

Only two of the men were talking. They were the two eldest, and they sat half turned away from the younger man as if they would rather not acknowledge his company. He did not seem to want to push himself forward either, but sat bent over the table gazing listlessly into the flame of the oil lamp. The golden light cast a ruddy glow over his fair hair which hung down to his shoulders. The two older men were talking about him, a fact which apparently he did not mind. But now and again he drummed his fingers on the tabletop, as though he were growing impatient and were only waiting for them to finish their conversation to get on with his business.

"What's he done with them?" asked one of the men. He was dressed in a sea-green toga over a finely woven yellowish tunic, and on his upper arm he wore a heavy gold ring. The man he was talking to had on a coarsely woven cloak of the same color as the unplaned tabletop and the ship's timbers around them. He gave the impression of belonging there, of being part of the ship.

"We shut them up in the hold," he answered. "As I told you before, he was standing down on the quayside a little while ago with these four scruffy fellows he had chained together. He'd noticed my ship was up for sale, and he wanted to barter his four slaves for her. So I told him I'd no use for slaves, but we could send for the town's slave dealer. Then he could sell his slaves to you and pay me my price for the ship. I want six thousand sesterces for her."

"She certainly isn't worth much more!" The slave dealer peered round the cabin and pulled a face. "It's to be hoped the slaves are in better condition than the ship—otherwise I can't give him six thousand for them."

"Three of 'em are young," grunted the skipper. "They're all right. But the fourth's a bit old and scraggy."

"What country do they come from?"

"One's a Gaul all right. The gray-haired fellow and the two others are Germans. There's not much doubt about that."

The slave dealer made a slight movement of the head. "I hear you're selling your comrades," he said.

This startled the young man. "I was sold myself once by a man whose life I'd saved," he said.

No one answered him. They regarded him as a nasty bit of work they would have to put up with until the deal was concluded—but not a moment longer.

"Whoever's strongest can do what he wants!" the young man suddenly exclaimed, banging the table so hard with his fist that the dust jumped up between the planks. "Only the strongest wins and gets rich!" he shouted.

The two older men looked at one another without answering. They remained sitting with their backs turned toward him.

"Good. Let's have a look at them then," said the slave dealer as he rose to his feet.

Up on deck the young man stopped and laid his hand on the slave dealer's arm. "Look," he said, pointing up at the sky, "when the new moon wanes I must be back home."

"A pleasant journey!" said the slave dealer. "No one here will miss you, I can assure you!"

"Don't you understand that's why I'm selling them? There's not much time left and I must hurry."

The slave dealer pulled his arm away and turned to the skipper.

"How will he manage without a crew?"

"That's his look-out!"

They stopped amidships and Odbjørn bent down to raise the hatch.

"Are they chained?" the slave dealer asked.

"Yes," Odbjørn replied, "they're chained to one another."

"Ah . . ." The slave dealer seemed to be wondering about something. "Just tell me—how did you go about getting them chained?"

"It wasn't difficult." Odbjørn stood still for a moment with his hand over his eyes as if he were trying to recall how it had happened. "First of all I let two of them into the plan, the idea being to sell the two Cheruscans to get money for the journey home, and so they gave me a hand chaining them. Then I took one of the others behind a warehouse—it was an easy matter to overpower him, and when he was lying chained on the ground I called the other one. And so . . ."

"Good . . . That'll do!" cried the slave dealer. He thrust his hand under his toga and grasped the hilt of his sword. "Let them out then!"

Odbjørn flung the hatch open. "Come on!" he shouted.

They heard the rattling of chains down in the darkness of the hold. The slave dealer and the skipper stepped back as they saw Ulver appear. Then followed Buekil and the two Cheruscans bound together by a chain fastened around their wrists.

"We'll settle the payment on shore," the slave dealer said.

The skipper nodded. "The boat's yours," he muttered as he sat astride the rail.

The slave dealer gave the hooded man a push with the flat of his sword. "Forward . . . !"

As the slaves passed Odbjørn they turned their heads away. None of them had uttered a word and they disappeared into the darkness of the quayside without looking back.

When he was left alone he set about examining the ship. It was no bigger than a river barge. Age and neglect had left the woodwork gray, and he could scrape away handfuls of rotten timber from the bulwarks with his fingers. When he opened the hatch a sickly stench rose to meet him, the stench of half-rotten turnips that had clearly been the ship's last cargo.

Along the ship's sides between the rowing benches he counted twenty oar ports. He found the oars stowed away under the half-deck in the stern, and he laid them out ready along the thwarts.

Then he climbed on deck and went ashore. He walked along the quay and onto the Roman bridge which, on its seven boat-shaped piers, spanned the Moselle. In the middle of the bridge he stood still, gazing at the town. Lights were shining all around him, from windows and door cracks, like hundreds of red eyes glowering at him from the gloom of the buildings.

When he returned to the ship he let go one of the moorings and left her tied up to the quayside by the stern rope only.

He sat down on the hatch, drumming on the deck with his foot. Then he lay on his back, but, catching a glimpse of the new moon as he did so, he sat up again with a groan of despair. A strange restlessness drove him backward and forward across the deck. From time to time he would stop and stand gazing ashore. Then he would lie down again on the hatch and listen to the quiet lapping of water as the current slipped endlessly past the ship's sides. He could hear river noises, but when he turned his head the surface of the water lay mirrorlike and motionless, like a pool of molten silver among the soft contours of the hills.

At length he fell asleep, and he did not wake until the new moon had disappeared behind the line of hills. In the darkness he heard the sound of stealthy footsteps like a gentle shower of rain, and at that moment a black shadow slid over the rail. Odbjørn jumped to his feet.

"Is that you, Ulver?"

"Were you expecting anyone else?" roared the shadow as it came to meet him with a hoarse laugh.

Odbjørn rushed towards him and threw his arms round him.

"Good, Ulver!" he cried in jubilation. "Have you

brought the Cheruscans back with you? And Buekil—where's Buekil?

"Buekil?" Ulver grunted, with a humorous grin spread over his hollow cheeks. "Here I come bringing you a score of oarsmen, and you ask after that miserable mammal-maker!"

"Is that me you're talking about, you gray-haired mountain sheep!" Buekil cried, as he pushed his way forward through the slaves who were standing huddled together by the bulwarks. "I'll tell you what, Odbjørn. Another time I'm not going to let myself be sold along with this old gray donkey . . ."

"Hold your tongue, you long-legged potsmith!" Ulver drew his sword. It was rusty and squeaked in the sheath as though it were full of mice and rats and such. "You just take back your 'mountain sheep' and your 'old gray donkey'!" he bellowed as he made a grab at Buekil.

Odbjørn separated the two fighting cocks.

"You do find it hard to get on together, you two! What's up now?"

"He dropped the chain, nitwit that he is!" Buekil poked his finger into his ear and shook his hand as though he were waving to Ulver over Odbjørn's shoulder. "There he was groping around for the chain and nearly losing himself in the dark!" Buekil complained. "If that slave dealer chap had turned around, he would have found out we were just holding the chain in our hands!"

"But he didn't find out!" Odbjørn laughed. "Now tell me what happened!"

"It went off fine!" Ulver said in his rumbling voice. "He led us out of town to the amphitheatre, and when we came into the arena he took out a bunch of keys and opened a trap door in the ground. Well, we heard snoring and chains rattling down in the cellar, and so we knew the lockup was full of slaves ready to be driven into the arena for the next gladiator fight. Well, so just as he turned around to drive us down the steps we all let go of that damned chain—he hadn't expected that! . . . Well, then, we bound him and flung him down into the cellar. Then we set the slaves free and brought them along with us. And so here they are," Ulver concluded, pointing to the silent group by the rail.

"Well, so that's all there is," added Buekil, mimicking his voice and jumping smartly out of reach as Ulver raised his hand.

"Cut away the mooring, Buekil!" cried Odbjørn. "And you, Ulver . . . take the steering oar and keep her in the middle of the river!"

For two days they drifted eastward with the current. Buekil assured them that sooner or later the Moselle would tip them into the Rhine at the point where he and Odbjørn had once spent the night in the Roman camp of Confluentes. But the doubt grew in Odbjørn's mind whether in fact the Moselle led anywhere at all. Sometimes it flowed to the north, sometimes due south. The river wound lazily and languidly in and out among the green hillsides, and one hillside looked exactly like another. At one point Odbjørn inisisted quite seriously that they had passed that way the day before.

"I wonder whether either of you two wise men of the East has ever seen a river flow backwards, or turn around and run back into the mountains?" Buekil asked. He looked at Ulver and Odbjørn in turn, shook his head and sat himself down amidships in order to be equally out of the way of Ulver, who was standing at the helm, and Odbjørn, who was hanging over the bows and craning his neck to see around the next bend. When the Cimbrians were in that frame of mind they were ready to quarrel over anything, he reflected, including whether day followed night or the other way round.

During the evening of the third day they reached an island in midstream. Buekil said they were now close to the spot where the Moselle flowed into the Rhine. The Romans would stop them there to inspect their river pass and check whether they had permission to sail past the Roman fort. They must therefore try to slip past at dead of night. Once they had reached the Rhine, Buekil thought, they would be able to float downstream into the German Ocean without running into any further obstacles.

Ulver nodded. From there he knew the way along the Frisian coast. They would soon be home then, he said comfortingly.

"It's thirty days at the most to the spring sacrifice," Odbjørn muttered.

"We'll do it!" Ulver promised. He was gazing straight ahead with a serious thoughtful look as if he were measuring the distance across the mountains to the Cimbrian coast. The calculations that occupied him must have been difficult, for his mouth stood half-open.

"Mind the last thought doesn't fall out!" Buekil put a finger under Ulver's chin and shut his mouth for him. Then he had to run for his life with the infuriated Ulver at his heels.

Odbjørn laid the boat to behind the island and they settled down to wait for nightfall.

As the sun disappeared behind the hills night began spinning threads of shadow across the river valley and its black blanket closed slowly over their heads.

Buekil could hear Ulver sharpening his sword as he sat over by the rail, and he could hear Odbjørn pacing restlessly backward and forward across the deck. Suddenly Odbjørn was standing in front of him.

"We'll sail now!" he said.

Buekil stood up, his face a blur of white mist in the darkness.

"If they catch us, it'll begin all over again," he said. "The long journey south—the salt mines and slavery."

"You're wrong! It'll end where it began—in the fortress of Confluentes. We're runaway slaves and we shall be condemned to death if they get hold of us!"

"Yes, you're right," Buekil whispered. His teeth chattered as if he were cold.

"Are you afraid?"

"I'm frightened to death," he admitted.

Ulver jumped down from the rail and came over to them with the two Cheruscans.

"Fetch a lamp," said Odbjørn.

"What are you up to?"

Odbjørn had shot back the bolt from the hatch. Buekil seized him by the arm.

"What are you going to do? Don't go down there!" he said excitedly. "Listen! They're a set of treacherous criminals, I tell you! They were all condemned to death in the arena for their crimes!"

"The Romans punish according to different laws from ours," Odbjørn answered.

"One of 'em's a Roman soldier who deserted from his unit!" Buekil called after him.

When Odbjørn was standing below between the rowing benches, he raised his lamp and peered around. The men lay sprawling on the thwarts, the handles of their oars resting under knees or armpits. As they pulled themselves slowly up, their sluggish movements reminded Odbjørn of the cunning treachery of a beast of prey. Rough coarse faces were turned toward him. Yes, Buekil was right. They were a sinister-looking lot, ragged and tattered, their limbs and bodies covered with swollen scars of cuts and gashes. He could well imagine all the pain they must have suffered, and it was pain, no doubt, that had lined their faces so deeply. Suffering had filled their minds with cunning submissiveness or bitter defiance.

On the upper benches he caught sight of the Roman soldier. With a derisive twist to his mouth, he sat dangling his legs to and fro in front of Odbjørn's face.

"Listen to me!" said Odbjørn. "We're close to the Roman fort at Confluentes. In one moment I will attempt to sail past. I was a Roman slave, too, and, like you, I escaped. If they catch us it'll mean death for all of us! But for me it's the way home to the Cimbrian peninsula."

He stopped and took a deep breath. The men sat tense and motionless, but their eyes were on the hatchway where Ulver stood barring the ladder. Odbjørn was suddenly aware of a movement behind him. He turned sharply and sprang to one side. The man behind him had raised the heavy handle of his oar above his head.

"Ulver!" he shouted without taking his eyes off the man.

"Yes."

"Get up on deck!"

"But . . ."

"Clear off!" yelled Odbjørn.

He heard Ulver stump up the ladder and a whispered murmur pass along the benches.

"Now listen! As I said before, my way takes me past the Roman fortress. The time's come for all of you to make your choice. Whoever wants to can be put ashore."

He heard them taking deep breaths as if they had come alive and were breathing for the first time. An excited whispering spread among them and died away.

"Would you rather be rid of us?" asked a voice.

"I've plenty of use for you at the oars, but I don't know whether I shall ever be able to pay you."

"Shall we be chained?"

"In my homeland it's not the fashion to chain men to the thwarts," he answered.

For a long time the men talked together in low voices. Then a voice spoke up from their midst.

"We'll sail with you to that land you spoke of."

"When we get out into the German Ocean it'll be heavy work at the oars," Odbjørn said.

"We'll go with you!" answered the voice.

"We may meet death any moment now," Odbjørn said.

"He'd already arranged to meet us in the arena," the voice replied.

"Good. You've made your choice. Now listen to what I have to say. . . ."

The men sat up straight and grasped their oars.

Buekil came running up from the bows.

"Now! . . . We're there now!" he whispered hoarsely.

Odbjørn jumped down a couple of steps and thrust his head into the hold.

"Stop!" he shouted. "And you, Buekil! Put the lamp out!"

Ulver crept over to the bulwarks and kept a lookout toward the bank. The ship was gliding silently through the darkness toward the mouth of the river. Drops dripped from the oars and hit the water with tinkling splashes, and as he stood listening on the ladder he could hear the oars-men's heavy breathing.

A little way off Buekil stood pressed against the mast, the lamp rattling in his shaking hands. Odbjørn was just going to tell him to put it down when he heard an excited whisper from the rail. Ulver was pointing toward the bank, and Odbjørn could just make out the black outline of the tower-crowned ramparts as they appeared on their bows and glided slowly along their starboard side. And now he seemed to hear a low washing of water. They must be

close to the mouth of the river now, near the point where
the rivers met. Very soon they would feel the current of
the Rhine tugging at their bows. He held his breath and listened. Buekil's hands were shaking so much that the lamp
rattled.

"Quiet!" he snapped.

And Buekil dropped the lamp. It rolled clanking across
the deck, and even before it clattered against the bulwarks
a loud shout came from the ramparts.

"Hallo, there! . . . Starboard your helm and heave to
in midstream!"

The shout made Odbjørn turn cold. He stood there
paralyzed, incapable of action, while the boat drifted on
toward the mouth of the river.

"Can't you hear! Stop!" The shout rang out in the
dark across the river.

"Ulver, run—take the steering oar from Haman!"
Odbjørn whispered.

There were several heavy bumps followed by the clattering of oars, and he saw a boat putting out from the
bank.

Buekil came hurrying along close to the rail.

"They're coming!" he whispered.

"Listen!" They heard creaking and a heavy thud, like
a felled tree crashing to the ground. And at the same
time there was a splash in the water in front of their bows.

"That was a catapult!" gasped Buekil. "They're shooting from the fort!"

The ship shuddered. A stone had hit the mast and before
it plunged into the water had torn away part of the rail.

"What are you waiting for?" cried Buekil. "Get them
rowing!"

Odbjørn gripped his arm.

"Not until the Rhine turns our bows," he hissed. He
stood bent forward as if he were listening for something
in the darkness.

"They're drawing nearer!" Buekil wailed.

"Then they won't use their catapults any more. Now!
. . . Did you feel that?" he cried. "The current's caught
us—we're in the Rhine!"

He let go of Buekil and stumped down the ladder.

"Oars ready!" he shouted into the darkness between the
rowing benches. "Now . . . !" he yelled.

The oars creaked and threshed the water into foam along
the sides of the ship.

"Now . . .!" he yelled. "Now!"

He kicked a tread out of the ladder and, grasping the
lump of wood in his hands, beat out the time against a
rowing bench. He increased the tempo. Faster and faster
the oars swept through the water.

"Come on now! Come on!" he roared.

He could not see them. But the darkness was filled with
puffing and groaning and creakings and rumblings.

"Now then . . . now . . . Come on!" The sweat was
running down his forehead. "Come on now . . . !" he
hissed in a hoarse voice as he drummed out the rhythm
against the rowing bench.

How long it lasted he wasn't sure, but he did not recover
himself until he heard a shout from the deck and Buekil's
head appeared in the hatchway.

"Leave off!" he yelled. "Stop . . . Stop! They don't fancy
following us," Buekil grinned. "They've obviously remembered they'll have the current against them when they
turn back! The Romans, you see, have grown fat and lazy
because Augustus never wages war!"

As it grew light they caught sight of two islands a little
ahead of them. They looked like two river barges that had
heaved-to side by side and cast anchor in midstream. They
put in to the larger of the islands and stayed there throughout the day. Not until nightfall did they continue their
voyage northward.

27

Graywind Returns to His Master

One night they sailed past the Roman camp at Vetera where the merchant Serbulus had sold Odbjørn into slavery. He stood by the rail gazing in the direction of the town, and in spite of the darkness he could make out the jetty from which the ferry sailed and the dark outline of the houses huddled together under the ramparts like chickens around a brood hen. He recognized it all again and he fell to thinking about Serbulus—Serbulus and the slave dealer, Æmilius—and Thorkim. As always when Thorkim came into his mind, he felt the piece of amber burn beneath his tunic as though it lit devouring flames of hate and revenge in his breast.

As he stood there recalling that night in Vetera when he had fled through the narrow streets pursued by Æmilius's slave drivers, he suddenly heard a subdued shout from the bows. In the darkness ahead Buekil had caught sight of a dozen ship's lanterns, their flickering lights looking like red pearls on an invisible string stretched across the river.

Roman warships lay at anchor north of Vetera, barring their passage to the German Ocean. Odbjørn's last hope was shattered.

From night to night he had watched the moon's golden sickle dwindling away until there was little more than the curved line of an arc left. Before very long the sky would be black and empty. Then the new moon would rise again and the spring sacrifice would be celebrated at the settlement. Thorkim would lead his men on to the meeting ground, and when the fire flared up before the image of Frey they would turn for the last time toward the heather-covered hills to see whether he, Odbjørn, would appear after all. Then they would laugh and shake their heads, and he would be forgotten the moment Hugwa the farmer placed his daughter's hand in Thorkim's.

"It's no use. I give up!" he said, weary and dispirited. "Turn the ship about!"

They turned about and rowed upstream, while Ulver and Buekil crept quietly around, casting glances at Odbjørn who sat slumped down on a coil of rope in the bows. A little to the south of Vetera they ran the ship into the River Ruhr and cast anchor.

"As we sailed past Vetera I saw a Roman galley lying alongside the jetty," mumbled Ulver.

No one answered him. He stepped close to Odbjørn and added that the galley had looked practically deserted.

"There were only a couple of watchmen on board," he said.

Odbjørn sat staring down at the deck.

"Buekil," Ulver called out, "did you hear what I said?"

Buekil turned and looked at him.

"Did you say something?"

"I said there's a Roman galley lying over by Vetera!" Ulver shouted, red in the face. "When it's dark we could sail across and throw the watch overboard. With two ships I could break through the blockade, but I haven't the men to sail the Roman galley! That's what I said!"

Odbjørn lifted his head.

"Men? Did you say something about men?"

"I said . . ."

But Ulver got no further. Odbjørn had jumped up.

"Buekil!" he called. "Do you think you could find your way through the forests to Arminius?" Buekil nodded. "Then off with you! Greet Arminius for me and say . . ."

A few days later Buekil returned.

He brought greetings from the prince of the Cherusci, and he had three score men with him. But that was not all. As he came toward them they saw that he was leading a horse. Odbjørn sprang forward with surprise.

"Graywind!" he shouted as he jumped ashore.

But there was no getting hold of the animal. He knew him well enough, but . . . First he struck his hoofs into the ground and stood stock-still, but when Odbjørn put out his hand to touch him he shied to one side and kicked out with his hind legs until there was a hail of clods all around him. Then he galloped off and came charging back with thundering hoofs. Backward and forward, around and around, ever nearer until finally he ran straight at Odbjørn and sent him sprawling to the ground. And when he got to his feet and rubbed his horse under the chin he was bitten on the shoulder so that he cried out with the pain of it. But Graywind intended no harm—it was all pure joy at seeing him again.

When Odbjørn sprang to his back, he carried him like the west wind up along the riverbank and into the forest. He turned back snorting and, with the wind whistling through mane and fetlocks, galloped in among the men, scattering them in all directions like chaff beneath the flail.

Ulver saw there was no curbing their restless excitement.

"Odbjørn!" he cried, as he jumped hastily out of the way. He got to his feet again as horse and rider turned and came charging back at him. "Why don't you ride home!" he shouted.

The horse drove his pasterns into the ground and stood as though on four quivering posts. Odbjørn turned and rode slowly toward him.

"What was that you said?"

"I said you're restless. Why not try getting home on your own? In the meantime, we'll take the galley over by Vetera, and try fighting our way through the cordon of Roman ships. I shall either reach home in time for the spring sacrifice, or else"—Ulver grinned broadly—"or else I shall float downstream into the German Ocean as dead as a drowned herring!"

Buekil, too, tried to persuade Odbjørn to ride home. He kept a respectful distance from Graywind and admitted that he wasn't much in favor of putting to sea with a wild animal like that.

"One gray donkey on board'll be quite sufficient," he said.

A moment or two later the light dawned; Ulver spun round and made for him.

"Let me go!" yelled Buekil, bending forward to shield a bundle wrapped in hide which he had been holding under his arm.

"What's that you've got there?" asked Odbjørn.

"That's something Arminius asked me to give you," he answered mysteriously. "But you won't get it until I see you again," he added, tucking the bundle carefully back under his arm.

Odbjørn now took leave of them.

"And don't go letting the Romans pin you in between two of their ships, like a louse between a pair of thumb-nails!" he warned them.

"Ride like hell!" Ulver shouted after him. "We don't

want to hang about on the Cimbrian shore waiting for
you!"

Night and day Odbjørn rode northward, galloping furiously. The stinging branches struck him like whiplashes,
raising weals across his face and tearing his clothes to
tatters. The echo of hammering hoofbeats rumbled hollowly through the murky German forests.

And when the forests came to an end the marshes and
the open plains lay waiting for him. Graywind's hoofs
squelched noisily through the bog and rattled across the
stony ground as the spray of marsh water rising about his
fetlocks gave place to a cloud of stifling dust around his
clattering hoofs.

Marsh and meadowland, hills and steep slopes, rivers
and streams, and flat interminable plains—the same
ground that he and Serbulus had traveled over on their
journey southward sixteen months before.

But the way seemed endless. For six whole days he rode
northward toward the land of the Cimbri. It was the nights
he counted and reckoned. When it grew dark he would
draw rein and let Graywind graze and rest while he wiped
the foam off his quivering flanks with a handful of grass.
He would whisper in the stallion's ear that the next day
would be the last, that the next evening they must be back
home. Then Graywind would have a chance to rest and
recover, and never again would he be ridden beyond his
strength. That he promised him, and Graywind snorted
into a tuft of grass and sighed deeply.

But the following evening saw no change in the countryside, and the night was the same as before. No, not quite—
for that night the sky was black like a jeweler's cloth of
black velvet covered with myriads of glittering pearls.
There were only the glittering, sparkling stars—the sickle
moon had disappeared.

Odbjørn flung himself on to Graywind's back and galloped into the darkness of the night. There was no longer time for rest.

"On!" he cried, as he dug his heels into the horse's flanks. He felt the animal tremble, his gray coat quivering and twitching under him. "Only tonight and tomorrow—then we shall be home!" he whispered.

He was racing north with the spring, but the spring was outpaced and left behind. In the morning Odbjørn and Graywind galloped into a driving snowstorm blowing straight into their faces. The heavy flakes of wet snow lay like a gray coat of mail over the breast of man and horse. Dazzled and blinded, he let Graywind stagger on through the tempest. About midday the snowstorm abated, and when he opened his eyes he saw black wands of heather sticking out of the gray slush. And then he knew he was not far from home. When the Emperor Augustus visited the East, carpets and palm leaves were spread before his feet. Yes, indeed . . . and for him the black heather-carpet of the heath lay spread out before the threshold of Hugwa's dwelling. Odbjørn laughed aloud, threw his arms round Graywind's neck and shouted into his ear, his heels beating like drumsticks against his flanks. Yelling and shouting, he sped on over the carpet of heather.

Toward evening he reached the beacon to the south of the settlement. The dream he had dreamt in his narrow prison in the sewers of Rome had come true. In the distance lay Hugwa's hall, like an ox bent-backed among the heather-covered hills. But it did not look quite as he had seen it in his dream. In his imagination Hugwa's hall had grown to the size of the temples and palaces in the city on the seven hills, and it now seemed as if the hall and the village and the farmsteads beyond had shrunk and shriv-

eled. It all seemed strangely small, as small as it really was
. . . if not smaller.

When dusk began to fall he lit the beacon on the hilltop,
and it was not long before he saw a horseman appear from
behind Hugwa's hall. He lay in the heather and followed
him with his eyes, watching him zigzag this way and that
over the great marshes, as he followed the paths that led
across the treacherous ground. Then the horseman leaped
across the stream and disappeared in a white mist of spray.
As Hjald's head appeared over the hilltop he rose to his
feet. Hjald gave a shout.

"Odbjørn!" He jumped off his horse and threw his arms
round his blood brother. "Welcome home!" he cried,
laughing and thumping him on the back. He held Odbjørn
at arm's length and gazed at him as if he had returned from
another world. The first thing that caught his attention was
the strange dress Odbjørn was wearing—a tattered tunic
and filthy sandals, the leather cracked and gray with dust.
Then he peered around as if he had hoped to find others
on the farther side of the hill—a numerous band of followers, perhaps. But all he saw was a horse, gray and dis-
heveled and flecked with foam. He tried, without great
success, to hide his disappointment.

"You didn't manage it, then," he muttered.

Odbjørn laughed. "I can see by the long face you're
pulling that they haven't come yet! But they're on their
way, Hjald! Sea rovers, I tell you! About four score of them
and two ships. . . ."

His friend nodded but did not look at him.

"Don't you believe me?" Odbjørn cried.

"Yes, of course! If you say so, then I believe you. But
I'm afraid your men'll come too late."

"What do you mean by that?"

His blood brother hesitated to answer.

"Hjald," cried Odbjørn, "you don't mean Groa and Thorkim . . . You don't mean that, Hjald?"

"No, no. Not yet . . . Groa's sewing her bridal clothes with the women in my father's farmstead. But she finds it difficult to thread a needle, I promise you, for she cries most of the time, Odbjørn. . . . It's like this, you see. Thorkim has nearly forty men under arms . . . and no one's seen anything of you. So bit by bit she's lost all hope of ever seeing you again."

"But I'm here now! Hjald, you don't trust me!" he cried. "You're keeping something back!"

Hjald looked up. "There's one thing you're forgetting," he said quietly.

"And what's that?"

"The day, Odbjørn." He sighed heavily. "Tomorrow when the sun sets we celebrate the spring sacrifice on the meetingplace. . . ."

28

The Spring Sacrifice

Tova lay awake, listening as Odbjørn turned and tossed in the hay. In the middle of the night he got up and led Graywind out of the hut. She heard the hoofbeats disappearing in the direction of the sand dunes.

And so everything was just as it was before he left. He had come full circle. Once again he was waiting for Ulver, and Ulver did not come.

He rode along by the edge of the beach, with the foam-crested waves rolling in out of the darkness and breaking round Graywind's fetlocks with the magic murmur of the sea.

He pulled up and listened. Somewhere in the night a seagull screamed. Was he mistaken, or had he heard a shout out at sea? He tried to catch the sound of voices and creaking oars above the noise of the surf.

He stayed on the beach until the darkness grew gray with the first light of dawn, and then he rode home. In the straw stood a tankard of steaming mead, and, oddly enough, it was not until Graywind stamped across the floor that the old woman began to snore behind her bed curtains.

The rumor of Odbjørn's homecoming had spread like wildfire. Thralls and other inquisitive folk—but they were mostly bondsmen—lurked around the hut in the heather to catch a glimpse of him. But no one saw him, for Odbjørn had crawled up into the hayloft and knocked a turf out of the wall. All day long he sat by the hole gazing out to sea, but the blue-gray expanse of water stretched away empty and deserted into the sky, and though he strained his eyes until they smarted he saw no ship appear on the horizon.

Aslak came rushing up, breathless and bowlegged.

"They're now piling up the wood for the fires along the slopes around the meeting place!" he panted, his breath wheezing and whistling as he spoke.

Odbjørn nodded, and told him and Ketil to be off and to come back and tell him what was happening in the village. When they started gathering at the meetingplace he would have to be there—he had pledged that to Hugwa—though the gods knew that as soon as it grew dark he would much rather go away again never to return.

When Tova heard him say that she gave a little cry.

Odbjørn turned away and gazed out to sea. A sharp wind blowing through the hole drew tears from his eyes, and at that moment Ketil came in at the door.

"What's the news?" asked Odbjørn.

The old man stood shuffling his feet and gnawing his lip until his beard wagged like a goat's tail on his chin. Then all at once he turned around and was on his way out again when Tova stepped to the door and barred the way.

"Tell me now!"

Ketil wriggled sideways along by the hayloft.

"There's a branch in the cairn out on the headland," he said.

So! . . . Groa had stuck a branch in the cairn, the secret sign they had used in the past. Groa wanted to talk to him, but Odbjørn felt he had no right to go to her—less now than ever before.

He peered out of the hole. The dusk was beginning to creep in from the sea, and beyond the sand dunes the foaming crests of the breakers were dancing like snowflakes in the dark. Suddenly he started, and put his hand out to the hole as if he would tear away yet another turf. But he let his hand drop. He had been mistaken; he thought he had seen what he most wanted to see.

Aslak came rushing up, shouting that Witulf the priest was now riding into the sacred grove with his followers. They would hear the sound of the rams' horns any moment now. They stood still and listened. Then they heard someone wheezing and coughing outside: it was Ketil slogging up the hill with the latest news. He pushed Aslak to one side and staggered into the hut.

"Thorkim . . ." he panted, gasping for breath.

Odbjørn started and turned pale.

"What about Thorkim?" he shouted.

"Thorkim's setting out with his men," Ketil groaned. "And the village folk are gathering on the meetingplace," he said. "And Hugwa and . . ."

He suddenly stopped short as the rams' horns from the sacred grove called them to the spring sacrifice—harsh strident notes rising and falling like a dog barking and yapping in the distance. Aslak and Ketil stumbled to the door, struggling to get out first.

"They're lighting the fires round the meetingplace now!" yelled Aslak from the other side of the turf wall.

They knew that. He and Tova could see them. Beyond the open door a shimmering red glow rose against the dusky blue of the evening sky. The doorway stood out red and quivering against the black wall.

"The time's come, Odbjørn," Tova whispered as she blew her nose on her skirt.

"Yes," he said. He cast a glance at the hole, but it was no good now. The time was up and he had lost.

He slid down from the hayloft, and Tova now produced what she had been tacking together as she sat over in her corner—a cloak of a muddy brown coarse-woven stuff, but whole and without patches. As she laid it across his shoulders, Aslak and Ketil rushed in and, putting their heads together, got busy in the hay.

"Odbjørn," said Tova, "you know Gyrd, Asulf's daughter."

"Yes, I know Asulf's daughter."

"Once, while you were away, Gyrd came up here and asked if I'd any news of you."

"You needn't trouble, Tova!"

He went over to Graywind and led him out of his stall. He stopped in the doorway and turned around.

"Didn't Groa ever come up here and ask for news?"

The old bondswoman was silent.

"I asked you a question, Tova."

"Groa came here practically every day and talked about you," the old woman said in a low voice.

Outside he caught sight of Ketil and Aslak. The two old men stood pressed against the outside of the hut. They had put on their coats of ring mail and strapped their swords about their gaunt hips. They must have grown smaller in all directions since the last time they had worn them, for their rusty coats of mail hung down their legs like loose-fitting women's skirts, their scabbards trailed along the ground, and their helmets were so big it was no easy matter to say which was which. Under Odbjørn's sharp eyes they seemed to shrink even more. And then they suddenly realized themselves that they did not really bear comparison with Thorkim's warriors.

"You stay here!" said Odbjørn. "Don't you dare show yourselves at the folk-meet!"

As he rode slowly toward the sacred grove he could see the tops of its trees rising above the hillside. That evening, the trees and the hills and the sky—everything—seemed red with blood. Along the sloping banks the fires burned one after another. The sacred grove and the open space where the people assembled lay in a ring of fire as though at the center of a flaming sun-wheel.

A little way up the hill Odbjørn drew rein and looked out to sea for the last time, but beyond the sand dunes lay a wall of darkness, and there was nothing to see.

"I'll leave first thing in the morning, and go south to the Cherusci," he thought. "I'll take service in Arminius's bodyguard, and when the dark forests close about me I shall forget all that's happened tonight—and I shall never come back again," he whispered.

As they saw him appear over the crest of the hill a breathless gasp went up from the assembled village folk. The chatter of voices died away, and in the oppressive silence that followed they could hear the fires crackling.

The lone horseman had drawn rein a little way up the hillside. He was alone, and alone he remained, He would have done better to have stayed away, ne'er-do-well that he was.

"Is that you, Odbjørn?" inquired a voice.

Odbjørn started. The farmer had ridden forward in front of the stone circle around the image of Frey, and behind him, standing by the side of Witulf the priest . . . Odbjørn felt a stab at the heart when he caught sight of Groa's pale form outlined against the dark pile of wood. At first he did not hear what Hugwa said, and when he tried to answer him his throat felt choked.

"I asked you—as a matter of form and for the sake of the

challenge—whether you could produce more men than those you see Thorkim has brought with him!" Hugwa cried.

Some way off, Thorkim had halted on the meetingplace. There were at least forty men in his company, all horsed and drawn up in rank and file behind him. Unlike the rest of them, Thorkim had not stared at him as he had ridden over the bank that surrounded the meetingplace. Thorkim had sat erect and motionless in his saddle, staring in the direction of the sacred grove, just as he was doing now.

"Answer me!" shouted the farmer.

"They're on their way!" Odbjørn cried in desperation. "They . . ."

He did not know how he managed to get the words out —perhaps because he expected to see Groa's eyes light up with hope. Perhaps it was the grin on the faces of the village folk that made him answer as he did.

"They're on their way," he stammered. "They're coming."

A roar of laughter greeted his words.

Hugwa stroked his face with his hand as if he were wringing a smile of amusement out of his beard. He paused for a moment to give the people time to laugh their fill. Then he sat upright in his saddle.

"As everyone knows, I promised to give Groa's hand to the one who could produce the most men at the folk-meet tonight," he cried in a voice that thundered across the open space. "You who are gathered here are witnesses that Thorkim has won the challenge!"

A resounding shout affirmed his words.

Hugwa made a sign to the priest. They saw a red tongue of fire winding and twisting among the stacked branches, and the next moment the flames blazed, raging up beneath the trees of the sacred grove. The image of Frey and the circle of stones lay bathed in a golden glow.

The village folk greeted the sacred fire with a deafen-

ing shout. Their excitement was boundless. The clashing
of sword on shield beat rhythmically above the din.

"Thorkim!" shouted Hugwa. "Thorkim, Hamund's
son!"

Without knowing it for sure, Odbjørn had spoken the
truth: "They're coming . . . they're on their way."

Ulver braced his chest against the steering oar and sang
out the stroke above the oarsmen's heads. For a long time
he had seen the ring of fire that marked the spring sacrifice
glowing like a red eye in the darkness. He knew what that
meant . . . it was now or never. If he arrived too late he
could almost wish he might never see Odbjørn again. The
two ships forged ahead over the sea, side by side, prow to
prow—one might almost imagine they were taking part
in a race. Then they reached the first of the sand banks.
Ulver shouted to them to stop rowing. He glanced astern,
waiting for the wave that would lift them over the bank.

"Now!" he yelled. "Now . . . Row like hell!"

Ketil and Aslak were lying among the sand dunes staring
out to sea. Suddenly they heard voices to seaward. Look
over there . . . !

The sharp point of a prow broke through the darkness
and then vanished. It appeared again, and this time . . .
This time it came on toward them. The ship drove at full
speed through the breakers in a gushing spray of foam that
rose like the white wings of a swan about the bows. Like a
broad-bladed battle-ax the prow cut into the pebble bank
along the edge of the beach, and as the keel sank into the
crunching stones the ship settled to one side.

The two old men had jumped to their feet. Ketil tugged
at his beard as he pointed out to sea where the prow of yet
another ship came plunging through the darkness. Aslak
bent double, whimpering like a dog, and then he suddenly
spun around and started off over the dunes. As he rolled

along on his bandy legs, Ketil followed, puffing and groaning.

"Aslak!" he yelled, coughing and spluttering. Their rusty coats of mail jingled like tinkling bells round their skinny hips. Up on the hillside Ketil threw himself forward and caught hold of Aslak's leg, bringing him smartly to the ground in a clatter of iron ring mail.

"You old fool!" Ketil hissed. "You heard him say he didn't want us at the folk-meet!"

Ah, yes, Aslak remembered now! He lay there coughing and spitting. Ketil was gasping for breath, too, wheezing and groaning like a pair of bellows.

Shortly afterwards they poked their heads carefully over the crest of the hill, their two bearded faces hidden in the grass. Their eyes blinked as they gazed down toward the sacred grove, and their panting breath whistled like puffs of wind among the grass stalks.

Odbjørn clenched his teeth. He felt it would be better to wheel Graywind around and gallop away from it all. His heart hammered against his ribs and he was burning hot. He had no wish to see what was about to take place over by Frey's image, but he was unable to drag himself away.

Hugwa the farmer placed Groa's hand in Thorkim's, and then . . . Then with cupped hands brimful of golden grains of wheat Witulf the priest stepped forward before the god Frey and offered the corn to Groa. But she did not take it. She kept her arms behind her back and shook her head so that her hair curled and waved down her back and over her shoulders like a golden stream of flowing amber. He watched her lay her hand on Thorkim's arm and bend toward him. She whispered something to him and Thorkim nodded.

Then suddenly it happened . . .

Thorkim dropped Groa's hand, wheeled his horse around and galloped away from Frey's image. Odbjørn started with surprise as he saw Thorkim riding toward him. What did he want?

What did Thorkim want? It looked as if he hardly knew himself. As he drew up he tugged the bridle so hard that his horse rose on his hind legs.

"Now then, you scoundrel!" Thorkim struck him with the reins. Thorkim was finding it difficult to control the horse. Confoundedly difficult. Thorkim was playing for time.

"Odbjørn," he said, staring at his horse's ears as if he had never before seen anything quite so odd as those two cone-shaped ears. "Odbjørn, I'm glad to see you home again."

Odbjørn frowned. Those were strange words coming from Thorkim's mouth, but more were to follow.

"I've not had a quiet hour since you left," he said. Odbjørn felt the piece of amber burning beneath his tunic. His fingers itched to pull it out and fling it in Thorkim's face—his one desire was to pick a quarrel and settle his account with Thorkim. His cheeks were flushed with a wild fury and something was banging away behind his temples.

What was it Thorkim had said? He looked up and looked Thorkim straight in the eye.

"Are you merely saying that to try to right a wrong you've done?" he asked.

"No, Odbjørn. I'm saying it because I can see no joy in her eyes. I've won everything—fame and wealth—while you, Odbjørn, you haven't grown a scrap in men's esteem since the day we left . . . And yet Groa's heart belongs to you—to you and no one else. Take her, Odbjørn. She's yours!"

Odbjørn was filled with a wild joy. So all Thorkim's wealth went for nothing! Then all at once he seemed to hear Arminius's voice. Arminius had said power was a rare thing, but power and wealth would not win men's hearts, only those of old graybeards like Hugwa . . .

"But what do you think Hugwa will say to it?"

"I and my men will stand by to protect your happiness and Groa's," Thorkim said. "The old man won't have much to say in the matter!"

Thorkim was pale, but he smiled.

"Well, Odbjørn, I'm giving you your bride. Don't you think you could offer me your friendship in exchange?"

Odbjørn turned toward him and looked steadily at him.

"Here," he said. "Here, Thorkim! Take this as a pledge of my friendship!" He handed Thorkim the piece of amber. Inside that golden stone the spider stretched groping legs towards the gnat.

"No, no!" Thorkim cried as he drew back. "I won't have that again!"

"Then let the gods have it so that it may never again sow discord among men!"

With all the force at his command Odbjørn flung the piece of amber in the direction of the sacred grove. They heard it tearing through the treetops.

"It no longer stands between us now," Odbjørn said. He rode up to Thorkim and held out his hand. But Graywind set his teeth in the chest of Thorkim's horse. The two animals reared and backed away from one another with a whinny, much to the amusement of Odbjørn and Thorkim.

"I can see myself in that horse—myself as I was when I left here!" Odbjørn laughed and stroked the horse's mane with his fingers. But Thorkim saw that his thoughts were elsewhere.

"She's waiting for you," he said.

Odbjørn rode slowly down toward the pillar of Frey. At the same moment a wave of excitement swept through the assembled village folk. A gasp went up, a single gasp from hundreds of throats.

"Look there . . . ! Up on the hillside!"

One after another they came into sight. A whole band of warriors came crowding over the earthwork. And still more followed them . . . more and more of them . . . And in front a thin stooping man.

A murmur of wonder rose from the village folk gathered together by the sacred grove. Look! The strange warriors were closing up behind Odbjørn and he wasn't even aware of them.

He had no eyes for anyone but Groa.

Groa dismounted and went to meet him. With her fingers she wiped something from her cheek, and she tossed her head back so that her hair rippled over her shoulders. She smiled. Her teeth gleamed moist and white like the shells on the beach, and her hair shone golden like the fires around them.

He knew now that what was worth having could not be bought for sesterces and chains of gold. Nor was the power of the sword of any use either. One could not gain a man's friendship with threats, nor could one, with golden amber and precious trinkets, win a bride worth the having. He realized that now. And his travels had been long and to little purpose, since it was there in his own home that he had found the truth of it.

Buekil held out a bowl to Groa and Odbjørn, a transparent bowl that turned everything green when you looked through it. Placed on a shelf by itself, it would be an ornament to any hall, and everybody would be able to see that in the house of Odbjørn and Groa bowls were made of other things than silver and bronze. Buekil stood there jabbering away to this effect.

"Here you are!" he said. "This bowl's a wedding present from the Cheruscan prince, Arminius! . . . Oh, well, if you can't be bothered," he said, letting his arm drop, "it can wait!" He turned around with a grin on his face and winked at Ulver.

A gentle breeze blew across the meetingplace, a soft breath of air spiced with the scent of flowers and new-mown hay and warm with the summer sun. It was nothing at all really. The mild wind was only a foretaste of what was on the way. The village folk distended their nostrils and took a deep breath.

Spring had come—spring that Odbjørn had overtaken and ridden past in the land of the Saxons. Spring reached the settlement the night they celebrated the spring sacrifice on the meetingplace.

Translator's Note

This is primarily a story of adventure and romance in days long gone by. The hero, however, becomes involved in events that really happened and meets half a dozen people who were actually alive round about the year A.D. 10. Having read the book, you may like to know more about those events and people.

The rapid expansion of the Roman Empire during the past 150 years had led to one conquest after another, as the Romans felt the need to secure their ever-extending frontiers. Fifty years before the victory of the German chieftain, Arminius, at Teutoburger Wald in A.D. 9 (described in this story) Caesar, in the course of his campaigns in Gaul, noted the incursion of German tribes across the Rhine. But as long as Rome remained split by civil war nothing was done about the long northern frontier of the Rhine and Danube which held the warlike and unquiet tribes of Germany precariously in check. After two generations of internal conflict, Augustus emerged in 27 B.C. as the strong man of Rome, and by 13 B.C. he felt sufficiently free from more pressing matters to send his stepson Drusus across the Rhine with the double purpose of subduing the potentially dangerous barbarians and of shortening the frontier by advancing it to the Elbe. The Cherusci of this story were subdued in 11–9 B.C., and military operations were continued for a further three years by Drusus's elder brother Tiberius, who later succeeded Augustus as Emperor.

The campaign was resumed in A.D. 6, when plans were made to bring it to a conclusion by overthrowing Maroboduus, King of the Marcomanni in Bohemia. These plans were frustrated by a large-scale insurrection in the provinces of Pannonia and Dalmatia, which at the time seemed to threaten the very existence of Rome. Fifteen legions and an equal number of auxiliary troops were needed before the insurgents were finally suppressed in A.D. 9. And it was no doubt this situation that prompted Arminius to rouse his fellow-tribesmen and their neighbors to throw off the Roman yoke that had lain uneasily on their shoulders for the past twenty years. Five days after the announcement that the rebellion had been crushed came the news of the disaster in the Teutoburger Wald. Three legions had been destroyed, as much through the incapacity and vanity of the Roman commander, Quintilius Varus, as through the leadership of Arminius and the warlike character of his men. The ageing Augustus, now over seventy years old, did in fact, as now in fiction, give utterance to the general terror of Rome in his despairing cry of, "Varus, give me back my legions!"

Arminius, who was indeed the son of Segimer, was born in 17 B.C., and had therefore spent his youth and early manhood under the domination of Rome. He was twenty-six at the time of these events, and had no more than twelve years to live. In A.D. 15, the first year of his reign, Tiberius once more sent a Roman army across the Rhine, this time under his nephew Germanicus Caesar. It is a sad thought that when, a year later, he was finally victorious, he led Thusnelda captive to Rome. She, too, is a character of history and was Arminius's wife. The victory was not followed up, however, and Germany never became a Roman province, but the danger to Rome had been removed for three or four centuries. The later years of Arminius's life were spent fighting against that Maroboduus whom the Romans had previously intended to overthrow and in quarrelling with his own people, probably for the reason suggested in this book, that he had his eye on founding a powerful kingdom of his own. He was murdered in A.D. 21.

Throughout the succeeding century the Cherusci declined rapidly in power and importance, chiefly through constant warfare with their neighbors, the Chatti; and when, with the decline of Rome, the German tribes again figure largely in history, their lands are inhabited by the Saxons.

In *The Challenge* Arminius is seen as a German hero through German eyes. The Arminius of history is known to us only through the writings of Roman historians. The traditions of the North know nothing of him, or of his people either. Nevertheless, some eighty years ago a gigantic statue was erected to his memory on the Grotenburg mountain overlooking the probable scene of his victory.

I have in this brief summary named all the historical characters in the book. The rest are fictitious, though there is no reason why men and women like them should not have lived and had similar adventures. If, here and there, some slight falsification of history may be detected—as in the law which Julius Caesar introduced to prohibit wheeled traffic in the streets of Rome, not at nighttime as in this story, but during the hours of daylight—it must be remembered that the author's chief purpose was to write a story. He has given us a tale of exciting adventure set against a picture of Roman life that is substantially correct and offers a great deal of accurate and interesting information.

L. W. KINGSLAND

Grimsby, England, 1961